HOUSE of IVY & SORROW

Also by
NATALIE WHIPPLE

Transparent

House of Ivy & Sorrow
NATALIE WHIPPLE
HARPER TEEN
An Imprint of HarperCollinsPublishers

HarperTeen is an imprint of HarperCollins Publishers.

House of Ivy & Sorrow

www.epicreads.com

Library of Congress Cataloging-in-Publication Data

Whipple, Natalie.

House of ivy and sorrow / Natalie Whipple. — First edition.

pages cm

Summary: "Seventeen-year-old Josephine Hemlock has spent her life hiding the fact that she's a witch—but when the mysterious Curse that killed her mother returns, she might not be able to keep her magical and normal lives separate"—Provided by publisher.

ISBN 978-0-06-212018-2 (pbk. bdg.)

[1. Witchcraft—Fiction. 2. Blessing and cursing—Fiction. 3. Grandmothers—Fiction. 4. Fathers and daughters—Fiction. 5. Dating (Social customs)—Fiction. 6. Friendship—Fiction.] I. Title.

PZ7.W57663Hou 2014 2013008052

[Fic]—dc23 CIP

AC

Typography and display lettering by Erin Fitzsimmons

14 15 16 17 18 CG/RRDH 10 9 8 7 6 5 4 3 2 1

❖

First Edition

To my Grandma Dorothy,

who, though she died when I was eight,

I've always believed was magical.

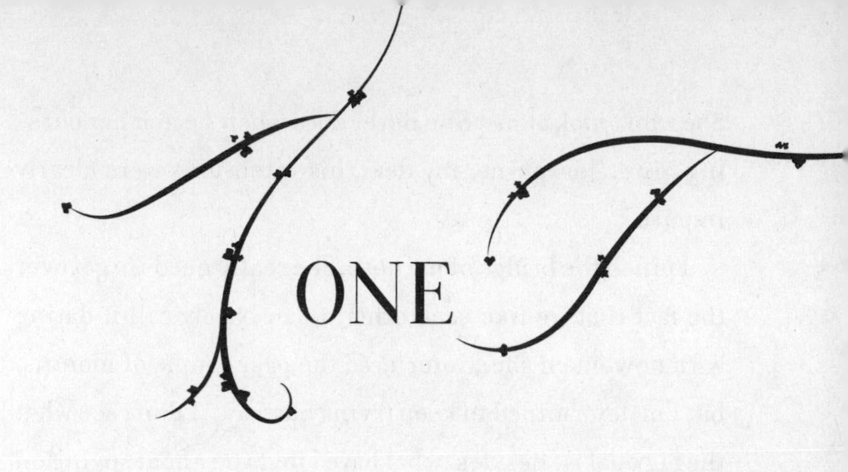

ONE

They say a witch lives in the old house under the interstate bridge. Always in the shadows, draped in ivy and sorrow, the house waits for a child too daring for his own good. And inside, the witch sits with her black eyes and toothless sneer. They say she can foresee your death in return for a lock of hair. She can make someone love you for the small price of a pinkie finger. And, of course, she can kill your enemy if you give her your soul. Some people think it's only a silly tale to scare children, but it's true. Every word.

I should know. She is my grandmother, after all, and right now I could steal her pudding stash for what she did to Winn. "Nana! He was just talking to me!"

She sits at her large mahogany desk, a variety of feathers and animal bones arranged precisely in front of her.

She won't look at me. She never does when I catch her cursing him. "Josephine, my dear, his intentions were clearly impure."

I pinch the bridge of my nose. She really needs to get over the fact that we like each other. I can barely call it dating with how much she's interfered the past couple of months, but I'm determined to keep trying anyway. "I don't see what the big deal is. Besides, what have I told you about spying on me at school?"

She frowns.

Letting out a long sigh, I sit in the throne-like chair her clients usually inhabit. "I'm safe, what with all the charms you make me wear. So can't you let me date someone without cursing him every time he tries to touch me?" I jingle my bracelet, which is riddled with runes and tiny organs encased in glass baubles.

"I know you're safe." Nana grabs her ivory cane and hobbles over to me. As she puts her hand on my shoulder, I can't help but feel ungrateful. "You are so precious to me. I cannot bear to lose you."

"You won't." My mother died when I was seven—from the mysterious Curse that's followed our family for generations—and ever since then I have been kept under tighter security than the president of the United States. It seemed important when I was young, but almost ten years later I want a little wiggle room. "And you can't give a guy a face full of pimples because he smiled at me, especially when they just appear like that. Your reputation is already bad enough, even though most of Willow's End doesn't believe you're real."

She cackles. Seriously—it's how she laughs. At least I've never heard anything else come out when she makes a joke.

"Nana, I mean it. Winn is a nice guy, and I really like him. Get rid of the zits."

"Oh, fine." She plops down in her chair, the old floorboards creaking even at her meager weight. She rearranges the feathers and bones, and then holds her hand over them. In the center, a flame sparks and consumes the feathers. "There."

I smile. "Thank you."

"In return, I need you to collect thirty spiders. I'm running low."

My smile is no more. Should have figured—there is always a payment. It's the number one rule of magic: you cannot get something for nothing. Nana lives and dies by that rule, even when magic isn't involved. "Fine."

Before I leave her apothecary, I grab a spare jar and fish out a frog eye from the bowl on her desk. Standing at the front door, I hold the frog eye in front of me and close my eyes. I picture the door I need: the one that leads to the ivy-covered home under the bridge. The magic pools in my hand, and I concentrate on what I desire it to do. It's work, switching doors. Usually I keep it set on the brown one that connects to the house in the heart of town—the house my friends think is real. It is, in a way, since it leads to the same interior as the other one.

The door I need is heavy and black, with a large bronze knocker in the shape of a gargoyle. It always groans when it opens, like most things in this house do.

Once the frog eye dissolves, I open my eyes. The brown door is now black and old and menacing. I turn the gilded knob, and the sound of freeway traffic overhead greets me. Checking to make sure the coast is clear, I cautiously step onto the front porch. Not that many people use this road anymore, since ours is the only house still standing out here. And "standing" is a loose term—it looks more like an abandoned ruin.

It's always cool under the bridge, even in the hot, humid summers. Sun gleams from either side, providing enough light to see. The tree in the yard is more moss than leaves, and the grass is thick and wet. I breathe in the air, full of dampness and magic.

That is, after all, part of why my great-great-grandmother moved here.

Normal people tend to think magic comes from inside a person. That's partially true. Witches can store magic in their bodies, but without a source to replenish that power they lose it. Magic—real, pure magic—is in places. It seeps into the ground, grows in the plants, lives in the objects that inhabit its realm.

This house, this land, is one such place that simmers with magic. And no matter what, we Hemlocks will protect it.

I don't have to go far to find my first spider. Half the front window is covered in webs, and I pluck one from its perch and drop it in the jar. In the corner behind the rusty swing, there are two more. By the time I step off the porch, I already have seven. The dark places under the stairs earn me eight more. I comb the ivy all the way to the back of the house until I get the rest. As I head to the front again, they struggle over one another in the slick, glass jar. "Sorry, guys, there's no escaping."

"Excuse me," someone says.

I look up, freezing in place. A man in a suit stands at the weathered iron gate, his hands in his pockets. He doesn't look like Nana's usual clientele, who come dirty and smelling of hard times, who are so desperate that magic pulls them here without them knowing. He reeks of money—or maybe that's the fancy convertible parked behind him that gleams even in these shadows. I take a few wary steps forward. "Yes? Do you need something?"

His eyes go wide as he takes me in. I grab the ends of my black hair, wondering if I have web in them. Nothing.

"What do you need?" I say again when he doesn't answer. For some reason he makes me curious to get a closer look, like I've seen him somewhere, even though I know I haven't.

He shakes his head, as if coming out of a daze. "Um, does a Carmina Hemlock live here?"

It's my turn to be taken by surprise. Who on earth would be looking for my mother after so much time? Before I know it, I'm saying, "She's dead."

"Dead?" he croaks. "When?"

"Ten years ago."

"Oh." He looks away, and for a moment I wonder if he might be fighting tears. "I'm sorry."

Something is off. There's a coldness on the other side of the gate. Something waiting. I can feel it reach for the iron bars, hear it hiss when the protective spell bans its entrance. This man brought darkness and evil with him. "You'd better go."

"I . . ." He stares at me, a strange sort of longing in his eyes. "Are you related to her? You look a lot like her."

"Leave." I take a few steps back before I dare to turn, and then I run for the house.

TWO

I slam the door behind me and lean against it. My heart pounds, though I'm not quite sure why. He didn't seem like a bad person, but there was something evil with him. It was wrong for him to be here, to see me.

After I bolt the door, I head back to Nana. "Here are your spiders."

Her white eyebrows furrow over her impossibly dark eyes. "What's wrong?"

So much for hiding my panic. "Nothing. There was just a man at the gate. I sent him away."

She goes to the window and pulls the green velvet curtain back, as if he'd still be there. "He didn't come for a spell?"

I shake my head. "He . . . asked for Carmina."

Her eyes snap to mine.

"He didn't know she was dead."

She shuts the curtain with far more force than necessary. "You are not to go out there again."

"Wha . . . wait, what?" I didn't expect her to be happy about the stranger, but this is harsh, even for her. "Why?"

"Not safe . . . not safe . . ." She goes to her cabinets, grabbing all sorts of eyes. Eyes—for which to see. Magic can be rather literal at times. "No good can come from those who seek the dead."

"Would you mind explaining?"

No answer. She's already in full incantation mode, the small cauldron heating on a Bunsen burner and all. Nana is an incredible witch. I watch in amazement as she goes through each phase at lightning speed, and by memory. I still have so much to learn from her. The liquid is almost finished by the time I realize what she's doing.

I groan. "Do I have to?"

"Yes, child, before it's too late." She motions for me to come over.

I grab the small knife on her desk as I go. Payment. Always. I hold my finger over the bubbling liquid and cut. It doesn't sting until the blood is already dripping. I watch, only because I have to know when to stop the flow. The concoction turns from green to autumn orange. I pull my hand back and search for a tissue.

"That's it. . . ." Nana waves her hands over the baby cauldron. In an instant a ghostlike figure appears—the man, with his sad eyes and nice suit, right from my fresh memories.

"No," she whispers. "It can't be."

I study her face, confused by her expression. I can't tell if it's horror or sadness. Then I look at the man again. He doesn't seem to carry the evil in this translucent form, but I know what I felt. "Do you know him? He seemed . . . weirdly familiar, but not."

She sucks in a breath and then waves the figure away. "I thought perhaps, but no."

"It looks like you—" Her eyes flash, and I stop. "Okay, you didn't."

"Regardless, only use the Main Street door until I say so. It doesn't hurt to be cautious." The clock chimes four, and she claps her hands together. "Time for pudding."

I try to hide my smile. Nana loves her pudding. It's one of the nicest-tasting toothless-friendly foods. She refuses to get dentures; she refuses most anything that comes from a doctor. But that doesn't mean her teeth fell out. Nope. She's pulled all but five herself—for what, I'd rather not know. Spells that use your own teeth aren't exactly the nice kind.

"Time for homework, I guess, since we still don't have TV," I say. No matter how many times she says no to cable, I still hope maybe one day she'll find my begging annoying enough to relent.

"Rots your brain!" she calls from the little fridge next to the normal one—the home of her pudding stash.

"I have plenty to spare!" I head up the stairs, which protest each step.

I glance at every picture frame on the way up, where the faces of my ancestors stare back at me. At least those who have lived here. When the Curse drove our family from New York, Great-Great-Grandma Agatha Hemlock put every penny she had into this house, knowing the magic here was too strong to leave. She put up crazy-strong magical barriers around the house and town. We thought we were safe—at least until the Curse found my mother.

My room is the second story of the tower, completely round and covered in floral wallpaper that I should hate, but don't. It's absolutely wild—big, bold flowers in faded blue and green. My cast-iron bed is just as ancient and cool. Most everything is white, since I figure the wallpaper has more than enough color. I flop onto my bed instead of heading to my desk. Reaching for the English book on my nightstand, I decide reading poetry is the least trouble.

But I can't stop thinking about that man.

I know Nana was lying to me.

I won't question her, though. We are blood, and that means so much more to us than to normal people. A witch's blood is the source of her power—the mark of her power. All the Hemlock women bear the same magical signature.

Nana, no matter what, has my best interest in mind. I am the only one who can preserve our family line. If she is lying, then she has a good reason.

My phone rings, and I dive for it. We may not have internet or TV, but my cell can usually eke out a few bars. It's my one technological indulgence.

"Gwen! Please say you're about to save me from doing homework on Friday night."

"But of course, Jo. Are you sitting down?" Gwendolyn Lee loves to be dramatic, but in a town as small as Willow's End we need it. Not sure what Kat and I would do without her.

"Lying, actually."

"Winn came into the deli after school, and he asked about you."

I sit up. "He did?"

"Yes. And he may have invited us to watch a movie at his house with some of his friends."

It's all I can do to restrain my squeal. So far we've only been hanging out at school, eating lunch together, stuff like that. I've been dying to go on a real date with him since I first sat next to him in art class eight months ago, but Nana's always made sure to ruin any moment he tries to ask. Going through Gwen—brilliant. Why didn't I think of this earlier?

"If you're kidding, I hate you forever."

"I'd never! I'll pick you up at six. We're doing dinner first."

"Okay." After hanging up, I head straight for the shower. Two hours is hardly enough time to get ready for the best night of my life.

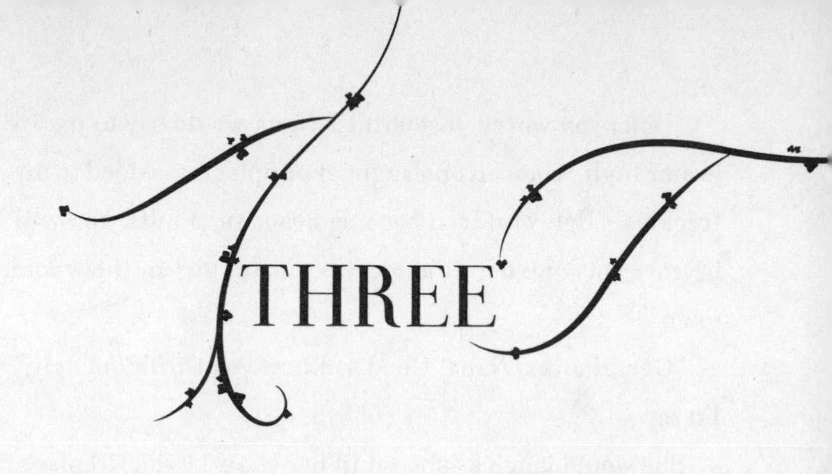

THREE

I check the hall mirror every couple seconds as I wait for Gwen and Kat to show up. I can't help it. Sometimes I have nightmares that I've gone back to the crazy-haired, freckle-faced, buck-toothed version of myself.

It was bad. Seriously bad.

Right after Mom died, I came home from elementary school bawling because Emily Harrison said I looked and acted like a boy. Admittedly, my wiry hair had turned into a frizzy nightmare without my mom's wondrous ability to tame the beast. Emily told all the girls that I must have gotten cooties, and for the rest of the day no one would sit next to me, let alone talk to me. Nana wasn't happy. Let's just say Emily started a lice epidemic the next day, and then everyone said she had cooties instead.

"Don't you worry, Josephine," Nana would say to me in junior high, when an onslaught of pimples was added to my freckles. "Ugly children become beautiful adults. You will be gorgeous one day—the most beautiful girl in the whole town."

"Gee, thanks, Nana. Good to know you think I'm ugly," I'd say.

She would laugh as she sat in her chair by the fireplace. "But not forever!"

I knew she meant well, but it was hardly comforting at the time. What if I really was doomed to be an ugly little mouse for the rest of my life?

Back then I didn't know that Nana is never wrong.

It practically happened overnight, like someone had cast a spell on me. I woke up the morning of my sixteenth birthday, barely a year ago, and my freckles had faded so much I couldn't see them under makeup. My hair started curling the right way, instead of whichever way it wanted. And it was like my face finally fit my gigantic teeth. I rushed down the stairs to the picture of my mother on the mantel. Taking it to this same hall mirror, I fought back tears as I stared at her and me together. "So I am your daughter after all."

As I fix a few stray curls, the floorboard creaks, and I jump. "Nana, you scared me."

"Are you going somewhere?" By the look on her face, I have a feeling I should have told her sooner.

"Out with the girls. We got invited to watch a movie at Winn's house. A bunch of people will be there, so you don't have to worry about anything." Not that she won't. Even though I begged her to stop, she'll totally spy on me.

"It's not a good idea, considering what happened this afternoon."

I put on my best pout. "But you said it was nothing. I'm not using the bridge door, and he's probably long gone in that fancy car of his. He definitely didn't live anywhere around here— probably not anywhere in Iowa."

One of her eyebrows arches. That was so not the right thing to say. "Strange that he would drive all the way here, then, just to ask for your mother. Who was murdered. By the darkest of magic. Without so much as a clue to who is responsible."

She has a point, but this is Winn we're talking about. I won't back down so easily. "Nana, is he dangerous or not? Two and a half hours ago you said he was nothing to worry about, and now you won't let me go out the Main Street door because of him? I have a feeling you're not telling me something."

Gwen's horn sounds from outside.

Nana sighs. "If you see him again, you are to come straight home. By any means necessary."

I give her a hug. "Thank you! Love you!"

I'm out the door before she can change her mind. Gwen

honks her horn three more times, though she can see me walking down the path. The Main Street house is much like the one under the bridge, except without the ambiance. No stained glass. No cobwebs. Just a perfectly manicured lawn and a white picket fence that blends in flawlessly with the rest of our sleepy old town.

"Hurry up!" Gwen calls from the window of her giant, decrepit truck. She inherited it when her dad got a new one, mostly because he was tired of driving her from the farm to work at the town deli. Since Kat and I are woefully devoid of transportation, Gwen's truck is the best we have.

"Where are we eating?" I squeeze in next to Kat, who rounds out our trio with her indifference and constant, endearing grouchiness. If it weren't for her, I'm pretty sure Gwen and I would fight all the time. Kat makes sure we know when we're being stupid.

"Marcello's," Gwen says. "According to Winn."

I lean my head back, unable to restrain my smile. Winn Carter is by far the cutest guy in our grade. It's practically mandatory for every girl in town to have at least a little crush on him. He is so gorgeous he had an older girlfriend, Chelsea Marlowe, who broke up with him when she went to college. This has been the first time anyone else has had a chance, and yet he hasn't made a move on anyone all year. Until me. Of all people.

"You have no idea how happy I am right now."

Gwen flips her blond hair. "You better be! It's about time you two take it up a notch. We need some official coupling around here. Tonight is the night!"

We both squeal.

"Oh, for the love," Kat says. But she's smiling, so Gwen goes on.

"That is not even the best part, honey." Gwen rummages around in her purse and soon produces a piece of familiar yellow paper—an order slip from the deli. "Here."

I take it from her and read it. Then read it again. And again just to make sure. "This really is the best night of my life."

Kat rolls her eyes. "What does it say?"

"'For Jo,' with his phone number and 'Call me anytime.'" He's tried to give it to me before, but Nana always gets in the way. I still haven't forgiven her for the time she made me throw up when he asked for my number. I barely missed his shoes.

"Whoa." Kat takes it from me, her mild interest saying everything. "This is big."

"So big!" Gwen laughs.

"I know." Suddenly I feel fluttery all over. I can't help but fear what Nana might do if he tries to make a move. She could curse him blind if he puts his arm around me. What if she strikes me down for holding his hand?

"Are you gonna barf?" Kat asks.

I shake my head, searching for a plausible cover. "Okay, kind of freaking out now. What am I supposed to do? Do you think he'll try something? I'm not exactly, uh, well versed in that stuff."

Gwen shrugs. "Just do what you've been doing. It's obviously working."

"But I haven't been doing anything!"

"Then don't do anything, duh," Kat says. "It's called being yourself."

I whimper. "Why does that seem so hard all of a sudden?"

"Stop it." Gwen parks in front of Marcello's, the only pizza place for thirty miles. "Josephine Hemlock, you are arguably the hottest girl in school now—"

"Believe me, we're just as surprised as everyone else." Kat pushes her long bangs to the side. "A year ago you were the ugly one of the group."

"Shut up!" I laugh.

"Don't interrupt my pep talk!" Gwen shoves Kat. "As I was saying, you will go in there and be your ridiculously charming, beautiful self. Winn will finally confess his undying love for you, and you will be official by the end of the night."

I cover my face, trying to calm my nerves.

"And then me and Kat will get dates, too, because Winn's friends will be around us so much that they'll realize how amazing we are."

"There's the real motivation!" I say. "Gwendolyn, you're evil."

"I don't want a boyfriend," Kat says. "Guys are idiots."

Gwen gets out of the truck, and we follow. "Whatever. Idiots or not, you know you want one. Someone nice and jaded who can share your negative view of the world."

"That could be refreshing. I hate being the only practical one around here." Kat opens the restaurant door, and it dings. The place is fairly busy, being Friday and all. There are only three restaurants in town—Marcello's, the deli, and the Lucky Star diner. There's also a bar, but it's hard to sneak in when everyone knows you.

"Jo! Over here!" Winn calls.

My face flushes as I follow the voice. There he is, his perfect smile in place. Lots of things make Winn attractive—the hardworking farmer-boy build, the dusty blond hair that curls by his ears, the stormy blue eyes—but it's his smile that gets me. His mouth. It sounds dirty, but he has an incredible mouth.

All I did the first month sitting next to him in art was try not to stare too much at his lips. But the way they pursed when he concentrated . . . I still get fluttery when I think about it. Then one day, we had to draw a display our teacher put up. It was a family of ceramic frogs.

Yes. Frogs. With red eyes.

"The one on the right looks like it wants to kill us all,"

I said under my breath, but not quietly enough, because Winn heard and laughed.

"That smile definitely means he's up to something," he said. "Frogs don't smile unless they have diabolical plans."

I nodded. "World domination, probably."

"For sure."

"All hail our demon-eyed overlords."

We both busted up, so much so that we almost got in trouble because we couldn't stop laughing. Winn drew one of his frogs with an army helmet, and it was over. My little crush was a full-blown he-is-the-most-awesome-guy-ever-born obsession. And by some miracle we've been friends ever since, building into whatever we are now.

I manage to wave at him. Gwen has to nudge me to get my feet moving, and then we're at their table. Winn stands. "Hey."

"Hey, uh, glad your face is . . ." I stop. *Of all the things I could have said, why am I starting with the pimple attack? Get it together, Jo.*

He cringes. "Oh, yeah. Must have been some kind of allergic reaction, because it disappeared as soon as I got home. Weird, huh."

"Yeah." It's scary how easy it is not to bring up magic. Nana says science was the best thing to ever happen to witches. Now there are all sorts of logical explanations for what we do, and people are always inclined to believe those first.

"Anyway . . ." Winn looks at his feet, and I feel horrible for embarrassing him. "I'm glad you could make it. Kind of last-minute plans."

"Not a problem. It was this or homework." I slide into the booth, immediately regretting the homework line. I'm not sure this being-myself crap is going so well, but then he laughs.

"Glad we're at least better than homework."

"Barely."

"Ouch." He smiles as he slides in next to me. Gwen and Kat end up by Winn's buddies, Adam and Billy, filling out the round booth.

"So." Gwen sits way too close to Adam, but he doesn't seem to mind. "Please tell me you didn't rent scary movies so you could watch us scream, because I'm really hoping you guys are cooler than that."

"We have a bunch of different stuff," Winn says. "Pooled all our Netflix orders, so you have your pick." The closest movie theater is like an hour away. Without Netflix we'd never see anything.

"Don't let Gwen pick." Kat grabs a breadstick. "Otherwise we'll be stuck with some sappy romantic comedy."

"Hey! What's wrong with that?"

The guys laugh, and I'm so distracted by my friends that Winn's shoulder against mine takes me off guard. "Your friends are funny," he says into my ear.

"I was thinking crazy, but that works, too."

"Crazy people usually are funny."

I smile. "True."

He pushes a menu in front of me. "What do you want?"

"Hmm." I pick it up, though I already know I want pepperoni and olives. It's been my favorite for as long as I can remember. "Are we doing the mini-pizza thing or sharing bigger ones?"

"Mini pizzas have crap toppings," Billy says. "It's like one pepperoni a slice."

"I'm for sharing," Kat says. "We can take whatever we don't eat."

The battle over toppings begins, but I manage to get a half pizza with my choice. As we wait for the pies, I'm surprised how well the conversation goes. Gwen has a way of getting people to talk. I love her for it.

"How are we doing against homework now?" Winn asks right as the pizza comes.

I purse my lips, pretending to think about it. "Pretty good, I guess."

"So maybe you'd skip it next Friday, too?" His eyes meet mine, all bright and hopeful.

"The night's not even over. You never know; it could go downhill. Are you sure you want to commit to another?"

"Really sure." His knee bumps mine, and a thrill runs through me. "You?"

“Oh, I think that would be—”

The door dings, and I can’t help but look at who comes in. Everyone is staring, because no one in town owns a suit like that. And somehow, his eyes find me immediately.

No.

Not fair. I don’t want to go.

But that dark something is there again. I can feel it slinking under the door, weaving its way through the room like a black spider.

“Jo?” Winn says.

It’s only then that I realize I’m standing. I have to get out. Even if I don’t want to, I must. It’s more important than Winn. More important than everything. “I have to go. Right now.”

He moves, though he doesn’t look happy. “Now? Why?”

I gulp down the fear. “I . . . I just do. I’m so sorry. Next Friday, though. If you still want.”

The man stands at the front door, so I head for the side exit. The shadows are wrong. The door is ice. Whatever this evil is, it’s too close.

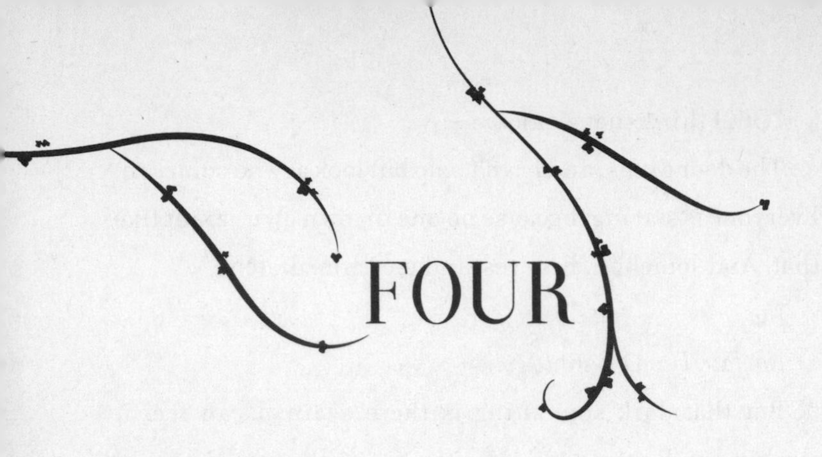

FOUR

Witches know darkness. People like to think there is light and dark magic, but that's not true. There is only dark. A black pool full of power and pain. The difference between "good" or "bad" witches is how responsible they are with the darkness. There are two choices: Control or Consumption.

Sometimes Control is hard. Nana says being Consumed is like being drunk on magic—you feel more powerful than ever. You are, but you lose yourself in the process. The darkness Consumes your soul bit by bit as payment, until you're a slave to the power you could once control.

Always a price.

The dark shadows are Consumption. Or at least something tied to someone who has been Consumed. I can feel their hunger. They desire to have me, call to me with promises of power beyond anything I have now.

It's wrong. I repeat the words over and over as I head into the night. The cool spring air nips at my arms, but it's nothing in comparison to the aura that man brings with him.

The Main Street house is four blocks from here, but I can't stand to walk that far. I worry the man is already making his way back outside, determined to talk to me again, and this time I don't have the protection of our magic-fortified iron gate.

I wince as I rip out a handful of hair. Then I wrap it around my palm until it looks like a pentagram. Closing my eyes, I visualize my room. The white drapes and blue window-seat pillows. My armoire and full-length mirror. The magic surges from my toes to my head. Soon I'll be safe from the darkness. A little bald, but safe.

The restaurant door slams behind me. "Jo?"

I let out a squeak at the voice, and my spell is broken. Whirling around, I find Winn standing there with a box. I let my handful of hair fall to the ground. "What are you doing out here?"

His brow furrows with concern. "Shouldn't I be asking you that?"

"Sorry." I slump. "I told you things could go downhill."

"You didn't get to eat." He holds out the box, and I melt a little. "Thought you should at least have dinner."

I take it, wishing so badly that I could go back in there and pretend nothing was wrong. "Thanks. You didn't have to do that—I haven't paid."

He shrugs. "I was going to pay for you anyway."

"Oh." He's killing me here. I can't help but think about how incredible this night could have been, and instead I have to run out on him. "I better—"

The door swings open again, and my jaw drops. Winn sees my expression, which I assume has crumbled into horror, and turns to look at what caused it. "Can I help you, sir?"

"I need to speak with your . . . friend," he says, his eyes intent on me, desperate and sad. The darkness seeps out of him, slowly making its way over. "I need to know if she's related to Carmina Hemlock."

"Leave me alone." I take a few steps back. "You have no business here. I won't talk to you."

The man comes forward. "But—"

Winn stands in his way. "She said she didn't want to speak with you."

"Winn." I tentatively put my palm on his back. "I have to go home. Now. Can you take me home?"

"Of course." He takes my hand and pulls me to his truck.

"Wait!" The man and his shadows follow. "Please! I don't mean you any harm. I would never do anything to Carmina's fam—"

"Get away from her!" Winn quickly unlocks the driver's side. "Climb in."

I do as I'm told, landing in the passenger seat right as he revs the engine. He peels out way too fast, but under the circumstances I don't mind. As Winn heads for my house, I realize the man might follow us. "Drive around a little. I don't want him knowing where I live."

"Okay." He makes a right on the closest street. "Can I ask what's going on? You're trembling, Jo."

"I am?" I look down, just realizing my arms really are shaking. My fingers are freezing. No, all of me is freezing. I rub my hands together. "I guess it's colder outside than I thought."

He turns on the heat. "I don't think that's the only reason."

My throat tightens. What am I supposed to say? Witches don't tell outsiders about our powers—way too much bad history with that. But I have to tell him something, especially since he's putting his neck on the line more than he knows. "He's . . . been asking about my mother. I think he figures we're related because we look alike. I have no idea who he is, but he gives me the creeps. It's like he's following me."

Winn purses his lips. "That doesn't sound good."

"No." I pull my knees up, hugging them to my chest. We drive in silence for a few moments. Night is starting to fall over the endless fields outside town. Soon they'll be planted, and by the end of the summer there will be corn, corn, and more corn. "Please don't tell anyone about this. It's personal. Family stuff."

"I would never. Secrets are my specialty."

I put my head to my knees. Talk about downhill. Suddenly I feel exposed, like Winn is one step away from knowing way too much about me. "I'm so sorry I dragged you into this."

"It's my fault. I'm the one who followed you out, though I gotta admit I'm glad I did."

I scoff. "Glad you got forced into driving me away from a possible stalker? You sure have a strange idea of fun."

"No." The car slows to a stop, and when I look up there's nothing but field in every direction. "Glad I could be there for you when you needed it."

I shouldn't be smiling right now, but Winn has a way of doing that. I grab the box from the dashboard. "And you made sure we had food."

He laughs. "Hope you don't mind that we stopped. Don't want to run my tank dry."

"We're probably okay out here." I open the box, suddenly starving. "We could wait a little to make sure he's gone, if you don't mind."

"I don't." He grabs the other slice, and we eat.

It takes a second for it to sink in, but once I realize we're alone in his truck, in the middle of nowhere, I panic for very different reasons. "Where are we, exactly?"

"Our southern field," he says through a bite of pizza. "Figured we could see him coming from here."

"Good idea."

"I have them sometimes."

I glance over, only to find him staring right back at me. I keep waiting for him to look away, but he doesn't. "What?" I finally say.

He shakes his head. "Nothing. Just can't seem to keep my eyes off you these days."

"What a line." Too bad my smile gives away how much I fell for it.

"Do you remember the county fair last summer?"

"Of course." The county fair is by far the most exciting thing that happens out here. "What about it?"

"That was the week Chelsea broke up with me. I was bummed and my friends dragged me to the fair so I could see that she wasn't the only girl out there." He puts his hand over his face. "I felt so lame that day. We were sitting in front of the band with some girls they'd dragged over. I wanted to be anywhere else. I would have taken the pigsty at that point . . . and then I saw you."

I startle. "Me?"

"Yeah. You were with Gwen and Kat, sitting on the grass eating ice cream and laughing. You flipped your sandals off and leaned back on a tree trunk, like you were completely comfortable and content."

I blush all the way to my ears. "I didn't realize you saw that."

"Well, you seemed way cooler than the people I was hanging out with. There was something different about you. I wanted to go over and say hi, but I couldn't get myself to do it."

"Why not?"

"Because . . . I don't know." He sighs. "I knew who you were, but only barely. You looked gorgeous in that blue dress, kind of intimidating. I almost got up to talk to you a hundred times, but I guess I didn't want you to think I was on the rebound or something. After that I kept wussing out. Every art class I planned to ask you on a date, and the words never came. Figured if I didn't do it before school ended I might never get the chance."

"You mean this entire school year you've been wanting to ask me out?"

"Basically." He winces. "Now you know, and I feel like a complete loser for telling you that story. Talk about stalking. This is the part where you ask me to drive you home and never speak to me again, huh."

I bite my lip, secretly thanking scary stalker man for getting me alone with Winn. "Well, you do have to take me home . . ." I scoot closer to him. "But I plan on talking to you a lot. You'll probably get sick of hearing my voice, especially since you gave me your number and everything. You really shouldn't have done that."

He smiles. *That smile, oh, why does it make me go all melty?* "I shouldn't have?"

"Nope. You're doomed now."

His hand comes over mine, and our fingers intertwine. "I think I'm gonna like being doomed."

"We'll see." I squeeze his fingers, bracing for a freak lightning shock from Nana or something. It doesn't come. "You really do have to take me home now, though."

"Guess I can live with that." He lets go to start the car, but then his hand is right back over mine. It feels so good, wiping away any chills I still had. Strange, how easy it is to lean my head on his shoulder when earlier tonight it seemed impossible.

But when he slows to a stop outside my house, I want to shrivel up and die. Nana stands on the porch, waiting to kill me.

"She doesn't look happy," Winn says.

"If I don't call you tomorrow, come looking." I reluctantly let go. "Good night."

"Good luck."

"Thanks, I'll need it." And with that, I open the car door and head to what may very well be my execution.

FIVE

Nana doesn't say anything as we go inside. Or when I follow her to the kitchen. She pulls a chocolate pudding from the little fridge, grabs a spoon, and eats while staring me down.

I am in so much trouble.

Gulping down my fears, I say, "I assume you were watching, so you have to admit that I shouldn't have gone straight home. That guy could have followed, and then he would have known both entrances to our house."

She takes another spoonful.

I hate when she does this. It's worse than a lecture. Worse than punishment. My guilt is enough of a penalty. I lean my head on the counter. "Nana, I'm sorry. Really."

The pudding cup lets out a crumpled cry when she crushes it. "You need to tell me exactly what was said between you and that man."

I look up, surprised that she doesn't sound angry. The spying spell doesn't include sound unless you want to throw in bat ears, and those are pretty hard to come by so we save them for important things. "He asked if I was related to Carmina."

"Did you say your name? Did he hear your name at all?"

"I'm sure he didn't." Then my stomach drops. "But I did say Winn's name. Is that bad?"

She sighs. "It's not good. You may have put him in serious danger—you know the power of names."

I suck in my tears and guilt. "I was so scared. I wasn't thinking straight. The man hardly said anything, but he carried . . . something. Shadows. Darkness. Anger. It kept oozing out of him. Not sure what it was, except it was bad."

She nods. "I could see it."

"What was it?" I reach out for her hand. "What is going on? I think I have a right to know. It's after me, isn't it?"

Nana is not exactly the kind of grandma who looks young, but with one sigh she ages another few decades. "I hoped this day would not come. Carmina and I worked so hard to prevent this from happening. But those shadows found him—and since his intentions toward us are good, he isn't repelled by our barriers."

"Who is he?"

Her look is flat. "Surely you know, Josephine. Separate

him from the darkness, and you will see."

I do as she says, picturing the man with as much detail as possible. He has dark hair and light eyes, but I can't remember the exact color. He is tall and lean, and his skin, while tan, has traces of freckles. I gasp. Mom never had a single one, and who else would care so much about finding my mother? He seemed familiar to me because . . . "He's my father?"

She nods. "Joseph Johnson."

I can't seem to find air. This is a day I never thought about because witches simply do not know their fathers. We don't do families like that. We have relationships, but they never result in commitment. We only have girls—girls who possess our bloodline and power. It is the mother, grandmother, daughter, sister bonds that make up our families.

Romantic love never ends well for us, though we need it like anyone else. The men we choose to be with are always in danger of becoming pawns, leverage. Which must be my father's case, because knowing who he is makes me want to protect him. Nana doesn't have to say anything for me to know what's going on. Someone is using him to get to us. Someone cruel and consumed with darkness.

"Carmina loved him very much," Nana says. I can feel the sorrow in her voice, the pain of losing her daughter and her daughter losing the man she loved. "She wanted so badly to stay with Joseph, and she took many risks to be with him as long as she was. But when she found out she was pregnant, she knew she had to protect you and him. She disappeared from his life and came home, though I don't think she ever got over it."

"He never knew where she went?" I ask.

She heads for the apothecary, and I follow. "Oh, he tried to find her. We did many things to ensure that he couldn't, since any knowledge he had would only hurt him. When she was Cursed, we put more barriers around him, for fear that he would be used as he is now. It seems our hunters finally found a way through."

"If only we knew who they were." There are other witch bloodlines. Some friendly. Others not so much. The Curse must have come from someone's magic, but no one will own up to it. Those who go looking for answers end up dead. All we can do is what we've done for centuries: Run. Hide. Hope it doesn't find us again.

"If only, yes. The shadows around Joseph are similar to your mother's Curse. I fear they have come for us, Josephine." She grabs the jar of spiders she made me collect. Spiders, which crawl and sneak and kill. What she plans to do with them, I'm not sure yet. "But if we are very careful, we may be able to free him. And if we are very lucky, we could discover your mother's killer as well."

My eyes go wide. "Are you saying we might be able to avenge Mom's death?"

"That's exactly what I'm saying." She grabs a bag of crow ashes and heads for her desk. Crow and spider—this spell must be something with bite. "Of course, it was safer to hide before, since making sure you came of age was far more important than vengeance. But if they're knocking at our door, they will have hell to pay for what they've done to us."

"We can't leave? Find another magical place to hide in?" Not that I love the idea of leaving Gwen, Kat, and Winn, but the Hemlock line is at risk here.

Nana's expression is positively grim. "It takes too much time to search and rebuild. When Agatha came here, there were still five witches in the New York house. Only one had been Cursed. By the time she established this house, none of them were alive."

"Oh." My heart doubles its pace. I don't have to ask more questions. The Curse has been a plague for generations, slowly killing family lines. The Sages, the Maggis, the Firebrands . . . they are long gone. And we might be next.

"I don't mean to frighten you, Josephine, but if this evil plans to snuff us out I cannot sit here and wait for it. Maybe we can find answers—and with those answers we could stop this, save other witching families from the Curse. We might be a small bloodline, but we are strong." She puts her wrinkled hand on my arms, squeezes once. "What do you say? Shall we fight back?"

I can feel the smile on my lips, which reminds me too well that I am no mild-mannered, normal girl. Murdering a witch is a grave, evil offense. We should not kill our own—there have been too many years of other people doing that for us. When my mother died, our sister witches gave their condolences, but we wondered which one of them had done the unthinkable and why.

My mother did not die without pain. I remember her cries, young as I was. I would sit by her bedside, holding her hand as Nana tried everything to remove the Curse. She did all the spells she could think of to stop Mom's blood from turning black, but it never worked. Whatever that poison was, it wasn't going anywhere. I remember the moment I knew Mom would die, though she never said it.

"You'll be okay, right?" I'd ask every day after school when I'd rush up the stairs to her room.

And every day, she would smile and say, "Of course."

But one cool fall afternoon, as the leaves were turning gold and red and orange, I came in to check on her. I asked what I always asked, and she said, "I don't know, baby."

That's when I knew, though I told myself she was just tired of being sick. Tomorrow she would say she was fine. It was only a hiccup in the pattern. But after that it was always "I don't know," until she couldn't speak at all.

Then she was gone, and it felt like I would never quite be whole again.

Truth is, I'm still not.

I stand tall, determined, as Nana and I stare at each other. It's time to fight, and vengeance sounds good right now. "What do I need to do?"

SIX

My phone's chirping wakes me the next morning. I grasp at my nightstand, wondering who in the world would text me at this ungodly hour. Especially on a weekend. It's barely daylight—like, daylight happened thirty seconds ago—and I've told Gwen and Kat they will suffer if they wake me up before ten. Gwen had a very awkward rash the week after she woke me up just to say some boy kissed her at summer camp.

I squint at the screen's brightness.

Still alive? It's Winn, btw.

Well, maybe I won't curse him.

Yes, but I don't remember giving you my number.

Almost immediately, my phone chirps again.

Asked Gwen. Figured it's OK, since I'm doomed already.

I squeal into my pillow. This can't be real.

Except don't text me this early. Gosh.

Early? I've been up for over an hour.

I laugh. Winn's family owns one of the biggest farms in the area, and like most farm kids he's always up before the sun doing chores.

I feel so lazy.

You could come help.

Not that lazy.

Ha. Gotta go. Field-plowing time. Call me later?

Of course!

Nana knocks at my door. "Josephine? Are you up?"

"No." I put my phone on vibrate, cursing myself for not thinking of it sooner. No doubt she has a lot of work for me to do, and it probably involves dead animals.

She opens my door, the light cutting a sliver through my dark room. "I heard the phone chirp. Was that your boy?"

"He's not *my* boy, at least not yet, thanks to you. Last night barely counted as a first date, so please don't give him warts."

"I was thinking more like permanent bad breath."

"Nana . . ." I whine. "I really like him, and you know he's a good guy. You've probably been stalking him since I mentioned we were in art together."

She sits at the end of my bed. "I keep forgetting how old you are."

"Yup, turned seventeen last week, remember? I think it's high time I be allowed to date. Kissing and all." I let out a long sigh at the thought, which sounds far more dreamy than I expected.

"He is quite handsome. Lovely smile."

"I know, right?" I say. Nana, despite the evil streak, does have a kind heart. And a soft spot for good-looking men.

"He reminds me of a young man I used to go out with, when your great-grandmother Geraldine still ruled the house. I was living in Rochester at the time."

I give her a surprised look. "I didn't know you lived in New York."

"Only for a summer. I spent some time with the Crafts; we'd grown to be good pen pals."

The Craft witches are probably our closest allies, for lack of a better word. Since Mom died, they've been the only family Nana has allowed in our house. Maggie Craft is a year younger than me, and she's visited off and on over the years to learn from Nana. "Is that how we became so close with them?"

She shakes her head. "Oh, no, we've watched out for each other since the crossing. After the fiasco in Salem, we both went over to New York in search of magical places."

"I see." Lots of witching families left Europe to escape

the Curse, us and the Crafts included. Many settled in Massachusetts, since there was a huge well of magic in Salem, but fights broke out and the Curse followed. Our families headed to New York. The Crafts have remained safe there, but the Curse found us again. Now we're in Iowa . . . and hopefully we can find a way to survive.

Her hand comes down on my leg gently. "I'm getting off track, like always. I meant to talk about Winn."

"Please don't make me give him up. I promise to be more careful. I'll protect him and us." I cross my heart. "I swear."

She snorts. "That's not what I was going to say."

I tilt my head. "Then what?"

Her sigh is heavy. "I wish I could tell you this will be easy, dear, but you are too smart for that. You like him. If I let you be more serious with him, you may come to love him. But there is a part of you that you cannot share, a secret you must always keep. Someday, you will have to say good-bye. It is our way. Don't ever forget that."

A lump forms in my throat. I can't think about it right now. The present is what matters, as Nana always says. Always enjoy the time you have. Don't mourn over things that haven't happened yet. There will be plenty of time for that later. "So you're saying I'm allowed to date? You won't interfere anymore?"

She tries not to smile. "For now. Be careful, though."

I sit up and put my arm around her bony, yet strong,

shoulder. "Careful? But I should probably get on with making you some great-granddaughters. . . ."

She digs her knuckle into my leg.

"Ow!" I say through my own budding cackle. "C'mon! Our babies would be beautiful!"

She waves her hands in the air, as if she's trying to unhear what I said. "We need to work on the spells to free your father. Start defrosting the rest of the crows in the freezer. Then prepare them for an obliteration spell."

I groan. Maybe I should have gone to help Winn with his chores.

It takes the entire weekend to prepare for the "exorcism," and by Monday morning we are nearly finished. First come the amulets laced with lily nectar, dove blood, and our own eyelashes, to protect us from the dark shadows. They should repel the blackness and fear long enough to do our work. Then come the reagents to help free my father from the spell that has been placed on him.

My father. Joseph.

It's strange, knowing Mom named me after him, like I had a piece of him all along. My mother never spoke of him, and I never questioned after she said, "Honey, our kind don't know our paternal heritage. I don't know my father either."

But he's family, and right now I don't have much of that.

Even if it's not traditional, part of me wants him to stay here and never leave. Though I love Nana, the idea of having a real live parent means more than I can describe. Then there's the other side—the side that is terrified about what he'll say about Mom. If this works, I'll have to hear stories that will make my heart hurt all over again.

"Josephine," Nana says. "Are you done with the measurements?"

"Almost." I hold my breath as I count. I have to get the exact number of snake scales into this vial of crow's blood. One over or one less will ruin the potion.

She grabs the first vial I've prepared—forty strands of mink hair mixed with minced crow liver. "Is something wrong? You don't usually work this slowly."

"I . . ." I feel stupid saying it out loud, but Nana and I have always shared our thoughts with each other. We're all we have. "Do you think he'll like me? My . . . dad?"

She laughs. "Of course. Who wouldn't like you?"

I set the finished vial in its holder. "But he didn't know I existed until a few days ago. Well, he still doesn't know, exactly."

"And look how intent he is on finding you." She holds out her hand for the next reagent.

"That's not the spell?"

"No, dear." She slowly pours the crow and scorpion ashes into the mixture. "That is why whoever did this sought him out. Our hunters needed someone who cared enough not to give up at the first sign of resistance or strangeness, and someone who we would care about as well. As far as I can tell, what our hunters have done is turn him into a living video camera. He probably has no idea he's cursed."

I nod, a slight pang of guilt hitting me. It must have hurt so much, me yelling at him like I did. Here he'd just found out the love of his life was dead, and the girl who looks way too much like her refuses to speak to him for no reason he can see.

"I don't get what these people who Cursc us want." I try to steady my hands, but it's hard with how angry I am. "Why would other witches want us dead?"

"Is it not obvious?"

Sometimes Nana makes me feel really stupid. She assumes that I have all her wisdom. I think it's her way of reminding me that I have a long way to go before I take over the house. "Not really."

"What happens when we are dead?"

"Oh." Duh. A witch Consumed by darkness wants as much magic as she can get, and that means she needs as many magical places as she can own. "That's not fair. Why can't they be happy with their own land?"

"That's not how Consumption works, dear. You cannot comprehend what darkness you are capable of when you give in to magic's call. Now, help me seal this concoction."

Putting my hand over the cauldron, I channel into Nana's spell to add my power to it.

I can sense each individual reagent, and I focus on weaving them together. As I draw the magic from myself, the ingredients swirl as much in my head as they do in the cauldron. This spell is strong—stronger than any spell we've worked on in a long time. My fingers tingle with the current. The power is intoxicating.

It whispers that I could be stronger if I let it fill me. It tells me I could solve all my problems, save my family, if I give in.

"Josephine," Nana hisses. "You push too hard and this spell could kill him."

"Sorry." I square my shoulders and focus on controlling the magic. *Control. Use the magic. Don't let it use me.*

The concoction stabilizes under our command, shrinking and shrinking until it's the size of a pearl and just as iridescent. Nana plucks it from the cauldron's black iron bottom and holds it out to me. "You know what to do."

I nod, taking it from her as the school bus honks.

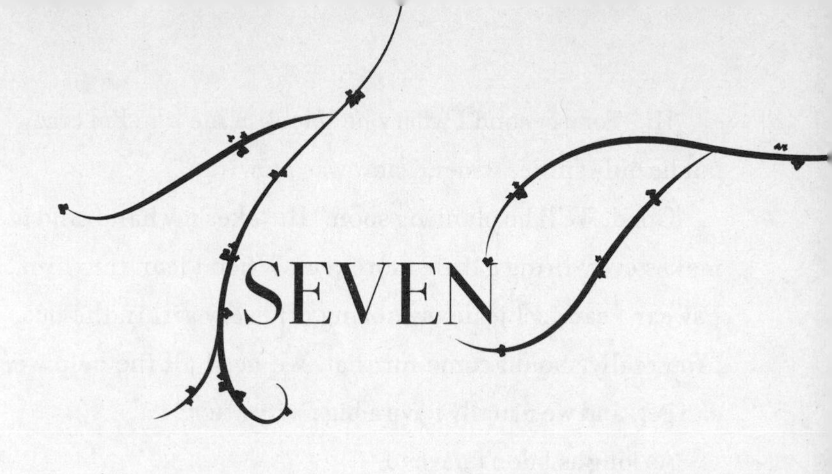

SEVEN

Willow's End is too small to have its own school, so all the kids in town are bused to Denison, which is thirty minutes away. Even older teens with cars take the bus because it's better than wasting gas. Climbing the three stairs, I smile at Mrs. Gunner like always. And then I face every kid in our entire town, my heart pounding as my eyes lock with Winn's. The seat next to him is empty.

Gwen and Kat are right behind him, doing a horrible job of hiding their excitement. As I head over, I can't deny that I'm pretty excited myself. This can't be part of my life—not when the other part is so supremely strange—and yet it is. When I sit down, the bus goes silent save for the roaring engine. I can feel every single eye on us.

"Hey," Winn says.

"Hi." For a second I worry he'll look at me like I'm crazy, but he only smiles wider. "How was plowing?"

"Good. We'll be planting soon." He takes my hand, and it makes everything a little more real. When I lean into him, I swear I can feel jealousy oozing off every girl in the bus. "You really should come for that. We need all the help we can get, and we usually have a big party after."

"As long as I don't have to—"

Gwen's face appears between us. "Can we come, too?"

Winn laughs. "If you want."

I roll my eyes, knowing too well why she wants to. Winn has older brothers—cute older brothers—who will definitely be home for planting, what with school ending in a few weeks. "Because you love farmwork," I say.

It is a known fact that Gwendolyn Lee is the most unfarmy farm girl ever born. Even as a toddler, her parents couldn't convince her dirt was a fun thing. She's like a city girl without a city. It's kind of adorable.

Gwen shrugs. "I love parties."

"You mean you love hot boys working," Kat says.

She laughs. "That, too! It's everything I ever dreamed of."

Winn shakes his head. "Wow, I had no idea my farm was that exciting."

"Well, exciting is relative," I say.

"Ouch." He bumps my knee with his. "You're not good for my ego, Jo."

I roll my eyes. "You like it."

He leans in to whisper. "I do."

I can't seem to stop smiling. I don't care if I look like an idiot—Winn's freaking holding my hand, and Nana isn't cursing either of us for it! Finally. Then the pearl comes to mind, and for a second everything is horrible again. I put my hand over my jean pocket to make sure the little bead is still there. Nana would kill me if I lost it.

When we get off, Winn follows me to my locker, as if he's part of the group now. I thought Kat and Gwen would disappear, but they seem to be enjoying this as much as I am.

"One rule," Kat says as I gather my books.

I raise an eyebrow. "Rule?"

"Don't make out in public. I will slap you both if you do."

My face burns as I glance at Winn. "Can you be more awkward, Kat?"

She puts her hands up. "It's only right to give warnings when violent punishment is involved."

"Rule noted." Winn rubs the back of his neck, and I kind of want to die. "We're, uh, gonna go to art now."

"Yes." I grab his hand. "I don't think I've ever been this excited for class."

He laughs. "Me neither."

The rest of the day goes like the bus ride, flitting between elation and dread. Eyes train on me at every turn, and this is not a day I want to draw attention to myself. I have a dark job to do, one that no one can see.

Soon enough, we're all back on the bus, and Winn says, "You know, you've never been to my place."

"I haven't?" I know this very well, since I've daydreamed about it more than I will ever admit to him. "We should remedy that sometime."

"Yes. I think you'd really like it. It has a magical quality to it."

The word makes me bristle, even though he couldn't possibly know. "Magical? Who says I like magic?"

"Who doesn't? Okay, maybe I'm hyping it up a little so you'll want to hang out with me this afternoon. We can do homework, and I can drive you home later."

I pout. How I wish I could say yes.

He tilts his head. "You can't?"

"I'm sorry. Nana wants to go bug catching, since it's warm enough that they're coming out. She likes to see how they mature over the summer." Most people think Nana is a retired entomologist, which explains at least some of the strange behavior.

"Ah, okay. Just tell me when you can hang out, then."

"Of course."

The bus stops at Winn's long dirt driveway before it gets to town, and he waves as he gets off. Gwen takes his spot. "I hate how adorable you guys are. You totally belong together, even if I'm kinda jealous."

"It's disgusting," Kat says from behind.

"Seriously," I say. "I disgust myself."

They both laugh.

I get off at my usual spot, just two houses down from mine, but I don't go home. I head for the only place where visitors stay overnight: Shirley's Bed & Breakfast. Taking a deep breath, I pull the door open and find Mrs. Shirley perched behind a tall desk. I wave at her, making sure to give my best and most innocent smile.

"How can I help you, Josephine?" she asks.

"Has a man named Joseph Johnson been staying here, by any chance?"

Her eyebrows disappear behind her curly hair. "Why, yes! How did you know?"

I shrug. "Has he left?"

She flips open a book, which I assume is filled with visitor information. Her finger stops, and she reads the line for what seems like forever. "Looks like he paid for a couple days at first, but Mr. Shirley wrote down 'indefinite' yesterday."

That makes me tremble. "Do you know where he might be?"

"I believe he's here. Would you like me to get him?"

I nod. "But don't say my name, please. It's something I need to tell him."

She gives me a funny look. "Okay, hon."

As she walks off, I take slow, deep breaths to calm my heart. I grab the pendant around my neck, three circles that look a lot like a Venn diagram, telling myself I'm protected. The shadows won't get me. Nana's amulets are airtight.

My pep talk works until he comes down the stairs, his eyes locked on mine. Everywhere around him is darkness, as if he's standing in a place void of light, and yet he smiles like nothing is wrong. I don't know what to feel, pulled in by the fact that my father is right there and repulsed by the fear of what's inside him. I wait for him to come to me.

"How did you know I was here?" he asks.

It takes me a moment to find my voice. "Only hotel in town."

"Ah." He points to the sitting room. "Can we talk here? You have no idea how much I want to speak with you."

The darkness reaches for me, like black tentacles, and it's all I can do not to scream. They creep forward, frantic with desire to have me. I take a few steps back. "How about we go for a walk?"

He glances at Mrs. Shirley, as if he thinks she's the reason I don't want to discuss things here. "That sounds great."

"Okay." I make for the door probably too quickly, but I want distance between those shadows and me. The amulet can only stand so much. There's no sense letting them at me so soon. There's still a lot to do, and I must save the magic I have stored since I can't go to the house.

The afternoon is perfect, warm yet breezy. The world is in full spring mode, with tulips and daffodils and ranunculus decorating every flower bed. The cherry trees are pink and fluttery, and the willows are bright green with new leaves. The sun shines overhead. And still, it doesn't penetrate the dark.

"It's a lovely day," he says. "I didn't expect it to be so pretty here."

"Iowa always gets crap, but I love it. Where are you from?"

"California."

"Really?"

"Yes. The Bay Area."

He drove halfway across the country to get here? I expected something like Chicago at the most. "Wow."

"It's not as exciting as it sounds."

I don't know what to say. I need to keep him with me, but if Nana is right about the spying spell, our enemy could use any words I speak. Or anything he mentions. It's best to get to the willow tree and get this over with.

This particular willow is a favorite place of mine. I've spent hours there with Gwen and Kat, hanging from the branches or sipping lemonade in the summer heat. It grows right at the edge of town, near a creek we'd put our feet in to cool off. It's huge, like a natural house complete with heavy vine curtains. And unbeknownst to my friends, there is a little bit of magic there. Not like our ivy-covered home, but enough to help in my task.

"Where are we headed?" he asks as we step into the field. The darkness trembles with excitement, as if it thinks I'm about to reveal a great secret. It sickens me, but I force myself forward.

"To the tree. Somewhere private."

"Oh." He looks at his feet. The ground is still muddy from the last rain, and some of it has found its way onto his expensive-looking leather shoes.

Great, my dad's a pansy.

"C'mon." I keep walking, hoping that he will follow despite his ruined footwear. The world under the willow is cool and damp and dark. I breathe in the magic, knowing my stores will be depleted very soon.

My father puts his hands on his hips, taking in the giant tree. "Wow, this is pretty cool."

"Yup." I smile, despite the darkness creeping toward me, and pull the pearl from my pocket.

He squints at it. "What's that?"

I take a few steps toward him, the shadows finally licking at my heels. They hiss as they try to touch me, angry that they can't enter. "This will fix you."

And with that, I grab him by the neck and shove the pearl into his eye.

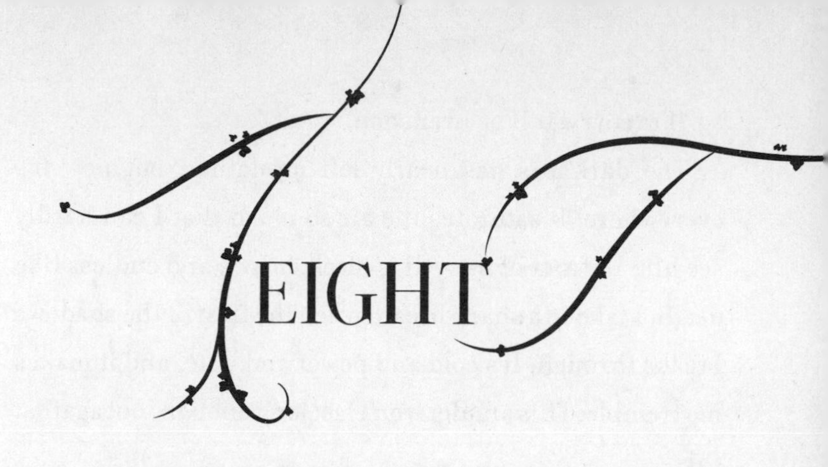

EIGHT

He screams, his hands instinctively going to his face. His fingers grab at mine, strong despite their shaking. The shadows curl around me like a thousand snakes as they try to break through the amulet. Blood trickles from his eyes as he crumples to his knees. I follow so my spell will stay inside him. The mossy dirt is spongy, and soon my jeans are wet. My father pushes against me, trying to throw me off balance.

As awful as I feel, I hold my ground. I have to. Already the darkness is leaving his body, his eyes being purged of the black curse on them. Shadows fight to enter me, to stop me from removing them. If it weren't for Nana's amulet, I'd be consumed by their power already.

"Why?" he moans, and all my insides shrivel up.

"I'm sorry. It'll be over soon."

The darkness has nearly left my father, but now it's everywhere. It saturates the air so much that I can hardly see him in front of me. All is black, heavy, and endless like death. I take in a sharp breath when the first of the shadows breaks through. It's cold and power and hate, and it makes me tremble. This amulet won't last long enough, not against this.

My dad goes limp, but the battle has just begun. I stand, my legs brittle like raven bones, and concentrate on pushing the darkness away from me. It jumps back, but it's strong and persistent. I'm not sure I'll have enough magic to get rid of it all. And worse, I swear it knows me. I don't know what that means but I don't like it. Without a noise, it tells me how badly it wants me.

It wants to consume.

It wants to hear me scream.

It will enjoy every second it tortures me.

No. Scare tactics won't work on me. I'm the one with the power here. Taking deep breaths, I draw on the magic in the tree and force the black away from my body. Slowly, slowly, it retreats. I can see my father on the ground, the soft swinging of the willow branches, the light peeking through the vines. The darkness swirls in front of me, like a storm cloud twisted up on itself.

And then it opens its eyes.

That is *so* not normal.

Limbs begin to form from the cloud, and I stand there, terrified and unsure of what to do. This was not in the plan. We thought my dad had a spying curse, not whatever this thing is. And by the way it looks at me, its hunger depthless, I have a feeling it's . . .

"Get back!" Nana cries from behind me.

I whirl around, relieved to find a door to our house standing there under the tree. Nana rushes forward, a dagger in hand. Not your normal dagger, of course, but one made from the jaw of a lion and dipped in white rose oil.

The darkness laughs—at least that's what I think the crackling sound is. Now it looks human, but not quite. It's more like the shadow of a person, if a shadow could stand in front of you and feel as heavy as iron. It lunges for Nana, but she ducks and shoves the dagger right into its belly.

Poof.

Not a scream or anything. It just *poof*ed, as if it wasn't a threat at all. I let out a breath, feeling lighter now that it's gone. Nana puts a hand to one knee, panting and trembling from the loss of magic. I feel the weakness in my bones, too, but she must have used much more magic than I did, casting whatever spell that was.

I go back to my dad. He looks awful, his eyes bloody and his clothing covered in dirt. I kneel next to him and put my hand on his cheek. It's warm and prickly and not at all dark anymore. "You're safe."

Nana clears her throat. "Josephine. We have another problem."

"Wha—?" I look up to find exactly what she means.

Kat.

She stands by the willow's trunk, frozen like a statue. I have no idea when she got there, but it must have been while everything was dark because I swear no one was around. I've been so careful not to give any clue about my heritage, and now she's seen enough to give her nightmares for years.

I take a shaky step forward. "Kat . . ."

"What the hell?" She shakes her head. "What the *hell*, Jo?"

I glance at Nana, unsure of what to do. Can I explain? Are we going to be concocting a mind-erase spell this evening? "I . . ."

Kat points to my dad. "What did you do to him? Did you kill him? Are you gonna kill me now?"

"No! It's not what you think," I say, though it's probably mostly what she thinks. "I'm not a murderer. He's fine—better than he was with that thing inside him."

Nana clears her throat. "Calm down, child."

Kat stares at her. "Calm down? You're the witch who lives under the bridge, aren't you? I thought that was a joke!"

"Your choices are simple." Nana waves the dagger at her.

"Come with us willingly, or come by force."

I didn't think it was possible, but Kat's eyes get wider. "Those are my only choices?"

"I suppose I could remove your vocal cords, if you'd like a third," Nana says.

Kat's hand goes to her throat. "Option one, please."

"Good." Nana pulls open the door. "Get your father, Josephine."

"Father?" Kat says it like it never crossed her mind that I had one, and then Nana shoves her inside.

"Be right there." I put my hands on my hips, trying to process what happened. This didn't go even remotely according to plan, but at least that evil spell is gone. Never mind the creepy shadow and one of my best friends walking in on an exorcism. I'll take one problem at a time, and right now that would be figuring out how best to carry my dad into the house when I'm barely strong enough to stand after using all that magic.

I end up grabbing him under the arms and dragging him. Once he's inside, I shut the door and breathe in the magic. When I have enough to feel better, I perform the spell to make the portal to our house disappear from under the willow. Then I run to the apothecary, where Nana has Kat in the chair. She looks so small there, like a child waiting to be scolded.

"Josephine," Nana says as I search for eagle feathers.

There's no way I can get him upstairs on my own, so a floating spell it is. "Would you consider this girl trustworthy?"

The question startles me. I figured Nana had only one plan—a mind erase. "Um, yeah. You know Kat. We've been best friends since we were kids. Of course I trust her."

"With your life?"

My eyes go to Kat, who's looking right back at me. I have no clue what's going on, but the answer comes easily. "Yes."

Nana nods. "After you're done tending to Joseph, come back down. Oh, and feel free to get him up to speed when he wakes up."

"Sure . . ." It's weird that she's okay with telling him, but I decide not to question it. Maybe she wants to pacify him until we decide what to do with him.

I float my father up to the spare bedroom next to my mother's old room. I almost put him in hers, but it seems like too much. I have a hard time walking by the door, let alone going inside. It's still the same as it was when she died: the bed unmade, her coat on the desk chair, a stack of yellowed papers waiting for words. One of the dresser drawers is ajar, a nightgown sticking out. We can't bring ourselves to clean it, as if it'll erase the last piece of her we have.

Once I get him out of the muddiest stuff and in bed, I wipe the blood from his eyes. Then I spend far too much time staring at him. I have his ears and his stubby fingernails. He snores lightly, like I always imagined dads doing.

He has to stay.

My stomach sinks when I realize he could have another family. I grab his left hand. No wedding band. Not that it means much—he could be divorced or he could have a girlfriend. I could have half siblings . . . a whole family that has no idea I exist, that will never know I exist. Shaking myself out of it, I stand. He'll be asleep for a while, and Nana and Kat are waiting for me. When I get back to the apothecary, I sit next to Kat and wait for Nana to explain.

"Your friend is . . . worthy," Nana says.

"Okay?" I glance at Kat, who doesn't seem as scared as she was at first. In fact, there's a hint of excitement in her eyes. "And what does worthy mean?"

"It could mean many things, my child." She pulls out a heavy spell book, and that alone sets me on alert. Nana never has to use the book, which means whatever spell she has in mind is not something we do every day. Hell, every decade. "But for now, it means she's allowed to keep her memories, so long as she goes through a binding spell."

My eyes go wide. "Binding?"

"It's rather simple. If she reveals our secret, she dies."

"Nana, that's way too harsh."

Kat shakes her head. "I'd never tell, so it's not a big deal. Better than forgetting this. I can't believe I never suspected anything. It's so obvious now."

I sigh. "Kat, this will hurt. You get that, right? Magic

isn't fluffy—there will be a sacrifice much worse than if you forgot."

"I know," she says. "A fingernail."

I shudder at the thought. "Why would you do that just to know?"

"Jo." Her look is flat. "You've always been the funny one. Gwen's always been the fun one. And I'm the peanut gallery."

"No! You're the voice of reason! Gwen and I would tear each other apart without you."

She rolls her eyes. "Whatever. I want to be a part of this. Haven't you ever wanted someone to talk to? How did you go so many years without this secret killing you?"

My throat tightens. "I . . . I had Nana to talk to."

"Seems lonely to me."

This ache forms in my heart, in the place my mother left gaping and bleeding. Loneliness is part of my life. It always will be in one way or another. And yet I can't help but love Kat for thinking of me, for wanting to take care of me.

"I want to do this," she says firmly. "You can't change my mind."

I nod, too sad to do anything else.

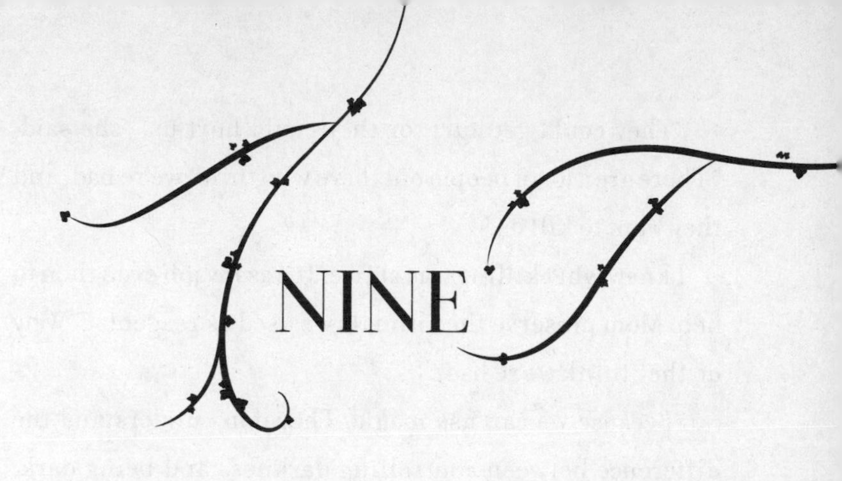

NINE

Kat and I sit at the kitchen table with heaping bowls of ice cream. It seems like an ice-cream kind of moment, something sweet to take her mind off the impending agony. That, and a good thing to fill awkward silences with, because all I really want to say is, "Are you flipping crazy? You know my grandma's in there preparing to rip out your fingernail, right?"

But she won't listen. She's definitely the most stubborn of our group—maybe the most stubborn person I know, save Nana.

"So, your dad's alive," she says between bites.

"Yup." Even if Kat's allowed to know about it, I can't seem to get my tongue moving. I still remember when Mom told me about secrets, about what could happen if my friends found out what I could do.

"They could get hurt, or they could hurt us," she said. "There are a lot of people out there who think we're bad, and they want to kill us."

I knew what killing was at five. It was my job even then to help Mom preserve the animals we used as reagents. "Why do they think we're bad?"

"Because we can use magic. They don't understand the difference between controlling darkness and being dark. We Hemlocks will never be dark, Jojo, never." She kissed my cheeks. "But still, you can't tell a soul."

Kat's spoon clinks against her bowl. "I always thought he died, since you never talked about him, you know? And with what happened to your mom . . . it didn't feel right to ask."

"I found out he was alive on Friday. Haven't technically met him yet."

She pushes her bangs out of her eyes. "Seriously?"

"Yeah, I couldn't talk to him—not with that thing in him."

"What was it?"

"Not sure." I gulp, the shadow's eyes coming back. How I wish my gut would stop nagging me about it. "It was supposed to be a spying curse, but I think it was more. Or purging it triggered something else. We don't know all the details, only that it might have to do with my mom's murder."

Kat's spoon stops moving, and she looks me in the eye. "She was murdered?"

I nod.

"And now whoever did it is after you?"

"Probably." I can't say yes, even though I know how much that darkness wanted me.

She leans back. "That's so evil, using your dad. How can you pretend you're okay through all this? I'd be a total mess."

I shrug. I'd never really thought much about it. The dark, lonely nights were part of my witch life, and it didn't occur to me that I could bring the sadness over to my small corner of normal. Or maybe I didn't want to. Hanging out with Gwen and Kat has always been a break from all the hard stuff. Why waste it moping?

A splash of cold hits my face, and I look up from my bowl. "You did not just throw ice cream at me."

"Talk! You're acting like I'm a stranger. It's pissing me off."

"Sorry." I wipe the ice cream off. "It's weird, okay? Nana has never done this. Never. It's always secret, secret, secret. I can't help feeling like something is wrong. I don't get why she'd let you know."

Kat purses her lips. "When I said I didn't want my memory erased, she told me that I'd always be in danger of dying or being cursed or revealing your secret. I said I could handle it, and then you came in. After that, she said you needed me, and she started telling me about how magic works."

I nearly choke. "She . . . what?"

"Is that weird?"

"Uh, yeah. Telling an outsider about magic is not done. Everything about this is strange. Not even my father knew Mom was a witch." I rub my temples, since it feels like a hundred alarms are going off in my head. Nana is planning something so far outside normal witchcraft that I can't guess.

"Sorry, I didn't know."

I shake my head. "Don't be. I should be happy about this. No, I am! I'm just worried about the *why*."

Because there's always a payment, and something as good as having one of my best friends know about me must come at a heavy price. I don't like that Kat's life will hang on a flimsy thing like keeping our secret.

The ceiling lets out a ghastly moan, and my heart leaps so high it feels like it might burst out of my rib cage. "He's awake."

"I'm assuming you want to go alone," Kat says.

I wince. "I probably should, though I'm kind of freaking out here."

She smiles as she walks to the living room. "You'll be fine. I'll read a book or something."

I head for the stairs, but I can't take a breath big enough to calm down. My dad's in there, and this time I'll get to say everything I've wanted to since I realized who he was. The door creaks in warning of my presence, and he shoots up.

"How are you feeling?" I ask.

"I can't see." His eyes dart back and forth, straining hard against the blindness.

I take a few steps forward, and he tenses like he's preparing for an attack. "It'll go away, but I'm not sure how long it'll take. That's . . . the payment for removing the curse."

His brow furrows. "Curse?"

"Yeah. Someone put a spying curse on you, because Carmina? She was a witch, and I'm a witch, too, being her daughter and all. You probably already guessed that. The daughter part. Not the witch thing; you had no idea about that. I mean, we're really not that—"

He holds his hand up. "Whoa, slow down. So you're Carmina's daughter? How old are you . . . ?"

He stalls, clearly waiting for me to say my name. A lump forms in my throat, because the moment I say it he'll know, and maybe he'll freak out and run away. I want so badly for him to want me, even if I shouldn't. "It's Jo, Josephine, and I'm seventeen. Just barely, like a week ago."

His face goes slack. "You're my . . . my . . . ?"

"Daughter? Yeah. If it makes you feel better, I didn't know who you were until you showed up either."

He shakes his head. "Is that why she left? Did she think I'd be upset?"

"No, not at all. She didn't want to leave you. Our kind . . . we don't stay with our, uh, partners. It's not safe for them, which you can see. Okay, you can't see, but that's kind of the point, right? The only reason any of this horrible stuff happened to you is because you knew her."

"Loved her." He puts his hand on his chest. "I was going to ask her to marry me, and then she just . . . disappeared. The police couldn't find anything. All her records and pictures and possessions vanished. It was as if she never existed. My whole life I've wondered what happened to her, hoped to God that she was happy and safe, and she's . . ."

His tears make my eyes water. "I miss her, too. Every day."

He motions for me to come over, and I tentatively sit on the bed. Slowly, he holds his hand out. "May I . . . ?" I take it, surprised at how easy it is. For a second, it feels like we're family. If Mom weren't a witch, we would have been. He puts his other hand over mine. "I wish I'd known about you sooner."

"Really? Even though I blinded you?"

It's the first time I see his smile, and it's mine. It's strange to see it on him. I'd never really noticed the non-Hemlock aspects of myself, or at least I never thought about the fact that they belonged to someone else. "Sounds like it was necessary. I had a curse?"

"Yeah, about that . . ."

The door creaks open before I find the words, and Nana comes in like nothing is wrong. "Ah, Joseph, you're up. Nice to meet you."

His eyebrow arches. "Who are you?"

"Dorothea Hemlock, your dear Carmina's mother."

"Oh, I see. So Josephine lives with you, then."

"Yes, indeed." She claps her hands together. "Speaking of, I have to steal Jo from you for a little, and I wanted to ask if you needed anything. Some water? Pudding?"

I put my face in my hand, restraining a groan.

"Water would be great,"

She shakes her head. "Get him some chocolate pudding, too, dear. Chocolate fixes everything."

"Even blindness?" he asks.

Nana lets out a cackle. "I see why Carmina loved you so much. Make sure to get plenty of rest. Your eyes will need it."

After getting some food and water for my dad, I head to the apothecary, where Kat sits in front of a small, round table. On the table rests a pair of pliers, neatly placed in the center of a white doily.

TEN

I've seen a man give up his ear for enough luck to save his family from foreclosure. I've seen a child sacrifice his sense of taste for three months to keep his dog from going to the pound. And I've seen a woman literally give up her right arm so her baby would live. But it's not the same when I know the person. I'm not sure I can watch Kat go through pain. My stomach turns, and all Nana has done is hand her a bag of ice to get her finger as numb as possible before . . .

I'm so going to lose it.

"Why do we have to do this again?" I ask. "I trust Kat. I don't need a binding spell to know she won't tell."

"It's as much for her protection as it is for ours. Once she is bound, you will know if she's in danger, and she'll know if you are." Nana drapes three necklaces over Kat's head.

"These are protection charms to dull the pain, speed healing, and prevent infection. Do not take them off until your nail has grown back."

"Okay." Kat puts a shaky hand to them. "Thank you."

Nana goes back to her desk, reading from the book. "Now, Josephine, you sit across from Katherine. We will use your skin for our part of the deal."

I raise an eyebrow. "Excuse me?"

She lets out a frustrated sigh. "This is a contract. We promise to protect her, and in return she promises to protect us as well. A nail to symbolize shielding, and a piece of flesh to represent the bond of protection. A fair trade."

"Of course, should have known," I say. "Where am I cutting and how much?"

Kat gulps. "This is so morbid."

"This is magic. It's not pretty." Nana turns to me, setting down a small pair of gold scissors. "A dime-size piece should do, from wherever you'd like."

"From wherever I'd like? You say it as if I'm excited to mutilate myself." I look over my skin, trying to decide where to cut. Avoiding joints would be smart. It should probably be a place easily covered by clothes, so as not to draw attention. But then again, a good scar is always a conversation starter.

Nana rolls her eyes. "It's hardly a scratch."

"Yeah, yeah. Let's get this over with."

She scoots the pliers toward Kat and puts a copper bowl between us. "The offerings go in when I say. Katherine, you will be expected to remove the nail yourself."

She nods, grabbing the pliers.

My mouth goes dry. As lovely as my part is in the spell, I want to trade. I don't want her to do this. I want to knock her out and erase her memory and let her go along her merry way.

"Jo."

I look up at Kat, who's trying to smile. "Remember that time Colby Turner was ragging on me?"

"Yeah." It was in third grade, during the worst of my awkward period. For some reason, my baby teeth stuck around forever, and I'd just lost my first front tooth. So I had this awful poofy hair, a face full of freckles, and a hill-billy gap. Most everyone called me Billy Jo.

Kat was a skeleton back then. Still is. The girl can take down a large pizza on her own, and nobody knows where it goes. Colby kept poking her where her spine stuck out when she hunched over. I don't remember what I said to him, but I do remember it was the first time I cursed someone on my own.

I gave up seeing color for a week; he had the runs for a week.

"I learned something that day," Kat says. "Let's face it: Everyone made fun of you, and you know what? I never thought to stand up for you. I don't think Gwen did either. We consoled you after, but we let it happen. And then you . . ." She looks down, seeming ashamed. "You stood up for me. You taught me how friends were supposed to act. So stop freaking out and let me be there for you, too."

I sigh. "Fine."

Nana tousles Kat's short, dark hair. "You darling girl. How come you never bring your friends over, Josephine? They're wonderful."

"Uh, the witch thing?"

"Oh, right." She goes back to her spell book, now propped on a stand. "Ash of the shepherd dog and golden eagle's tears."

It's a very short reagent list, but eagle tears aren't easy to get ahold of. Nana goes to the special cabinet behind her desk—the one with the most valuable and rare items. Then she grabs a bottle of ash from the shelves. She pours a little mound of the ash in the copper bowl, then drips four tears on top. As she holds her hand over the mixture, it liquefies into a silvery pool.

"The flesh to be protected," she whispers.

Before I think too much, I'm cutting at my forearm. It definitely doesn't feel good, but I try not to be a baby about it because it's much easier than Kat's part. Once I have the chunk, I place it in the bowl and it foams. Grabbing a bandage, I wait for the next part in a fit of nausea.

"The shield to protect." Nana eyes Kat. "Do it quickly. Hesitation will only make it hurt more."

Kat sucks in a breath, her tiny frame stretched as tall as it can go. She removes the ice from her left pinkie finger and clamps the pliers down. She closes her eyes. Her muscles flex.

That's when I look away.

She screams once, and it's cut short by a gasp of agony. Regardless of being cold and numb, it probably still hurt like hell. I look back just in time to see her place the nail in the bowl. Her finger gushes blood, and her hands tremble as she grasps the bandages. Her strained breathing fills the silence as we watch the liquid turn gold.

Nana holds up the bowl. "Drink, and become bound."

I take the bowl and drink. "Huh, tastes like honeysuckle."

"Really?" Kat says.

"Yeah. Go figure."

She takes the bowl from me and sips. "Not bad."

We freeze at the same time, so I figure she feels what I'm feeling. A warm sensation, like sunbathed grass, tickles at my legs. It fills in every piece of me, bit by bit, and by the time it gets to my head I'm keenly aware of Kat's well-being. Her finger kills, but other than that she's . . . happy. Definitely not in any danger.

She gasps. "Wow, it's like ultra-sensitive intuition."

"Yes." Nana shuts the book. "Almost as strong as blood."

I watch her, and all my instincts scream that she's hiding something. Honestly, I don't want to ask. Not now. There's been enough trauma today. Which means, of course . . .

"Time for some pudding!"

ELEVEN

My father sleeps almost all of the next few days, and we let him, though there is so much we need ask. He's so weak, and I feel bad pushing him more than necessary. Nana says it's okay, since our hunters can't see us anymore.

But this evening, Kat and I help my dad downstairs, and we spend all of dinner talking about magic. They have lots of silly questions like "Why don't you teleport everywhere?" or "Can't you conjure your food?" Most of which can be answered in one way: sometimes the payment isn't worth it. If I teleported everywhere, I'd be freaking bald. We use magic when the benefit outweighs the payment, when it's necessary, and, of course, when others pay us to help them out at their own risk.

"So all of Willow's End has a magical barrier over it?" Kat

seems to be having a hard time wrapping her mind around it. "How? What does it do?"

"It warns us if there are any threats to us," I say as I clear plates from the table. "If someone who intends to harm us tries to get in, it blocks them. The head of house is tied to the spell, so she can sense any attempts to breech it."

Nana nods. "Our home works much the same way, but the spells are even stronger. No one can step foot on our land without our permission, if they can find it in the first place. Only the truly desperate can be led here without effort, which is probably why Joseph didn't have any trouble finding the address."

"I was pretty desperate," he admits.

After we clean up, Nana pulls out her best pudding for Joseph—pistachio, butterscotch, chocolate peanut butter, devil's food. She orders it through the mail, and every month we get a big box of exotic flavors.

"Isn't that one divine?" Nana sits next to him, seeming way too happy that he's here.

He nods. "I had no idea pudding could be more than a second-rate dessert."

She slaps his arm. "Bite your tongue, young man."

"This is so strange." He searches for his water glass, and I push it into his hand. "Thanks. It's frightening how much of Carmina I can hear in your voices. I'd always thought she didn't get along with her family, since she refused to introduce me. Never would have guessed it was against the rules."

"Not against the rules, necessarily," Nana says. "You could say it is . . . distasteful. Most of us consider it selfish to risk the lives of those we love. Carmina even considered erasing your memories to protect you, but there were simply too many."

"No offense, but that's a load of crap." He takes a long drink while we stare at him. I'm not sure if I'm offended. At times I totally agree. "If you want to protect something, you keep it close. You don't push it away and hope nothing will happen. I could have been here for her, maybe not as protection, but as support. And it seems like this house is impenetrable, if whatever was in me can't enter."

"It's probably good you can't see Nana's face right now," I say. She looks positively murderous. I didn't even make the comment, and I'm cowering.

Nana finishes off her pudding, letting the silence work its dark power.

My phone decides this is the perfect opportunity to ring. I check the window and see it's a text from Winn.

We really need to have an actual date.

I smile.

I'm game. Friday?

"Who's that?" my dad asks, since Nana is still fuming.

"Umm . . ." So it turns out no matter how much you know

your dad, it's hard to announce that you are in a relationship.

Definitely, Winn replies.

"It was probably Winn, the boy she's dating," Kat says for me.

His eyes widen. "Oh."

"Back to the matter at hand." Nana puts her fingers together, as if she's plotting. "There was a time I would have made you blind for good if you said such things."

My jaw drops. "But—"

She holds up her hand to silence me. "Joseph, now that we've made you welcome and you've healed some, we must discuss the evil that sent you here. I need to ask why you decided after all this time to come here. Every detail you can recall could be important."

He sighs. "I wish I had more information. A letter was sent to my office—that's it. There was no return address, and the handwriting looked like it was done with an old ink pen. Inside, there was a picture of Carmina. On the back there was just 'Willow's End, Iowa.' No exact address. But it was enough for me."

"They knew we were here?" I say, shocked. *How did they find our town?*

"Do you still have the letter?" Nana and I ask at the same time.

"It's with my stuff at the bed-and-breakfast."

Nana looks at me. "Fetch his things after school tomorrow, but don't touch the letter."

"You mean . . . he's staying with us?"

"Can't have him going out there and getting cursed again." She pulls herself up with her cane. "I'm beginning to think some traditions would be better left forgotten, and it seems he wants to stay anyway."

He smiles. "I do."

"Good night, then." *Click* goes the cane, then a long creak, over and over, as she ascends the stairs.

"I better get home, too. My mom has texted me twice. Let me know if you need anything." Kat gives me a hug and leaves, her footsteps echoing down the hall.

"At least you can always hear people coming in this place," my dad says.

I let out a little laugh. "But . . . can you stay? I mean, you have a job and a life and, well, don't you have a family or friends? You don't have to stay out of obligation, really. We protected you for almost two decades, and we can again."

He shrugs. "I can work things out. It might not be easy, but the answers I've always wanted are here. As long as I have an internet connection, I'm sure I can talk my company into letting me telecommute for a while. I do half my job on conference calls anyway."

I'm not sure if that means he's in a relationship or not, but I decide I'd rather not know for now. "We don't have internet."

"I can fix that."

I smile. "If you can get Nana to install internet and a TV, I will love you forever."

He snorts. "Your love comes cheap."

"You think convincing her will be easy? How little you know." I'm surprised it feels this natural to talk to him, like there's a connection between us already.

He sips at his water. "I don't know. I think she likes me."

I shake my head, refusing to admit it's true. Nana is so easily charmed by men. It's a wonder she didn't have more daughters from the way she talks sometimes.

My phone beeps again.

I was really hoping you'd call me today.

"I'd better do homework," I say to my dad as I type.

Will in like 10 min.

"Do you need anything?"

"I'm figuring out how to get around." He smiles. "The house will probably cave in if I fall, so you'll be tipped off."

"True."

As I head upstairs, I can hardly wait to talk to Winn. But as I pass Nana's door, she calls for me. I open it as softly as I can. She's at her writing desk, a quill in hand. The quill isn't her sticking to some anti-technology thing. Though she's admittedly old school, that's how we speak with other witches. "Are you writing the Crafts?"

She nods.

"Why?"

"A few inquiries about the strange shadow we saw. I can't get it off my mind."

Here we go. Out comes the serious stuff. I shut the door. "Me either. Have you ever seen something like that?"

"No. It was very dark magic. Perverted. Insane. Whoever created it has to be entirely lost to the blackness, far more than we can comprehend." She keeps scribbling as she talks, and I picture the Craft sisters watching as her scrawl appears on their enchanted paper. "I don't want to jump to conclusions, Josephine, but I think you sensed what it might be."

I suck in a deep breath, the reality of what she's saying hitting harder than ever. If she felt it, too, then I can't pretend it away anymore. "The Curse?"

She nods. "We barely escaped the trap, my dear. It almost had you."

"I know." It comes out in a whisper, the image of that shadow and its desire to consume me all too real even now. This is why witches run. But it's too late for that option. They already know where we live, might even have us surrounded.

"I will never let it take you. I will die protecting you if I have to."

The reality of our situation hits again, and I have to force myself not to shake. "Is that why you let Kat and my father in? You think their comfort can replace you?"

Her pen stops for the slightest moment, and then she keeps going. "We need to read the histories for any clues. We've been attacked many times, and our bloodline will survive this as well."

My throat tightens when I realize what she's *not* saying. Her entire purpose is making sure I live, and that's how it has to be. "Of course *we'll* survive."

She looks up at me, her smile sad yet confident. "That's my girl."

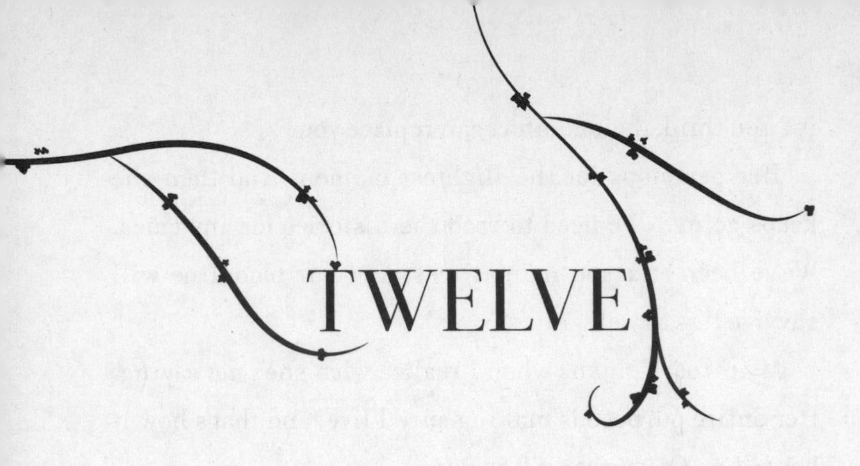

TWELVE

There are just over two weeks of school left, and they feel utterly useless. At lunch, everyone flees campus as if they can't stand looking at the cafeteria one more second. Winn and I sit under a tree with our friends, opening our recently bought fast food. The chains here in Denison are a treasure to those of us who live in towns too small to have them.

"Let's skip the rest of school," Gwen says as she stretches out next to Adam. "It's so nice today."

She has a point. The weather is perfect: warm and not too humid. Give it a month, and Iowa will turn into a steamer. The corn seems to love it. My hair? Not so much.

"We do have finals," Kat says.

"I kind of want to pass my classes, what with that whole college thing in a year." Billy runs his fingers through his dark hair, and it sticks up all over. He totally pulls off the cool-guy indifference thing. He's always seemed like such a poseur, but at a closer look he's more like a well-dressed intellectual.

"Psh." Adam spits French fry as he talks. "It's review all week until Friday. Not like we're missing anything. Study later."

"Or we could let our teachers tell us all the crap on the test, and have the rest of the day to chill without studying," Winn says.

I bump his shoulder. "I like your thinking."

"Good." He grabs me around the waist, which surprises me, but I don't mind at all. "Because we're hanging out today, even if I have to go bug catching with you and your grandma."

I laugh, at least until we get pummeled with greasy food wrappers. "Hey!"

"I warned you about the PDA," Kat says. "A few days and you've already forgotten."

I point at her. "You specifically said making out. We're nowhere near that."

"If only," Winn says, and I shake my head.

"Still." Gwen sips her Coke. "It's a slippery slope."

I roll my eyes. "Fine, but we're so allowed this. It's not even a full-on hug."

"I agree." Winn squeezes my waist, and it makes me laugh.

Kat sighs. "Just don't push it."

My eyes meet hers, and that intuition thing kicks in. She only said that because she knows how happy I am; otherwise she would have thrown more stuff at us. "I swear we won't."

Gwen eyes us, then zones in on Kat. "You're getting soft, girl."

Kat ignores her. "Billy, would you mind reading through my English paper? I really need a good grade, and you're always getting the highest score."

He nods. "Sure, on the bus?"

"Perfect."

"Subtle, Katie." Gwen moves so her legs are in the sun. The boys probably don't get it, but Kat and I know she's pissed. I can guess why—she thinks she's missing out on something. Her jealousy over Kat's healing necklaces has been pretty obvious, and it makes me feel awful. She hates not being in the loop, which might become a serious problem now that Kat is.

"Good idea." Adam scoots beside her, pulling up his pant legs to reveal some seriously pasty skin. "Gotta get ready for bathing-suit season."

Gwen tries not to smile, but she can't resist humor. Adam's pretty funny. Not as cute as Winn, but not bad, with his wavy brown hair and strong frame. If he's game, my bet is that we'll be punishing them for making out in public before Winn and I do.

After school, I get off the bus with Winn, and we walk hand in hand down the long dirt drive to his family's big house. I've driven by here all my life, but I've never actually been to his farm. The yard is beautiful, filled with old trees that shade our way. The smell of grass floats in the air, and wildflowers dance in the soft breeze. Underneath all that, there's the faintest hint of magic, like at the willow tree.

"So what are we doing today?" he asks.

I already planned this, and yet it's still hard to say. "Funny story, actually."

He raises an eyebrow. "Yeah?"

"Remember that guy who was kind of stalking me?"

His hand tightens around mine. "Is he giving you more trouble?"

"Not exactly. Turns out he's . . . my dad."

Winn stops and stares at me, as if he's waiting for the joke. I'm not sure what else to say. Nana might not be happy I told him at all, but I can't lie to him about everything. And if my dad is staying here, people will find out at least that much. "For real?"

I nod. "My mom never told him she was pregnant, but I guess he recently went looking for her and found out about me."

"Wow." He shakes his head, as if pushing away the shock. "And you're okay with this? I mean, that's pretty crazy for him to just show up."

"He's . . . really nice. He loved my mom a lot. She was the one who left, so it's not like I can blame him for not being there. The second he found out, he came looking, which has to mean he's a decent guy."

"So you're happy?"

I smile. "Yeah. I think so."

"Good." He pulls me into him, which takes my breath away. I've been hugged plenty of times, but this isn't the same. I can't explain except for holy-crow-this-feels-so-good. Putting my hands on his back, I sink into him more. He lets out a small laugh as he says, "Of course, this isn't so great for me, is it? I kind of liked that I never had to meet your father."

"Trust me, Nana is way scarier than him."

"I doubt it." He pulls back a little and looks at me. "So what does that have to do with what we're doing?"

"I've been commanded to get his things from the Shirleys. He's a little sick, and Nana has decided he shouldn't overexert himself." I wince, suddenly feeling bad for asking Winn to run my errands. "I figured it would be easier if I had your truck."

He smiles his gorgeous smile. "I see how it is. I'm your personal chauffeur."

"Nuh-uh." I lean my head on his chest again. "You also make a nice pillow."

"Are you saying I'm fat?"

"Yes."

Laughing, he takes my hand and we head for his truck.

"Mr. Johnson is your father?" Mrs. Shirley exclaims when I explain why I'm there. "Well, I'll be. Not that I don't believe you, honey, but I have to call him before I let you in. Can't have guests thinking I'd allow a stranger in their rooms."

"Of course." I point to the bright pink floral couch in the sitting room. "We'll be over there."

She smiles too sweetly at our clasped hands. "I'll be right with you."

"That's gonna get old fast," Winn says when we're out of earshot.

"No kidding. I feel like I have something on my face." That's the thing with small towns. The littlest pieces of information are a big deal. Between dating the cutest guy around and my mystery father showing up, everyone will be talking about me for weeks.

"Hey, at least they have good reading material." Winn grabs an agriculture magazine. "Oh, a whole feature on organic farming."

I smile. Most of the teens around here are dying to get out and see the world, but Winn is not that kind of guy. He loves the family farm, this town. I never expected to find that attractive, but I do. Maybe because that's how witches are, forever tied to the land that gives us sustenance.

"You're cute when you go all farm boy," I say.

He laughs.

"Jo!" Mrs. Shirley calls. "You're cleared."

I hop up and grab the key from her. "Thank you."

We climb the old stairs, which are a lot like mine but without the creaking. The walls are papered with an atrocious pink polka dot, and all the paintings are gaudy floral monstrosities. It's like a five-year-old princess was put in charge of decorating the whole place.

I stop at the door with a framed, pink three on it and turn the key. When I open it, I really, really wish I hadn't brought Winn, because there's magic in here. Bad magic.

THIRTEEN

There are two things I see as I step into the room. One, enough floral to suffocate a tenderhearted grandmother. Two, black smoke, curling and twisting in small plumes over a computer bag. It stops for a moment, as if it recognizes my presence, and I'm sure that's where the letter is. Obviously, it still holds some of the spell it put on my father.

"Sure packs a lot for a guy," Winn says as he goes to the biggest suitcase.

I nod, my attention locked on the blackness that seems to be looking right back at me. "He dresses nicely. I haven't asked, but I think he's rich."

"Score." Winn goes to the bed, where a smaller bag is laid out. The darkness bristles when he gets closer, this time uncoiling its tendrils toward Winn—at which point I practically lose it. I have to get him out and purge that spell; otherwise Winn will have to get a pearl to the eye, too. That would be fun to explain.

"Winn." I put my hand on his back as the darkness inches its way over the bedspread. "How about you take those two down? I'll take the computer and do a quick sweep to make sure we didn't miss anything."

He turns around, his arm slipping around my waist. "The way you say my name . . . it kind of drives me crazy."

"Winn," I say without thinking, and he pulls me closer. The shadows reach out for his jeans, so I spin him around, attempting to remain flirty. "Seriously, we need to get out of here. I will not have this tacky room be the location of any significant moment with you."

He laughs. "Okay, fine. Good to know location is important."

"Very important." I pick up the smaller suitcase on the bed, the black mist hissing at me. "Here."

"Thanks." He grabs the big bag, too, hefting it instead of using the rollers. "See you downstairs."

"Yup."

Once he's out of sight, I shut the door and face the spell. All I can hope is that it isn't as potent without a host, because I'm not prepared this time. I need to sacrifice something, and it'll have to be big. Sight is out of the question—I need that. Hearing, too. Touch would be obnoxious. It's so hard to walk when you can't feel anything. Taste and smell aren't enough unless I want to give up half a year.

There's only one doable option.

I run to the bathroom, relieved to find an empty glass. Filling it with water, I squirm as the darkness slithers over the rug. It's pissed. Not that hot, murderous passion that came out of my dad, but not fluffy bunnies by any measure. It wants to do as much damage as it can.

I pour water into my mouth until my cheeks bulge. Using every ounce of magic I have in my body, I push my voice up my throat. It tastes cinnamon sweet, like apple pie, as I let the magic do its work. My hand goes to the counter for support. Being totally empty of magic feels awful—especially without the willow for backup like last time—but I need it all. The spell must be gone before I touch that bag.

When the water is so sweet I can hardly take it, I let myself crumple to the floor. The darkness seems to smile at my weakness. It crosses the threshold to the bathroom. One tile. Two. When it hits the pink rug, I spit out the water. The spell squeals in pain, disintegrating like a lit fuse until it ends up right back at the computer bag.

I wait for a second, silently panting and praying it worked. Losing my voice for nothing would suck. The bag seems clear, so I take a few wary steps into the bedroom. I toss a pillow at it. No reaction. It's gone. It has to be.

That doesn't make it easy to touch. I keep imagining a

black shadow jumping out the moment I take the handle. Counting to three, I force myself to do it. My heart races even though nothing happens, and I rush down the stairs as fast as my weakened state will allow.

Winn frowns when he sees me. "Is everything okay?"

I shake my head, patting my throat.

"Oh. You should have said something earlier if you were feeling sick." He takes my arm to support me, which has me wondering how awful I look. "Maybe you caught what your dad has."

I nod.

"Better get you home."

As we drive, I already hate that I can't talk. What a punishment. Even if it's only a few days, it feels like torture. Winn helps me up to the door, and Nana opens it after one knock. No doubt she knows what happened. "Tsk. I told her she seemed flushed this morning," she says. "On the couch there, Winn."

"You know my name." He sits me down, and I breathe deeply to get the magic into my body.

"Josephine and I are very close. I've known for a while how fond she is of you."

I glare at her, wishing I could do more. This is not the time to be voiceless.

He smiles. "Really?"

"Yes, since she was—" I throw a pillow at her. She looks

positively indignant, but thankfully she stops. "Anyway, if you could get the luggage, Winn, we'd appreciate it."

"Of course."

When he's out the door, Nana sits on the coffee table. "That was some brilliant thinking, my dear. It would have been disastrous to let that letter be for one more hour. I hate to think about the Shirleys walking in on it."

I give her a weak smile.

She pats my hand. "Soak it up. Once you're full you won't feel so awful."

Being home does help. The magic in the walls is rejuvenating, like floating in a warm bubble bath. I don't know how abstainers can go without refilling, but I suppose that's because I've never had the option. Some witch families are big enough that members can choose to lead human lives. Even if I had that luxury, I can't imagine never using what was inside me.

Winn tromps back in, the three bags in hand. "Where should I put these?"

"Second-floor hall would be perfect," Nana says.

With all that luggage, it sounds like the staircase will buckle from the weight. I think Winn curses, but it's hard to hear over the house's protests. Then he reappears. "I'm pretty sure I almost died."

Nana cackles. "I have some things to attend to, but I trust you'll be responsible."

"Yes, ma'am." Winn kneels by the couch, taking my hand. It's ridiculous how cute he is, looking all worried for me. There's something in his eyes that changes their color from stormy to cloudy. "Feeling better?"

I move my hand, indicating so-so.

He smirks. "I guess that means no date tomorrow, doesn't it?"

I frown and mouth, "Sorry."

"Don't be. We'll just do it next week." He pushes back one of my curls, and my skin tingles. "I know we seem to have horrible luck, but I always have the best time when I'm with you."

Eye roll.

"I'm serious." He purses his lips, hesitating. "And you make the dullest stuff entertaining. I probably would have torn out all my hair in art if it weren't for you."

A new rush of excitement washes over me for where we could be headed.

He squeezes my hand. "I should let you rest."

I shake my head, not wanting him to go. I've barely had a chance to be with him as it is, and now yet another day has been cut short by magic.

"That's very considerate of you, Winn," Nana says, having just entered the living room again. From the tone of her voice, I know she has something important to tell me.

FOURTEEN

After Winn leaves, I hop up, trying to ask her what's wrong, though nothing comes out. She raises a bushy eyebrow at me. "I can't read lips, dear, but come. You must see this."

In the apothecary, a picture of my mom—which I assume was in the corrupted letter—hangs from a string that I'm pretty sure is tendon. From what, I'm not exactly sure. Nana claims I should be able to tell the difference between different animal tendons, but seriously, they're all white and stringy. Two ivory clips hold it in place. Since there are blood marks on it, I figure she's already performed the revelation spell.

"Watch the wall," she says, holding up a candle behind the photo.

An image appears, kind of like a projector, but it isn't

Mom's picture or the words on the back. It's an image in harsh black and white. A man sits at a desk, hunched over something I can't quite see. I point to the ceiling, hoping she'll get that I'm guessing it's Joseph.

"No, child. Look closer."

I sigh, which doesn't have the same weight when you can't hear it. Stepping right up to the projection, I squint to try and see anything that I missed. It's very simple. Man with dark hair in a dark suit at a desk. He might be reading. He might be . . . I stop. There is the smallest hint of something. I place my finger on it.

"Yes." Nana pauses, as if she doesn't want to go on. She holds the candle closer to the paper, and the image enlarges. "Tell me that's not what I think it is."

I stare at the little piece of fluff. Finally it clicks. That's a quill. He is writing. This isn't my dad—this is the man who put the curse on Mom's picture.

My blood goes cold.

Looking back to Nana, I can tell we're on the same impossible wavelength now. I pray she'll crack a smile, tell me it's a joke—anything to stop this terrifying train of thought. She doesn't.

There's a loud knock on the door, almost frantic sounding. I automatically go to answer, since Nana always makes me anyway. I catch the hint of something, like a dream just fading.

Someone is worried about me.

Kat. Of course. I pull open the door, and there she is, small and trembling like a wet mouse. "Gwen would not let me go. I swear the girl has a sixth sense for when someone's not telling her something. I'm so sorry I couldn't get here sooner."

I hold up my hand, hoping she gets that it's no big deal.

She tilts her head. "Something happened, though. I could feel it."

I wave my hand for her to come in and we head back to Nana, who is still analyzing the picture. She glances over. "Ah, Katherine, good to see the binding is working."

"Felt like I was going to have a heart attack if I didn't find Jo," Kat says.

"You probably would have."

Kat and I exchange a glance.

"Let's get you up to speed." Nana points to the image on the wall. "This is the person who wrote the letter that cursed Joseph, which we were able to retrieve thanks to Josephine giving up her voice for several days. There is something very wrong with this picture. We must figure out how this happened, and fast."

Kat's wide eyes narrow as she takes it in. "What's wrong with it?"

I point to the feather.

"That's weird?"

Nana taps the photo. "Witches use quills to put spells on paper. Very easy to transfer potions and magic that way. What this implies is that a man put the curse on the photo, which is impossible."

Kat sits in the chair. "It is?"

I plop down next to her, hating that I can't express how seriously messed up this is. Nana is acting way too calm for Kat to understand that we're in a situation I've never heard of in all of witchcraft. And clearly Nana hasn't heard of it either, which is the scariest thing of all.

"Men cannot use magic," she says. "This image is either false, or it destroys everything known about our world. And unfortunately, I'm inclined to believe the latter."

"Why? It could be a fake. Or maybe a woman who is really burly?" Kat looks to me for reassurance, but I can't give her any.

Nana heaves a sigh. "What with the unknown nature of the Curse, it would make sense for it to be something this evil and perverted. A man wielding the darkness? Heaven help us all. I have never felt so out of my depth. What can we do against something we have no knowledge of?"

I grab a pad of paper from her desk and scribble out, *How did he get magic?*

"I wish I knew, dear. I wish I knew. Since men cannot absorb and carry magic like we can, I am at a total loss as to how this man obtained his abilities. But from what we've experienced, it must have been by very dark means."

I put my head in my hands. When we set out to defend ourselves and find Mom's killer, I figured we'd discover some evil witch with a taste for blood or a score to settle. Not this. How in the world are we supposed to fight now? We barely know what we're dealing with, let alone how to get rid of it. And whoever this man is, he has even more reason to kill us now that we know men are probably behind the Curse.

Then I catch sight of my mother's picture, and my heart aches. I take it from where it hangs, my hands shaking. She's so young—maybe even my age. She sits at a café table, wearing a sundress and smiling as if she's madly in love. I wonder if my dad took this picture, and if so, how it got into the wrong hands.

I can't stop fighting. I have to know who would go to such lengths to ruin our lives. And if at all possible, find a way to end it.

We need help. We need to tell other families, I write.

Nana purses her lips. "It's hard to know who to trust. He had to have gotten the magic from somewhere, and the most likely is a *someone*. If we inform the wrong people we could be in worse trouble."

"But . . ." Kat trails off, clearly feeling out of place.

"Go on," Nana says softly. The way she respects Kat makes me smile, though it also makes me nervous.

"There must be some families you do trust, and if the Curse impacts them they deserve to know."

"This is true." Nana smiles. "The Curse has followed us for generations—he can't be the first man to wield magic. Witches are secretive, and perhaps these men have kept their existence from us as well." She stands. "The histories. I will ask our most trusted friends to scour their histories for anything. You two will read our own. It's been so long since I have read them, and I may have forgotten a vital detail."

I nod, even though reading the histories is no easy task. Kat seems excited by the idea, but she has no idea what we're up against.

FIFTEEN

With the mute thing I'm dealing with, going up to the attic to read histories would be suicide. Every witch in every family must keep a history, which is a fancy word for a diary. It's important to know our past, but of course we don't want other people knowing. This makes the histories a labyrinth of danger, frustration, and, admittedly, more than a giant's share of teenage angst that spans centuries. Of all the places in our house, it's the most protected with magic.

It'd be hard enough to watch Kat and disarm all the trap spells *with* a voice. The books will have to wait until I'm better, so I take Kat with me for another task: translating

"Come in!" my dad says before I knock on the door. He sure has the house's creaks down.

"Hi, Mr. Johnson," Kat says.

His eyebrows shoot up. "Oh, hello. I thought it would be Jo."

"She's here. But she can't talk, since she used her voice to get rid of a spell on that letter you had." Kat takes the desk chair while I stand by the bed, hesitating. "She's about to sit next to you, if you couldn't tell."

"Okay."

I sit with my notebook, scribble out a question, and hand it over to Kat. "She wants to know if you recognized the picture that the location was written on."

"Oh, yeah." He puts his hand to his mouth, the memories seeming to flash across his face. "That was the day I met Carmina, actually. My friends and I knew her roommates. She had just moved to the Bay Area, and we all went up to San Fran to show her the city. The second I saw her . . ." His smile has so much pain behind it, pain I'm very familiar with. "It was over."

Maybe it's good I can't talk, because I'd sound all weepy. I write another question and Kat reads it. "Do you know who took the picture?"

"It had to be one of her roommates, because I recognize the setting, but me and my friends didn't have a camera that day. They were taking pictures at some point, though. I remember her posing." He sighs. "That was over twenty years ago. We were in college then, and she moved around a couple times before we lived together. . . ."

I tilt my head. They lived together? Wow. Nana was serious when she said my mom stayed with him as long as she could. "Her roommates were Eva, Taiko, and . . . Stacia."

Last names? I write, and Kat repeats.

He laughs. "I remember Eva's because it was Corona, and we'd tease her about it. Taiko's was something long and Hawaiian. She was from Maui. And Stacia's was Black—she and Carmina were really close."

I jump at the name. Black. They're the largest witching family around. Not that any of our families are super big, but they have cousins and that seems huge to me. I haven't met any of them since I was a little girl, because Nana basically cut off all contact with other families once my mom was Cursed. But Mom loved to tell the story of how we once went to a big Halloween gala when I was four. Every other little girl was a Black. One of them, a snotty redhead with perfect ringlets, said, "Hemlock? I've never heard of that bloodline. Are you sure you're a witch?"

I scowled at her. "Of course I am."

"Prove it."

"Fine." I cut off one of her curls and turned it into a butterfly. She wasn't very happy about that. Mom told me that we might be a small family, but our magic was still as strong as anyone else's.

But maybe not all the Blacks were like that little redhead. Stacia Black could have been a lovely person. And it makes sense that Mom would bunk with at least one witch, especially if she was so far from home. If Stacia is a witch and knew Mom back then, then Stacia probably has information we're missing, information Mom wouldn't have told my dad.

"What, Jo?" Kat asks.

I grab the pen and paper. *Black is a witch family name. Stacia could have been a witch, and maybe that could be a lead.*

"Huh," my dad says when Kat tells him. "I would have never guessed, but that's the point, isn't it? You blend right in."

"No kidding," Kat says. "I grew up with Jo, and I never had a clue. She was just fun, sweet, crazy Jo."

I scrunch my face, embarrassed, but my dad smiles. "I bet. Sounds like—"

Boom.

The house rocks, every plank crying out its creaky song. Plaster rains from the ceiling, and a few pictures clatter to the floor. I put my hand over my heart, as if that will steady it, and wait for the world to stop swaying. The house hasn't fallen yet, but there's a first time for everything. Kat uncovers her head. "What the hell was that?"

Better find out, I write.

"We're going to investigate." Kat opens the door. "We'll see you later, Mr. Johnson."

He waves. "Hope to see you soon."

When Kat and I get down to the kitchen, everything is out of order, but that's not what has my mouth hanging open. Three women stand there, brushing themselves off as if they've come in from a rainstorm. They all have long golden hair, braided and looped intricately, and wardrobes that look either hippyish or medieval peasantish.

The Crafts. Nana must have asked them to come fast, because they usually use the front door.

Maggie turns, her big eyes lighting up. "Jojo!" she squeals as she careens into me. "This is all so crazy! I don't know how in the world you deal with so much and you can still smile and everything!"

I forgot how fast and incoherent she gets when she's nervous. Or excited. Or hopped up on caffeine. Last time she was here, she got ahold of one Dr Pepper and, wow. She ended up raiding our newt-tail supply and used it to toilet paper all of Main Street. Nana was not happy, but at least she had the foresight to get our house, too, so no one blamed us.

"What's the bad news Nana Dottie is writing cryptic messages about?" Maggie continues. "Mom and Auntie keep giving each other weird looks. You know, the ones where they know more than you do but they don't know if they should tell you?" She shoots them a glare. "I really hate when they do that."

She's never going to be quiet. It's hard enough to stop

her when I have a voice.

"It's been so long since I've seen you and it's so disgusting that you're prettier than—"

Kat clears her throat, and finally Maggie notices her. "So you're a witch, too, Maggie? I feel kind of stupid for missing that one."

Maggie smiles. "Hey, Kat. Long time no see. Are you having fun learning about magic? I heard all about the binding."

"It's been interesting so far, and not that long since I've seen you. A year maybe?"

Since Maggie visits often, my friends know her. They think she's my cousin, which is kind of true. Close as I'll ever get.

Maggie points back to her family, who eye Kat warily. "This is my mom and auntie. Gran stayed behind to man the house and watch Molly, my baby sis, who is the cutest little girl ever. You should see—"

"Mags." Her aunt steps forward, and immediately the air quiets from her authoritative presence. "We're here to get information, not give it." She appraises Kat in a way that makes me want to protect her. "So you are the one who received the binding?"

Kat tries to stand tall, but that's not much when you're five foot nothing. "Yes."

"I'm Prudence." She holds out her graceful hand, and

Kat takes it. "You have a lot to learn."

"I know."

Prudence scowls. "Good. And this is my younger sister, Tessa."

Tessa's smile is warm, just like Maggie's. "Welcome to our world, dear."

"Thanks." Kat nods in my direction. "Also, you might want to know Jo can't talk right now."

They all give me a surprised look, so I motion for them to follow me to Nana, who already has the picture rehung and waiting. She fills the Crafts in on the situation, and they stare at the image in horror. Even Maggie's perma-smile has faded. "Are you certain you've never heard of such things?" Nana asks.

"Positive," Tessa says. "That is . . ."

"An abomination," Prudence says. "If a witch did this, she should be publicly punished."

"While it makes sense that a witch would be behind this, we have no proof that one is. Carmina could have crossed paths with one of these evil men during her travels. I don't know. I'm afraid we have nothing to go on, and I'm not sure it's wise to alert any other families of our situation," Nana says.

Tessa nods. "With the threat so close, how can you know which way to go?"

"You thought you were doing a good thing cleansing

Josephine's father," Prudence adds. "And it almost cost you everything."

Nana sits in her chair, looking lost. I walk over and hug her. Her brow furrows. "What is it, dear?"

Kat clears her throat. "We went and asked Joseph more questions. Turns out he knew where that picture came from. He said one of Carmina's roommates probably took it—Stacia Black."

Tessa and Prudence gasp at the name, clearly familiar with whoever Stacia is. Which makes sense, considering they were my mom's closest friends.

Nana hugs me. "Of course! You darling girl."

Tessa smiles. "Stacia was so kind—definitely not your average Black witch. She and Carmina became really close. If anyone else knows more about Carmina's life, what might have happened, and who performed the Curse, it'd be her."

Prudence folds her arms. "I haven't seen her in years, though. I think Carmina mentioned a long time ago that Stacia was pregnant. Seems they lost touch after that—she wasn't at the funeral."

Kat, Maggie, and I lap up the information. This is all news to me. "If they were close, why wouldn't Stacia go?" Maggie asks.

Tessa shrugs. "It's easy to lose contact after you have a child—I remember how very protective I was of you, Maggie. I didn't take you from the house for years—not until you were four or five."

Nana nods. "If Stacia did have a daughter, she wouldn't have risked taking her to the funeral of a witch who died from the Curse. We have to find her now. It might be a stretch to think she has any answers, but . . ."

"She's your only hope," Kat says, as if reading my mind.

Nana's eyes are dark, so sad that they don't reflect light. "Exactly."

SIXTEEN

I don't bother going to school Friday or the following Monday. I can play the sick card until my voice comes back, and Nana needs my help fortifying barriers and tracking down Stacia Black. That, and Maggie needs supervision. I love the Crafts, but I'm sure Tessa and Prudence left her behind to "help" so they could get some peace and quiet back in New York.

"So there's this boy at the community center in the town an hour from our place, and he's the cutest guy in the whole wide world, but every time I think he's going to ask me out he swipes my pass and says, 'Have a great workout.' What's that supposed to mean anyway?" She dips her quill into the potion and continues writing. "At least you kind of live in a town—I'm in the freaking middle of nowhere. This is the closest interaction I've ever had with a boy."

The Crafts' house is in upstate New York, where the forest is so thick it's suffocating. But the magic there is rich and vibrant, like the leaves in the fall. The first time I visited their place, my head wouldn't stop spinning because it was so different from our land.

"I just want a boyfriend, you know? They tell us we're responsible for preserving the bloodline, and then they refuse to let us date! What the crap?" Maggie is homeschooled, which might be why she can't get enough of being around new people.

Try as I might, I can't bite back the smile as I think about Winn.

She stops writing. "Wait, what's with that goofy grin?"

I wave it off, though I can feel my face warming.

"Josephine Hemlock!" She shoves me so hard I have to grab the kitchen table to keep from falling off my chair. "Why didn't you tell me?"

I give her this look that I hope says, "Hello? Can't talk here."

Maggie mock glares. "Fine, I'll let it slide as long as I get to meet him."

I nod, dipping my quill back in the potion. Nana gave us a list of witches to send letters to. We have no idea where Stacia is, which means we can't send our words directly to her. Much like the door spell, we have to know the location in order to send or go there. Either that, or we need to have met the person recently to tap into their wavelength.

The letters are all the same:

> *Dear Friend, We are in need of assistance, if you are able. Having finally gathered the strength to go through my Carmina's things, we've discovered that she has something that belonged to her close friend Anastacia Black. We have not had contact with Ms. Black since before Carmina's death, and are unaware of her location. If you know where she is, we would very much like to return her valuable possession. Sincerely, Dorothea Hemlock*

I don't like lying, but Nana said if other witches find out that the Curse is after us they might be too afraid to affiliate with us at all. And if we mention we think our hunters are men? Everyone would write us off as crazy.

Nana's cane clicks down the stairs, and when she appears she looks absolutely haunted. "Forgive me, Josephine, but I still can't do it. I can hardly touch the cover."

She leans against the wall, spent, and I know exactly what she's been trying to do—read my mother's history. Each book has its own unique enchantments, but every single one is made so that you can't open it until you're ready to face what's inside. And since Mom should still be alive and writing in her history, Nana and I haven't been able to break past that spell. It would bring too much sorrow, and thus Mom's book remains clamped shut.

I was okay with that up until we needed the information inside.

Nana sits at the table, and I give her a hug. She pats my arm, leaning her head against mine. "How are the letters going?"

"We have . . ." Maggie scans the list. "Twelve down, eighteen to go. But my hand is killing me so can we please take a break?"

"Two more from both of you. I'll make an afternoon snack."

Maggie groans as Nana heads for the fridge, but we both get back to work. The faster we write, the faster we can find Stacia. And then we can discover if she has any bit of information that could crack this mystery and save Nana and me from my mother's fate.

My phone buzzes, and Maggie practically mauls me to see the screen. "Is that your boyfriend?" She frowns when she sees the name. "Just Gwen. Boo."

I roll my eyes as I open the message.

Tell me you're better. We need to hang out asap. I miss you!

I've only been sick 4 days! I'm that important?

Yes ☜ Btwn Winn and this you've disappeared. Can I at least come visit?

Talk about a stab to the heart, but it's true. Gwen, Kat,

and I usually hang out every day. I didn't see much of her last week, and I'm willing to bet Kat didn't either since she's here half the time. Gwen must be bored out of her mind.

I don't want u to catch this. I'll call u 2 nite, k? I should have my voice back by then.

You better. Or I'll be forced to seek comfort in Adam's arms.

Is that a threat?

Shut up.

Fine :P

I close my phone, locking away the guilt over lying to her. I'll make it up to Gwen the second I can.

"What'd she want?" Maggie asks, scribbling furiously.

I shrug. Picking up the quill, I finish off the letter I was working on. It's for Lorena Starr, one of Nana's friends from her childhood. I remember stories about how Lorena would visit here, and she and Nana would curse the boys who picked on other kids. Now Lorena is the head of her house, tied to her home and the responsibility of protecting it. They are the keepers of knowledge that younger generations need. I might be important for preserving the Hemlock bloodline, but Nana is just as vital. Without her, I'd know nothing.

I watch Nana as she stirs soup at the stove, an unsettling feeling coming over me. I push it back. Worrying will get us nowhere. We both know the risks of seeking out this dark man and his magic, but there's no turning back. Like she said—it's us or them.

But the feeling won't go away. My heart pounds too fast, and my hands are so clammy I wonder if I really am getting sick. Then I freeze, realizing what's going on. It's not Nana I should be worrying about. It's Kat. The panic hits me like ice water.

Something is after her.

My chair crashes to the floor when I stand. I rip out a handful of hair and close my eyes, picturing Kat's room—the black-and-purple bedspread, the punk posters, the glow stars on the ceiling. My fingers go numb as the magic pulls me to her house. I can feel myself shifting planes, and when the hair in my hand turns to ash, I'm there.

But Kat isn't.

I say her name, though nothing comes out. The house is completely silent, since her parents both work at the town hall. I swear the bus would have had her home by now, and it seemed like my gut was saying to come here.

Glass shatters downstairs. As I run for the kitchen, I know what Kat meant when she said it was like she was having a heart attack. It feels like my chest is about to explode. It feels like I'm going to die. And if I feel like that . . .

Kat stands in the middle of the room, swatting at something on her face. When she turns I see what it is—a bubble of water covering her mouth and nose.

SEVENTEEN

No matter how much water Kat wipes away, the bubble stays in place. I've heard of the spell—it's an easy combination of fish scales, raven hearts, and dew gathered from tombstones—but I've never seen it in action. How simple it is—almost comical in appearance, and yet terrifying in practice. When our eyes meet, hers start watering.

I've never seen Kat cry.

I want to tell her it'll be okay. That's the least I can do to calm her, and I can't manage it with my stupid voice gone.

Her pale skin begins to turn blue, which makes the pain in my chest burst into something part agony, part will to survive. I rush to her side in time to keep her standing and scan the kitchen for any reagents I can use to stop this. It has to be something pure, something with life to purge the death.

The orchids.

Kat's mom loves her orchids. They're all over the house, and she treats them like babies. I once heard her singing to them as she sprayed special water over their leaves. She'll freak when she finds them all dead . . . but it's my only option.

Kat might weigh nothing, but when she goes limp in my arms the weight brings me to my knees. After lowering her to the floor, I hold my hand to the orchids on the table. I use my magic to suck out their life, and they shrivel into black husks. Their power radiates through my hand, pure and clear and hopeful. I rush for the next group around the TV, then the batch in the living room, until I have enough orchid life in me that it assuages the pain in my chest. The magic begs for me to keep it for myself, but I quickly push back the thought and run to Kat.

I put my trembling hand to her mouth. It's cold and wet, still submersed in the bubble. The moment I release the orchid life, the water turns black and hot. My scream goes unheard as the death spell sears my hand, fighting against the life. It sputters and hisses, turning into steam the color of ash. I gag on the smell, putrid like the decaying carcasses we keep in the basement.

Before I lose my hand entirely, I force the rest of the spell out as fast as I can. The bubble gets hotter and hotter, until it's all melting steam. When it's gone, I pull back my hand, which is burned so bad there's blood at my knuckles.

But Kat comes first. I put my head to her chest so I can hear her heartbeat. It's there, but she's not breathing.

I never did learn CPR, but I have to at least try. I open Kat's mouth and put mine to hers. Her chest rises as I breathe out, and I wait for her to cough and sputter back to life like they do in the movies.

Except she doesn't.

As I breathe into her mouth again, my panic intensifies to the point that I can barely get air myself. I promised to protect her, and I've already failed. I should have never let her do the binding. This is what happens when normal people get caught up in magic.

She can't die. I need her.

"Wake up!" I scream despite being mute, shaking her because I don't know what else to do. "You're supposed to wake up!"

She coughs, and black water spews from her mouth as if she gulped down a whole lake of it. I hold her up, and she keeps going until I worry a lung will come out next. When she's spent, she says, "I really thought I was going to die."

Tears break free as I wrap my arms around her. She almost did. I don't know if she understands how close it was.

"How did you stop it?" she asks.

I point to the table, where the orchids look like charred husks.

"My mom's gonna kill me." She looks at me, and I'm

surprised to find her smiling.

"I guess it doesn't really matter." She leans her head on my shoulder. "Thanks, Jo."

I squeeze her arm once, and then hold out my burned hand, which looks even worse now. Her eyes go wide. "Holy crap. What do you need? Ice?"

I nod.

Once she gets that, she cleans up the black water. I feel awful that she's doing it all, seeing as she's the one who almost died, but my hand still feels like it's on fire.

How did this happen? I write on the fridge's whiteboard.

Kat looks me in the eye, her fear washing over me. "It was a letter in the mail. I swear it looked totally normal, but the picture inside . . ." She points to the counter, where a shiny photo reflects the fluorescent lights. "I touched it, and that's when the bubble came."

From here, I can tell there's no darkness left on the image, but I still approach it warily. Another cursed picture. If I had any doubt that this was related to our hunters, it's gone now. I look down, and my friends stare back at me. This was taken the day we ate outside under the tree. Gwen is in the sun, chatting with Adam and looking like a freaking goddess. Kat's sipping her drink, staring at the sky. There's a big black *X* over her face.

The threat couldn't be any clearer.

But there's something that might help, except it's as horrible as it is helpful—Winn is looking at the camera, his eyes locked in suspicion, while he holds me possessively. My oblivious smile looks silly, and I hate myself for not noticing whoever took this picture. Winn clearly did.

I turn the photo over, and chills run down my spine as I read: *I spy with my little eye . . . a girl who has a lot to lose.*

My breaths come fast and short as I process this simple little line. Whoever wrote it is pure evil. They can't get through the magical barriers around the town and my house, so instead they hit me at my weakest point: the people I care about. It feels like they're telling me to surrender now before it gets worse.

Kat stands next to me. "Don't worry. We'll get them first."

I force a nod and write, *We need to tell Nana.*

"Right. Just let me change." She heads for her room, and I follow closely behind. No leaving her alone. Ever.

I run my thumb back and forth over the picture as I wait outside her door. How will I protect them all? It seemed overwhelming enough to worry about Kat, but everyone I know? If the evil is this close, there's no telling when or who it'll attack.

"Let's get out of here," Kat says when she emerges, now wearing a purple-and-green striped shirt.

We head downstairs and out the front door, only to find another problem standing right in front of us—Gwen. She puts her hands on her hips, her anger crystal clear. "Sick, huh?"

EIGHTEEN

When Gwen first talked to me in elementary school, I was sure I was a charity case. She was such a pretty, outgoing little girl. Everyone loved her. Everyone wanted to be her friend. Boys and girls alike would flock around her at recess, hoping she'd choose them to play with. She hopped from crowd to crowd, as if she were trying on friends and none were good enough. Then in third grade, after my mom died, she sat down next to me and Kat at lunch.

"Can I eat with you?"

"Sure," I said. She was Gwendolyn Lee, after all. No one rejected Gwendolyn Lee.

Kat swallowed her sandwich bite, eyeing Gwen. "Is this some kind of joke?"

Gwen shook her head. "Why would I do that?"

"Because everyone else would," I said. It was true. A girl like her shouldn't be with outcasts like us. It had to be a dare. Or some punishment for losing a bet.

Gwen frowned. "I just wanted to sit with you."

"We don't need you," Kat said. "We don't care about being cool or popular."

"I know." Gwen sighed, like even at eight years old she understood how the world worked. She understood that everyone else was trying to get somewhere by being her friend, and all she wanted was people who really cared about her.

So we let her stay, and she's never left. In fact, she might value our friendship the most. That's why, as she stares at us with hurt eyes, I want to bury myself in a grave.

"Funny thing, Jo," Gwen says as I hide my burned hand behind my back. "I was coming here to grab Kat so we could storm your house with get-well treats and good gossip, whether your grandma liked it or not. But here you are."

"Gwen . . ." Kat glances at me like she knows what's coming.

Gwen points at her. "You, shut up." Then she turns on me. "So you're too sick to see me, but you can come all the way to Kat's house to hang out with her?"

I stare at the ground, wishing I could say something. But no, all I can do is let her think what she thinks, which is closer to the truth than I want it to be.

"I made her," Kat says. "She had some of my notes . . ."

Gwen holds up her hands. "Whatever. You think I can't see what's going on here? I always knew you two were closer, but I thought you'd at least wait until graduation to cut me out."

"What?" Kat takes a few steps forward. "Gwen, that is so not what's going—"

"Then explain those necklaces!" She points to Kat's charms, the ones to help her fingernail heal. "We've begged Jo for those, and she's always said her Nana only makes them for family!"

Kat grabs them, her desperate eyes on me, as if I'll have a good explanation. It does look bad. Even if I had a voice, I still wouldn't have a reply.

"You guys are totally shutting me out, and after all we've been through I think that's a pretty shitty thing to do." She stomps back to her truck while both of us watch helplessly. As she drives off, my throat tickles.

"Perfect," I say. "*Now* I get my voice back."

"We could go after her," Kat says.

I shake my head. "We don't have time. Nana needs to know about this, and then we have to find Winn." I hold out the picture. "He had to have seen who took this, which means he could describe the person."

"Good point."

I sigh. "Too bad it doesn't help me know which person

they'll attack next. You'd think they would have gone for Winn first, since he saw. But it's like they knew somehow that you were bound to me, and therefore most important."

Her eyes go wide. "You think?"

"Yeah." We speed-walk in the direction of my house. "We'll have to figure out how to protect everyone after I get more info from Winn."

"Nana!" I yell once we get back. "Nana!"

"She's gone." My dad emerges from the kitchen, wiping his hands on a towel. By the way he stares, I know he can see again. I feel like a dork for blushing, but he hasn't seen me since he found out the truth. Somehow, it's like the first time he's truly looking at me. "You got your voice back."

"Yup. And you can see."

He smiles. "The house looks a lot nicer than I imagined. It sounded on the brink of collapsing."

"She likes to talk back. I imagine her as my cranky old aunt." I point toward the apothecary. "Did you say Nana left? She hardly ever leaves."

"She took Maggie to fortify the barriers around town again. They had a whole bag of bones and some bottles of snakeskins."

"Good." I'm glad Nana already knows what happened and is doing what she can to protect my friends. As long as Gwen doesn't leave Willow's End or get a horrible letter in the mail, hopefully she's safe for now. "A dog skeleton, to sound warnings. And snakeskins to poison magical trespassers."

"Did something happen?" he asks. I hold out the picture for him, and he inspects it with this funny half frown. "So that's your boyfriend? The one from the pizza place?"

"Uhhh, kind of?" Cue awkward silence. It keeps smacking me across the face like this—the whole "I have a father" thing. "He's not my boyfriend. At least not yet. I don't know. We're just dating."

"Okay." He hands the picture back, not seeming convinced. "Whatever it is, it's fine. I guess. As long as you aren't, uh, never mind. None of my business."

"Yeah . . ." I can't look at him, positive he's implying what I think he's implying. "That's not really the point right now."

"But he has his arm—"

I point to the big *X* on Kat's head. "Whoever put that curse on you? They tried to kill Kat, and—"

"Your hand!" He takes my wrist, inspecting the red skin. "Is this how you saved her?"

I wince at his touch. "Part of it."

"That's what Dorothea must have meant. Come to the kitchen." He disappears, and I start to wonder if either of us will ever finish a thought without interrupting the other. But once I see what's on the table, I smile. Nana set out a balm for my hand and extra charms for my bracelet. He pulls out the chair for me. "Seems like your grandmother knows everything."

"Almost." I sit, putting my hand in the bowl. The creamy mixture is cool and soothing. It smells like roses, though that's only to cover up what's really in it. My guess is some kind of blend of animal innards and healing herbs. "Look at the back of that picture."

He flips it over, and as he reads his mouth gapes. "Jo . . ."

"I know." I stare at my hand, my whole soul feeling sick and tired. "It's like whoever is doing this is . . . having fun. I have to protect everyone in this picture before it's too late. Nana has the rest of town covered, but my friends need even more."

"What do we do?" Kat puts her chin in her hands and glowers. "I wish I could help. What's the point of being here if I can't help?"

"Kat . . ." I wish I could give her an answer. "Do you know Billy's address, by chance? Winn mentioned they were studying there tonight, but he's way outside town."

She shakes her head. "Ugh, I'm so useless."

"Don't say that. I'd hate to be doing this on my own right now." I pull out my phone with my good hand and call Winn. As it rings, my heart pounds faster and faster. *Please, please pick up. It can't be too late.*

"Hey," he says, and I can hear the gorgeous smile that goes with it. "Are you feeling better? Say you're feeling better."

Despite all my concerns, I grin like a fool. So relieved. "I'm feeling better."

"Good, I'll come get you, then."

"Are you sure? You're at Billy's, right?"

"Very sure. And I was just about to leave for his house, so perfect timing."

I laugh. "Awesome. I kind of need to beg Billy to read my paper—he did such a good job with Kat's, and I'm way behind on my stuff now."

"See you in twenty?"

"Perfect. Thanks, Winn." I shut the phone, a plan already clicking into place. "Kat, you're about to be very useful, more useful than you probably want to be."

Her brow furrows. "What's that supposed to mean?"

I give her my best cackle.

NINETEEN

"It's simple," I say to Kat as I paint the potion onto her palm. There's no way we could pull off giving Winn and Billy some kind of charm necklace, so I figure the best bet is to put the protection spell right into them. It won't be permanent, but it should ward off most bad magic and reduce the effects of anything truly horrible for at least a day. "All you have to do is touch him on the skin, and the spell will transfer. He won't even notice. Just don't touch anything before, or it'll get the spell instead."

Kat gnaws on her lip as I cover her fingers with the clear liquid. She doesn't daintily bite—no, she chews to the point you wonder if she'll start bleeding. "I don't know, Jo. I'm not a flirter; I can't touch him."

"Yes, you can!" I laugh. Kat never gives herself enough credit. She may be shy, but she is beautiful in her own right.

Punk beautiful, with her heavy bangs and porcelain skin. "You totally had a vibe going with him the other day at lunch, and he's all thin and hipster. You'd look good together."

She stares at her hands. "I don't want to date Billy."

"I'm not asking you to date him—I'm only saying you could if you wanted. One touch on the arm does not a relationship make."

She sighs. "I guess this is what I get for wanting to be helpful."

"That's the spirit." Winn honks his horn, and I jump. "Better go."

I certainly don't mind scooting in right next to Winn when we get in his truck. As he wraps an arm around me, I press my hand into his forearm. The spell transfers, and I feel a little more at ease. Then I notice the ends of his hair are wet. Oh, for the love, he just showered. "You didn't have to get all cleaned up to study."

He laughs. "Actually, I did. I was out in the fields testing soil and compost. You and Kat would have opted to sit in the truck bed if I came straight from that."

I tilt my head to look up at him. "You test the soil?"

"Any good farmer does. If the pH levels are bad, it can damage the crop. Or sometimes there will be too much of a particular chemical, so you need to plant a crop that'll balance the levels out. We rotate our fields all the time."

"Huh."

"Huh?" He pokes me. "Having grown up around a bunch of farmers, I thought you'd know this stuff!"

"Hello?" Kat says. "Jo and I live in town, and Gwen pretends she doesn't live on a farm. I've never even touched a tractor, nor do I plan to."

"Exactly," I say. "I have Nana's bug legacy to uphold, Gwen dreams of being a stylist, and Kat has her poetry."

"Poetry?" Winn leans forward to look at her. "You write poetry?"

She folds her arms. "I plead the fifth."

He glances at me, and I hold up my hands. "Hey, that's all I know. Kat doesn't show her poems to anyone."

We turn down Billy's dirt driveway, bouncing at each deep hole left from the winter snows. His house has its charms. The porch stretches all the way around, big and roomy. It's a nice shade of blue, with navy shutters. As we get out, I text Gwen in hopes that I can get her here so I can keep her safe.

We're @ Billy's if you wanna come. We want you to. Sry for what happened.

Winn rings the doorbell. "Texting Gwen?"

"Yeah. I think she's mad at me, though." Sure enough, her text says it all:

No thx. Too tired to play 3rd wheel tonight.

I show her answer to Kat.

"Ouch," she says.

"I know, right?" I sigh. Gwen won't let this one slide, and I have no idea how to make it up to her. I need to before our hunters hurt her.

Winn rings the doorbell again, which is when I realize we've been on the porch longer than the average wait for someone to answer the door. My heart speeds up, the thought of Billy hurt or dead suddenly at the forefront of my mind.

"Did you tell him we were coming?" I ask.

"Yeah, I called him." Winn knocks a few times. "Sometimes he can be a little spacey, though."

"Really?"

Winn smiles like he's remembering something funny. "Guy's in his own world half the time, but it's always entertaining."

Honestly, I don't know much about Billy, except that he's Winn's friend and his parents are some of the few people around who don't grow corn. They have apple orchards. Every mother and grandmother in the area waits anxiously to buy them for fall pies. Well, minus Nana. She's a horrible baker, which is strange considering she mixes precise, nefarious potions all the time.

"Maybe you should call him again?" Kat asks.

Winn frowns. "His car is right there. He has to be here."

We all knock at once until my knuckles hurt.

Just when I think I'll have to bust the door down and

save another person from death, Billy answers. His hair is the usual perfect mess, but he's breathing hard, and his face glistens with sweat. "Sorry, couldn't hear you over the music."

Kat and I exchange a relieved glance. What was he doing? Dancing? I try not to laugh, though the thought of Billy dancing is pretty funny. He's seems so laid-back.

Then, like a pro, Kat shoves Billy. "We were starting to think you were dead! Did you forget we were coming?"

The spell wraps around his arm as it drains from her hand in swirling plumes of blue mist. He's safe. At least safer. He shivers, but other than that I'm sure he has no idea what happened. He stares at Kat, surprised. "Sorry?"

"Whatever." She stalks past him and we follow.

"Got that out of the way quick," I whisper. "And after all that complaining."

She smiles. "I figured it was kind of like ripping off a fingernail."

I laugh, but it's cut short when Winn's arms come around my waist from behind. Is it wrong that I like how he grabs me without asking? It gives me permission to do the same. He plants his head on my shoulder, and I can't move even if I wanted to. "What're you two whispering about?"

"It's a secret."

"Hence the whispering," Kat says.

"Anyway . . ." I pull my paper from my messenger bag

and hand it to Billy. "Thanks for the help. Here we were all talking about not skipping school this week, and I missed Friday and Monday."

"Not a problem. It shouldn't be too hard to get you caught up." Billy plops down on a maroon couch in the living room, already frowning at my writing, which probably sucks. I'm not great at school in general. Maybe because I've always known what I'll be doing the rest of my life, and you don't study it in college. It's more important for me to memorize spells and potions than long math equations.

"Good." Kat kneels by the coffee table and opens her giant binder. "Because if she had to study during lunch tomorrow I couldn't prove to her that we don't have a stalker."

"What?" Winn says as he pulls me into the love seat.

I try not to smile. And she thinks she's useless. "I swear, Kat, the day we went out to lunch there was someone with a camera across the street. No one else was by us, so what were they photographing?"

"A car? The road? A penny left in the street?" She pauses, and then goes for her special notebook. The poetry one. I suppose that was . . . inspiring.

"Hmm, a penny or Gwen sunbathing?" I ask.

"I didn't see anyone," Billy says. "Did you, Winn?"

He purses his lips.

Billy's eyes go wide. "Seriously? You saw someone?"

I knew it, but waiting for Winn to admit it is torture. I want so badly for him to give us some kind of clue.

"He wasn't exactly hiding. If you looked over you would have seen him staring at Jo." Winn tenses, and so do I. He wasn't just holding me close that day; it was like some gut reaction to protect me.

"Why didn't you say anything?" Billy asks.

"He . . . I don't know. The dude was creepy. He looked right at me, and it felt like he'd have no problem stabbing me in the heart if he felt like it."

The hair on my neck raises. Winn doesn't know it, but I'm pretty sure he was silenced with magic. That guy put a fear spell on him, told Winn he was dead if he pointed him out.

"What did he look like?" Kat's voice trembles.

"That's the thing." Winn holds me tighter. "He looked totally normal—dark hair, tall, young—"

"Young?" I say, disturbed by the idea.

"Yeah," Winn says. "But then for one second he didn't seem right, like he was a real creep underneath."

There's silence, as if we can feel the sincerity in his words and what they might mean. Normal humans may not be able to see magic, but sometimes they can feel it—like the niggling sense that something is off, though you don't know what.

This young guy had to be the one who took the cursed

picture, but if that's true, then he's also not my mother's murderer. And that means there's more than one of these evil men after us. It could be a whole crew, for all I know.

Billy sucks in a breath. "Maybe we should skip school tomorrow."

I couldn't agree more.

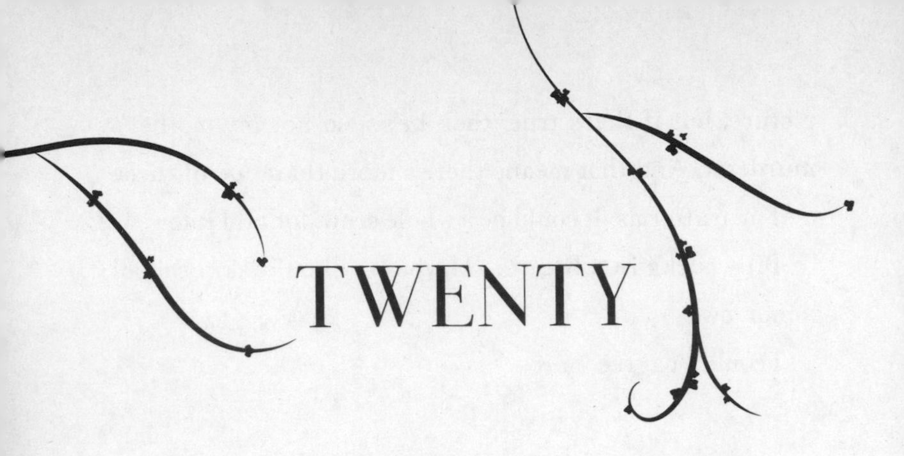

TWENTY

It takes every ounce of willpower I have to leave Winn tonight, but there is so much magic to prepare if I want to protect my friends, and "Nana expecting me home for dinner" is the easiest excuse I have. He hugs me after Kat gets out of the car. "Why do you always have to go?"

That frown of his is so not fair. He looks like a puppy locked up in the pound, begging me to take him home. "Seriously, Winn, it's in our best interest to keep Nana happy. What if I got grounded?"

He sighs. "That would suck."

"It would." I lean into him, soaking in the sensation before I have to get back to more witch stuff. "But we're still going on a real date, right?"

He hugs me tighter. "Right. And this time there will be

no stalkers-turned-fathers or sicknesses to get in the way. You're mine for a whole night."

My face warms. "Well, not a whole night. That would definitely get me grounded, even if we spent the entire time playing Trivial Pursuit with your parents."

"Yeah, uh, that is not even close to what we'll be doing."

I pull back to see him better. "Wait, you already have it planned?"

"Of course." Winn puts on his heart-melting smile. "Do you want a preview?"

The hairs on my neck prickle. It doesn't take a rocket scientist to know where this is going, especially when his face is so close to mine. "I like previews."

"Good." He leans in more, so close that I can feel his breath on my cheek. My heart pounds as I wait, and I hope kissing will be as awesome as people claim. At the last moment, Winn pulls back and holds up a piece of paper. "Because I'm really excited about this coupon—two for one at the diner!"

I grab the coupon and hit him with it, even though we're both laughing. "You jerk!"

"Hey!" He scoops me up so we're right against each other, and suddenly it's quiet again. "I just don't want you to feel pressured. Of course I want to kiss you, but that's not the only reason you're my girlfriend."

I suck in a breath. It's the first time he's said "girlfriend," and it feels incredible. "You know you said the *G* word, right? Are you sure?"

He nods, but the tiniest flicker of doubt shadows his eyes. "Unless you don't want to be."

"Winn." My cheeks hurt from smiling so much, but I can't seem to help it. "Of course I do! I've been dying to call you my boyfriend."

He's going to kiss me. I can feel it in the air, in the way he looks at me, in the way my heart beats at my rib cage. He leans in again, and as I begin to close my eyes there's a loud knocking on the window. We jump apart, and I whirl around, finding a disturbingly happy face. Maggie.

I let out an irritated sigh. "Guess that's my cue."

"Who's that?" Winn asks as I grab my bag.

"My cousin. Her school gets out a little earlier, and she's visiting for the summer." I open the door. "Maggie, this is Winn."

She swoons over him. "My, oh, my. You done good, Jojo. You done good."

Winn gives me this look like he's not sure if she's for real, and I cringe because she totally is. "See you tomorrow," I say.

"I'll call you later." He reluctantly lets go of my hand, and I force myself to get out and walk up the path with Maggie, who keeps looking back at him.

"He's the most beautiful boy I've ever seen," she says when we get inside.

I slide down the front door, wishing I'd had a few more minutes with him. "I know."

Kat appears from the living room. "Are you done sucking face?"

"We didn'—"

That's when my dad decides to come down the stairs. We stand there, silent, and he stares at us. "Were you talking about me?"

"Nope," I say, and all three of us burst out laughing.

He raises an eyebrow, clearly unsure of how to deal with a gaggle of teen girls. "Okay . . . well, Dorothea put me in charge of dinner, so you're warned. I'll have something barely edible for you in about half an hour."

I pull myself up from the ground. "Sounds good. We're going up to the histories, since I can finally talk again. Whatever you do, don't come find us when the food is ready."

"Why?"

I look up at the stairs, which from this angle seem to lead to mystery. "Trust me: you don't want to know."

Kat and Maggie follow me to the iron, spiral staircase that leads to the tower's third story. The railing is cold on my hand and slightly rough. At each step, the air gets thicker; the heat seems to pool up here as if it's attracted to the concentration of magic. It tastes earthy and powerful on my tongue.

We stand in front of the door, which is gilded in spells.

Gold-dust filigree—studded with bone carvings and preserved forget-me-nots—dedicate this place to the lives of the past and remind us that the information we've gathered must not be lost. In the center of the door hangs a heavy braid laced with shiny beads—a braid containing every Hemlock witch's hair since we began.

I remember the day Nana pulled me up the stairs to add my mother's. We were still in mourning, and I sobbed as I watched my grandmother lace sapphire beads onto my mother's black lock. She weaved it into the other strands, sealed it all with the purest olive oil, and then rebraided the whole thing, officially adding Mom to the long list of the dead.

I put my hand to a sapphire bead. I haven't been up here often since that day—only when Nana makes me try to open Mom's history or to write in my own. I should probably read the histories more, but I trust Nana to tell me what is necessary. Besides, no one could possibly get through them all.

"Kat, when we get inside, don't touch anything," I say.

"Seriously," Maggie whispers. "Nothing. It's too dangerous."

Kat nods, her gulp audible in the ancient silence.

I put my hand to the brass knob, and the spell calls for me to undo it. I push the required magic into the metal.

Click.

TWENTY-ONE

When the door creaks open, we're greeted by a surly boa constrictor. He coils around the nearest chair, eyeing us as if he's famished. His tongue flickers in and out, and then his eyes glow hot purple. Kat grabs my sleeve, and I laugh.

"Don't worry; it's an illusion." I pluck a few eyelashes and flick them at the image. It vanishes in a puff of pink smoke, leaving a pleasant scent like peaches. "Of course, it would have killed you if you didn't know how to get rid of it."

"Ours is a giant boar that will gore you to death if you don't give it enchanted mushrooms," Maggie says.

I groan. "I hate that thing. It's creepy."

Maggie rolls her eyes. "It's a pig."

"I'm beginning to understand why you didn't take me

up here when you were mute." Kat's hands are glued to her body, like any sudden movement will send a scythe at her head.

"So," Maggie says as she scans the rows of shelves, all filled with Hemlock tomes. They look intimidating even to me, hidden in the dim lighting. At least Great-Great-Grandmother Agatha took care to put them in order from oldest to newest. Having a time line should help us find things more easily. "What exactly are we looking for?"

"Hmm, that's a good question." I shake my head, trying to clear it. I always forget how intense the magic is up here, history after history enchanted with its own spells. It's like being surrounded by thousands of math problems your brain is begging to answer, except if you get one wrong you could grow a huge wart on your face. Or get covered in frog slime. Or lose an ear. It depends on whether the witch had a sense of humor or a dark side.

"What are those?" Kat nods at the three old desks, each with a heavy leather book on it.

"My history, my mother's, and Nana's," I say as I point to each desk. "I should probably get mine up to speed at some point. I think the last time I wrote in it was a year ago."

Maggie shakes her head. "Aunt Pru says it's our duty to keep a detailed account of our lives, what we learn about magic, and the changing world. She'd have my head if I neglected mine so much."

I walk to my mother's desk and read her name, neatly carved into the front. "Maybe she'd understand if Tessa were dead."

She bites her lip. "Sorry."

"It's fine." I'm too focused on my mom's history to be mad. Hers is the one we need—all the answers are probably right here between the pages. I reach my hand out. If I could open the cover . . .

A shock of electricity shoots through my arm before I even touch it. I recoil, mad at myself for not being able to come to terms with her death like I should.

"Maggie can't open it?" Kat asks. It's only then that I realize she's beside me.

I sigh. "No, only a Hemlock witch can—one who's prepared to read what's inside. After I open the books, anyone can touch them, though."

Maggie puts her hands on her hips, surprisingly serious for her. "So if we can't read Carmina's, what do we read? Where do we even start?"

"Well, we're looking for clues about these male magic users, how they came to be," I say. "So that means we need to read about the times our family has been hunted and Cursed, or anything else that seems out of the ordinary for witches in general."

Maggie nods. "Yeah, that narrows it down. A little."

"We should split up," Kat says. "Someone should start

from the beginning, someone at the middle, and someone near the end."

"That could work, but . . ." I tap my foot. There has to be an efficient way to do this. I snap my fingers. "Okay, Kitty Kat, you start at the beginning, since you have a lot to learn anyway. Mags, you find the Salem incident—that's when things got pretty bad for all witches in America. Maybe something will stick out. And I'll start with Agatha, who built this house. If someone wants it, maybe she'll have clues about who."

They both nod.

"This way." I lead them down the narrow aisle between shelves. The histories take up the entire attic. The farther we go, the more tattered the books become. We try our best to care for them, but we can't stop time. At least I don't think so. If we could, I bet we'd have to do something terrible like sacrifice people. No thanks.

A few books hiss or wail as we walk by, which has Kat even more on edge. She squeaks when a ghost girl with no eyes comes oozing out of one. "What pretty eyes you have," the girl sings to Kat. "Give them to me, and I will show you my secrets."

"Jo . . ." Kat backs into Maggie, who shoves her right through the ghost to me.

"It's okay. Witches can make ghosts. Way easy defense because they have always freaked people out."

Maggie smiles wickedly. "Plus it's fun."

"That, too." I reach into my satchel for the common items I grabbed. Eyes. It's like every spell requires them.

The ghost reaches out to Kat, brushing Kat's bangs away with a pale, translucent hand. "I've never had green ones before. Perhaps they have special powers. . . ."

"Here," I say, holding out two pig eyes in a plastic baggy. "I think these suit you better."

The ghost takes them happily, and then she's sucked back into the journal she came from. I take it from the shelf, since I had to go to the trouble of unlocking it anyway. Mary Hemlock, 1634–1698. "Hey, lucky us—she was alive during Salem!"

"Really?" Maggie looks at it. "Shoulda guessed, trying to freak us out with such theatrics."

"She was probably the head of the house at the time, since the trials were in 1692." I look at the book spines nearest Mary's. "Here's Emily Hemlock, who is probably her daughter . . . and Charlotte comes next, oh, and Teresa. Looks like Mary had a few daughters."

"So your family was fertile at one point." Maggie already has Mary's book open. She flips through the pages slowly, and I get the sense that she enjoys histories much more than I do.

"Shut up." Most witches struggle with infertility, having one child or two. Three is extremely lucky. Nana says that's how it is. She tried for a decade to have Mom, and apparently Mom was with Dad for a while before . . . Okay, stopping that image now. "Just because the Crafts are having a couple of fruitful generations doesn't mean you're immune. It happens to all families at one point or another."

"Do you guys always talk this openly about fertility and passing on bloodlines and other reproductive topics?" Kat asks.

I laugh. "Yeah, pretty much."

"It's really important," Maggie says. "My mom might make me wait until I'm old enough, but making babies is how we keep our magical lines going. How could we not talk about it or want it or look forward to it?"

Kat nods slowly, seeming to mull it over. "Fair enough."

After I open the Salem histories for Maggie, I head for the oldest books, which Kat will have a fun time reading. They are from twelfth-century England, and pretty crazy. "I'll dispel the first three for you. Call if you get through them all."

"Okay." She takes a deep breath. "They won't kill me after they're unlocked, right?"

"No." I smile at her worried face. "Actually, I thought it'd be worse. Seems like most of them have touch spells; so as long as you don't bump anything, you're good. And I'm right here if you get clumsy."

She nods. "You already saved my life once today."

"True." I look down at my hand, which has significantly improved thanks to Nana. I can still feel some pain, but it appears to be normal at least. "And I'll save it as many times as I have to."

"You're like a superhero."

"Yeah, if superheroes used the powers of darkness."

I pull out the very first history—Golde Hemlock, 1153–1201. Hers I have read, and it's fascinating how she was born with magic, though her mother didn't have it. That happened occasionally—still happens sometimes—when a mother-to-be gives birth in a place brimming with magic. The dark power takes the child for its own. Golde slowly discovered her powers, and then one day she found another witching family, the Sages, who took her in and taught her their ways.

The Sages were also afflicted with the Curse, even then. Nana told me that their family died out from it right before many witches left for the Americas to escape it. Sometimes I wonder if that's why it's also followed the Hemlocks so often, because Golde learned from the Sages.

The lock is simple to break: just a heat enchantment dispelled by blowing magic onto it. I hand it to Kat, and she carefully opens the leather cover. Inside, the parchment is yellow and slightly brittle. Then she tilts her head. "Uh, is this English?"

"Middle English." I pull out a piece of glass that's round

like a monocle, but without the chain. "This is a translator. Look through and it'll make sense."

She takes it from me. Now I can tell she's excited, because she's already reading. "That is amazing."

"It only took about a hundred animal tongues to make, so don't break it."

She cringes. "Lovely."

I open the next two books for her, and then head back to the newer histories. Agatha's isn't very far from the reading area in the round tower portion of the attic, which is well equipped with plush chairs and silky pillows. What little light we get under the freeway streaks through the windows. I take her history off the shelf, surprisingly nervous to read it firsthand. Nana has told me the story many times, so I never bothered to look up the source. Immediately the book sticks to my fingers, like the best superglue in existence. Funny. You'd definitely know who took it.

I rummage in the satchel for a vial of enchanted slug mucus. As I pour it on my hand, I realize I should have brought antibacterial wash, too. Oh, well. I settle into a deep red recliner and crack open the book.

Agatha's journal is fairly boring early on. She lived in New York as a child, near the Crafts, which isn't too surprising. The Hemlocks had a good piece of magical land up there that we stayed on for hundreds of years. It gets interesting when Agatha gets older—she's restless and wants to travel, so she takes a long trip to Europe and visits some of the most magical sites in the world. That's when it gets bad.

August 31, 1890

Nice, France

Fanny wrote me today with distressing news—Mama has been Cursed. They don't know how, but she has been complaining of weakness, of not being able to hold magic like she used to. I feel as if it's my fault somehow, for leaving the house. But then why am I not the one Cursed?

It makes no sense, but I must return home. I will miss my travels. Being penned into that house scares me almost as much as the Curse, but it seems I'll be head of the house sooner than I ever wanted, now that Mama has been sentenced to such a harsh fate.

My heart breaks for Agatha because I know exactly how she feels. I'm in the same position, except I don't have a sister. I always wished for one, someone to share the burden with when I got older.

I keep reading, and it gets worse. Agatha's aunt also gets Cursed. That's when Agatha and Fanny set out separately to find another magical place to live. They try to cover as much ground as possible, but most of the eastern American magic spots have been claimed.

July 13th, 1894

Iowan Plains

Today I found a miracle. I have soaked in the magic at Stonehenge, at the Giant's Causeway, in the Transylvanian forests, at Mont-Saint-Michel, but it's not until now that I have tasted magic that makes my whole being feel alive. And in Iowa!

The place is not much to look at, and it is hot as Hades. It is a wonder that such a plain speck of earth could hold so much power and promise, but I must have it. I will have it. This will be our new home, where Fanny and I can be safe from the Curse. I cannot stand leaving this place for one second, fearing that someone else may claim it before I return. So I have written to Fanny wherever she may be, and we will build anew.

The magic—it is deep and dark and strong, and I know the Hemlock family will be safe here for many generations.

I read on, enjoying the descriptions of this very house being built. It took many months, and apparently a lot of money for the period. Money isn't really an issue for us if we need. Years of family treasures, plus the ability to conjure precious gems, helps.

My heart doesn't speed up until I find another surprising entry:

May 3rd, 1895
Willow's End, Iowa

Glorious news! Fanny has discovered another highly magical spot in this area, and we are working to secure it. Buying land here has become increasingly difficult in the last year, as there seems to be a town springing up from nowhere. They are calling it Willow's End, due to all the willow trees that have been planted to combat the terrible summer heat. Let us hope they grow quickly, for the sunny months are upon us.

I've never heard of another magical place in the area, and I can't help wondering why we don't know about it. Surely Nana would have mentioned this to me if she knew. As I read through the next few years, Agatha mentions Fanny building another house in the area off and on. They have plans to have many daughters, to rebuild the Hemlock name to what it once was. Everything seems absolutely perfect until:

January 27th, 1900
Willow's End

Fanny is dead, and I feel as though someone has stolen half my heart. I tried to secure her house, but it has become curiously bound to the people who moved in. I think perhaps the spell was supposed to bind to me if I'd gotten there soon enough, but it was the day of Fanny's death that my daughter decided to enter this world.

It is lucky Geraldine came easily, for I had to do it on my own. Now we are the only Hemlocks in existence, and I've never felt so alone in my life.

My throat goes dry. I tear through the pages, searching for any more information about this mysterious "other house," but Agatha says nothing, save she misses her sister. She never mentions if Fanny was also lost to the Curse, and it seems strange that she wouldn't mention that. She specifically talked about everyone else being Cursed, and yet not Fanny?

How did she die, then?

Witches don't usually die from sickness, since we can fix almost any bodily ailment. Same with accidents. There are only two things that could have happened to Fanny—old age or murder. She was younger than Agatha, so that leaves murder, either by the Curse she concealed from Agatha or something else.

Or *someone* else.

Could she have discovered what Nana and I have? Did she know about the men with magic?

I jump from my seat too quickly, the book hitting the floor with a loud smack. Fanny's history—there has to be more information in hers. There is something weird about this. I can feel it.

But it's not on the shelves. I check the histories nearest Agatha's about forty times before I allow myself to believe it's missing. How could it be missing? I deflate when I realize that it's not missing; it's just not here.

It's at Fanny's house, wherever that is.

TWENTY-TWO

I stand at the front door, and Nana hovers over me to the point that it's suffocating. But I let her because I have to go to school today. I still haven't been able to protect Gwen or Adam past the barrier, and the thought of them being attacked next makes me ill. As much as I want to stay in Willow's End, it'll be easier to find them at school than orchestrate some scheme to make them stay in our ultra-fortified town.

"This will heighten your magical senses," Nana says as she drapes a charm over my neck. It glistens like abalone shell. "And this is the strongest spell repellent I have. Also, one to boost your magic so you don't have to use as much."

"How long did it take you to make these?" I ask. She forced me to bed after dinner, insisting that I needed my strength today.

"For-freaking-ever," Maggie moans from the living room couch. "I should know, since we only finished an hour ago."

"We do what must be done, Margaret." Nana holds out several extra necklaces and a bag of spell pearls that look like candy. "These charms are for Gwendolyn and Katherine, for protection and hiding and solidarity. You must stay together. Try to feed the boys these pearls—they have everything they need. But mind you, the spells won't last as long as the charms, if you catch my meaning."

"Nana . . ." The thought of guys digesting spell pearls isn't a good way to start the day.

She holds her hands up. "Pleasant or not, you must know. Margaret and I will make more and—"

"Why can't I go to school with Jo?" Maggie pulls herself up. Her long braid is messy, strands of hair sticking up in every direction. "I could help protect them."

"Too complicated," Nana and I say at the same time. Getting her a school guest pass, having her shadow me in classes, not to mention how Gwen might see Maggie as yet another person I was paying more attention to—the trouble outweighs the benefits.

Maggie pouts.

"I need you here to help with more potions anyway." Nana unlocks the door and looks me straight in the eye. "I'll be watching. If you see anyone suspicious, do not let them get near. If you were Cursed . . ."

I hug her. "I know. I'll be careful."

The bus honks, and I have to run to make it in time. As I scan the rows, I spot Gwen's bright blond ponytail. She has her face turned away from me, since she's chatting with Winn and Adam behind her. Kat and Billy are across from them, flipping through papers on who-knows-what.

I make my way to them and drape the charms over Gwen's head. "I owe my grandma a hundred beetles for these."

She lets out a little squeak, touching them with one finger. Then her hand wraps around them, and she looks at me with the same sad eyes she wore the first day she sat with us. "You didn't have to do that."

"Yes, I did." I sit next to her. "Nana gave those to Kat. I had nothing to do with it, but I should have thought about how you'd feel, and didn't. I'm sorry."

"I probably overreacted." Gwen smiles a little as she inspects the bauble filled with swan down.

"You think?" Kat throws a wad of paper at her.

"Don't say we're cutting you out again," I tell Gwen. "Because it'll never happen, ever."

Winn pats Gwen's arm. "Told you it was nothing to worry about." I raise an eyebrow, and Winn recoils. "Uh, she kind of yelled at me in text last night about stealing you away and ruining your trio."

I turn to Gwen. "Seriously?"

She sinks into her seat. "I was really mad! And I already

yelled at you and Kat, so . . ."

"I reassured her that I would never intentionally damage your friendship," Winn says. "Hope that's okay."

"Of course it is," I say.

"There's only one problem with all of this." Adam leans on the back of our seat. "Why didn't you call me, Gwen? You could have cried on my shoulder."

She gives him that look, the one that any guy would fall for. "I don't have your number."

He holds his hand out. "Gimme your phone."

When he takes it, I elbow her. She bites her lip, and that's all I need to know she's totally smitten. Despite Kat's claims that Gwen and I are giant balls of hormones, we've really only had a few crushes, and Gwen's the only one who's had a boyfriend until now.

"There." Adam hands the phone back, his smile surprisingly charming instead of mischievous. "Now if you ever want to ditch these losers, you have a place to go."

"Losers?" I hold out the spell candy. "I was going to let you have some of my nana's best homemade sweets, but if you think so little of me . . ."

He snatches the bag. "You're cool, Jo, even if you're dating a complete dork."

Winn takes the bag and shoves Adam off the seat. "That's it. Go sit next to Gwen, since she's the only one deserving of your presence."

"Damn straight." He pops a few candies in his mouth as he sits.

"These are pretty good," Winn says through a mouthful. "Billy, you gotta try some."

I breathe a tiny sigh of relief. At least they have some defense for the day, even if I have no clue how much it'll help. It sure would be nice to know what we're up against. Protection or not, I can't seem to stop looking over my shoulder. I fear our hunters are closer than we're prepared for.

Winn touches my arm, and I jump. That's right: I'm in art, and nothing is wrong, unless you count being forced to sketch a rocking chair with one seriously creepy doll on it.

"Are you okay?" he asks. "You're quiet. You haven't said a word about how that doll looks possessed."

I can't help but smile. "I guess I'm a little on edge about what you said yesterday."

"About the guy who took our picture?"

I nod.

He puts his arm around me, and I feel slightly better. "Don't worry. If we see him again, I'm calling the cops. I don't care if the guy is scary or crazy or what. I'm sorry I didn't say something that day."

I lean into him, glad for the comfort even if Winn is essentially powerless. If only cops could help.

The day is extremely uneventful, which makes it even

harder to focus on anything besides who could be watching me. It's all so normal, and yet not. I used to feel safe here. I can't feel that way now.

Ten minutes before school lets out, I start to think maybe we'll be okay. Maybe Nana and I blew things out of proportion. But then my heart stops, and every hair on my body raises.

Kat. Again.

My hand shoots into the air. "May I use the restroom?"

The teacher nods. "Take the hall pass."

I rush out the door toward the physics room, where I'm sure Kat is furiously taking notes. Putting my hand to my chest, I wish I could get my heart to slow down. But as I round the corner, the sensation is immediately gone, replaced with shock.

Dark hair. Cunning eyes. A suit.

He smells of magic, of power deep and limitless. I shiver as we stand there, staring at each other. I can feel his wanting, like a rope around my heart. He craves me and the power I hold. And like Winn said, he's a boy. An achingly beautiful boy who can't be much older than I am.

Maybe he's not the one who killed my mother, but that doesn't mean he won't kill me.

TWENTY-THREE

"That binding spell is pretty convenient," the boy says in a surprisingly soft voice. "All I have to do is think about killing your friend and here you are. Better than a phone, really, since you have to answer."

Instead of replying, I put my hand to the charms around my neck, pulling the magic into my fingers.

"Don't worry." He smiles, as if he finds this all extremely amusing. "I'm not going to Curse you . . . yet."

"So comforting." Kat would be out here if I were in real trouble, but I continue with the spell anyway. The magic makes my hand tingle with power. The charms are definitely working, because I don't think I've ever felt so strong. This stupid boy has no idea what he's up against.

"Seriously, you really don't want to do that."

"Oh? If you're the one who took my picture and tried to murder my friend, I definitely do." I let electricity spark from my fingers. My hair will turn permanently gray if I let the spell shock him to death, but that seems like a small payment.

He sighs. "Details, details. I knew you'd stop that bubble curse before your friend died—that's why I picked the one who was bound to you. I do have a cover to maintain, you know."

"That makes it okay?" I'm so angry I can barely contain myself. "Whatever you are, you're evil. You've tormented us for the last week and a half! No, for hundreds of years, and—"

"I know who killed your mother."

My eyes grow widc, and the spell fades back into my body. "W-what? Who?"

His grin turns smug. "Give away my best protection against electrocution? I don't think so."

"Then what are you doing here?"

He shrugs, coming a few steps closer. I force myself to stand my ground. I won't cower—not even if he can Curse me. He looks me up and down, and then says, "Just wondering what all the fuss is about."

"Who's fussing?"

His laugh is like a whisper, barely there and yet powerful enough to make me shudder. "It's cute how you think I'll tell you. But they weren't kidding." He takes in a deep breath, and the ecstasy on his face is sickening. "That is some top-quality magic, and it comes in such a pretty package."

The lightning surges to my fingers again. "Maybe I should show you what it can do."

"All in good time, Josephine."

I hate the way he looks at me, that he knows my name and says it so intimately. I flick a few sparks at him, and they zip right to one of his pretty brown eyes. In my peripheral vision, I can see a lock of my hair turn silver. "Don't. Push. Me."

He pulls out a handkerchief to wipe the blood. "Impressive, the control you have not to release the entire spell."

"I'm sure you know nothing of control." The spell begs me to do it, to let go and watch him fry to a crisp. It would be so easy, but I can't give in. He knows who killed my mother. Even if it's a lie, I can't risk losing a single lead.

Now his face goes truly cold. "You have no idea how hard it is to restrain myself from tasting your power, but I'm not a fan of taking what's not offered. Unlike some."

I tilt my head, completely confused. "Huh?"

He pulls the handkerchief from his eye, and it's as if I did nothing to him. "There's a lot you don't know. Let's just say people aren't telling you the truth."

My eyes narrow. "Yeah, I'm gonna believe some nameless, evil guy."

"Would my credibility improve if I said my name was Levi?"

"Could be a lie."

"But it isn't."

I grit my teeth, so angry I could scream. Maybe he's telling the truth, but I really don't need to be reminded by a freaking stranger that I don't know what's going on. I am well aware of that already. "Look, if you're not going to kill me or help me, then get the hell out of here. I already have enough to deal with."

"I could help you." Levi puts his hands in his pockets, seeming almost like a normal boy. He looks at me, hope in his eyes. "If you help me."

I scoff. "Nice try. That work on the last girl you terrorized?"

He smirks. "Yes, actually."

The bell rings, and the classroom doors burst open. I freeze when Kat and Winn emerge from the physics room. They immediately spot my horrible new acquaintance, who frowns when he sees them. I run to Winn and wrap my arms around his neck.

"You!" Winn's glare is ice, and he holds me tightly.

Levi appraises Winn carefully, as if he should know him somehow, and then lets out a laugh. "Interesting boyfriend you have here, Josephine. What's his lineage? There's something . . . off about it."

Winn's eyebrows raise, and I think I sense fear. "I don't know what you're talking about, but you better stop stalking her before I call the cops."

"Cops?" Levi turns to me, like we're in on some kind of joke. "Wouldn't that be fun?"

I ball my fists before the magic spills out again. It barely works, and Levi seems to notice because he takes a step back, as if he's honestly afraid of what I'll do to him. He should be. "That would be my cue to leave," he says.

"Wait!" Winn calls, but Levi keeps going. Winn turns back to me. "Are you okay? He didn't try anything, did he?"

"No, I'm fine." I snuggle into him, wishing this were the last day of school so I could never leave Willow's End again. "Why can't some guys take a freaking hint?"

"I don't know." Winn visibly relaxes, probably thinking Levi was trying to hit on me.

"What is with the full-frontal hug?" Gwen says when she appears from around the corner with Adam.

"Some creeper was hitting on Jo," Kat says.

Gwen laughs. "Hate to break it to you, Winn, but you're gonna have to get used to that. If you haven't noticed, she keeps getting prettier."

"No kidding." Winn finally lets me go, but only enough so that we don't look like we're mauling each other in public.

"I have the same problem with you, so it's even," I say,

though my mind is reeling from who I just met. Nana and I theorizing that male magic users existed was scary enough, but Levi made it all too real.

Girls hitting on Winn—I wish that were the only thing I had to worry about right now.

"Nana!" I yell the second I get home.

"Here!" Maggie calls from the dining room.

I drop my bag, wondering what they're doing in there. We never use that space—only the kitchen table. Everything in the dining room is original to the house, as pristine as it was when Agatha moved in. The table is dark cherry, each leg carved with hemlock flowers, small like baby's breath but deadly. The fancy cupboard matches the table and contains fine china with gold-plated edges. And if that's not elegant enough, the chandelier is stunning, with its draping flower crystals.

Nana and Maggie peer out from behind the thick velvet curtains. "Josephine," Nana says. "We have a visitor."

My heart sinks, envisioning something terrible, like Levi standing at the gate. If he got through our defenses we're doomed. "Who?"

"More like what," Maggie says.

I join them at the window. The front lawn of the house under the bridge is the same as always, shady and overgrown. I haven't been out there since my dad showed up, and

I ache to walk through the damp grass barefoot, searching for snakes and salamanders. "What are we looking at?"

"Under the ivy by the gate," Nana says.

I squint at the shadows. There—two glowing eyes. "A cat!"

Nana nods. "Our first clue to where Anastacia might be."

TWENTY-FOUR

Cats and witches have always gone together, and for good reason. Felines possess the same ability to hold darkness, but on a smaller scale. Most witches have at least two or three, which they use for various purposes. Cats are beloved companions to us, as faithful as dogs but much smarter. I've always, always wanted one, and seeing this cat's eyes makes me long to keep it here forever.

But Nana's violently allergic.

One strand of cat hair will make her entire face swell up. When she was born, Great-Grandmother Geraldine had to say good-bye to four beautiful Russian Blues. We still have a picture of them on the mantel.

"Once you discover why it has come," Nana says, "get back inside, shower, and then tell me what we've learned, both from the feline and that horrid young man you met."

"Of course."

I grab a frog eye from the apothecary and head back to change the front door to the black one. I savor the brass knob's grimy feel, excited to open it. It lets out a positively gleeful groan, and the world outside crashes into me, all power and shadows and age.

Unlocking the gate, I click my tongue and hold out my hand. The cat emerges from the bush immediately. It's a pretty thing, sleek and sandy in color. It saunters over like we have all the time in the world. I don't mind—I'm just excited to hold it.

It hops into my lap, and I run my hand over its silky soft fur. "What's your name, pretty cat?"

"I am Rose," she says in a delightfully rich voice. "I am here to deliver a message from my master to Dorothea Hemlock."

"Who is your master?"

"Sylvia Black." Rose's purr tickles my fingertips as I scratch under her chin. "She has heard that you are looking for her daughter."

My heart skips with hope. "Dorothea is allergic to cats, but I'm her granddaughter, Josephine. Are you authorized to give your message to me?"

Rose nods. "My master knows not of Anastacia's whereabouts since she is traveling. But if you would like to visit

Sylvia, she is willing to attempt contact with Anastacia for you. Her house is in Georgia, on an old plantation called Blossom Ridge."

"Well, that's something. Thank you, Rose."

"You are very welcome."

I scratch behind her ears, and she purrs. "Do you need anything before you leave? Milk? Food?"

Her ears perk up. "Milk would be lovely, but I can find my own meals."

I reluctantly put her down and crack the door. "Maggie! Grab a bowl of milk, will you?"

"Sure thing!" When Maggie brings it out, she smiles gleefully at the cat. "Oh! You are so pretty. It's weird to be in a house without cats. I don't know how Jo survives."

I fold my arms. "I don't. It's horrible not having them around. I miss them, and I haven't ever had one."

"It is a shame," Rose says. Then she sticks her face in the bowl, lapping up the milk. Maggie pets her as she drinks, this longing expression on her face. I wonder if I look the same.

After we take a few more turns petting Rose, I force myself to stand. "We need to get back to work."

Maggie frowns, but frees Rose from her hug. "Come back if you can."

The cat licks her paws. "Thank you for the milk." Then she runs through the gate and disappears behind the ivy.

As I climb the stairs for my shower, I hear Nana ordering Dad to vacuum the entire front hall and all the way up to the second floor in case we tracked in cat hair. I wouldn't be surprised if she made him clean the walls, too.

A shower and comfortable pajamas do wonders for my stress level. It feels like the last week and a half has been months, with so much happening that I can barely stop to breathe.

"Jo! Hurry down here!" my dad calls frantically as soon as I shut off the shower. I sigh. From one crisis to another.

He's at the front door, seeming perplexed. "So I can hear a knock, but when I open the door no one is there."

I laugh. "It's the other door. One sec, let me change it over."

Nana seems impatient when I enter the apothecary to grab more frog eyes, but she says nothing. She taps her fingers on the desk, and the sound makes me pick up my pace. I put my hand to the front door, and my father watches with curiosity.

"There we go," I say when the Main Street one appears.

He touches it. "That is incredible. It's like you're a witch."

"You think?" I open the door, and our visitor makes my jaw drop. I thought it'd be Kat or Gwen. Maybe Winn, though he said he had plow duty again. But never in a million years did I expect to see this.

It's a cable guy.

"No freaking way," I say.

The man looks between us. "Did I get the wrong house? I'm looking for Joseph Johnson?"

"Right here." Dad raises his hand. "Do you need any help with the equipment?"

"That'd be great. The TV is pretty heavy."

"Thanks for hauling that out for me, by the way. We're so far from everything here, and it wouldn't have fit in my car." Dad follows him to the big white truck, and I stand there in total shock. I don't know how he did it, but I'm so excited I can barely contain myself. They lug a huge rectangular box through the front door, and he smiles at me. "Where should we put it?"

"Oh, um, the living room, probably," I say.

The cable guy brings in a bunch of other stuff and gets to work. Dad looks at me nervously. "You like it?"

"Uh, heck yeah. I can't even believe it."

He laughs. "We should be online in a few hours. I hope you don't mind, but I bought you a laptop, too. I don't know how you've been writing your school papers, but I figured it would help to have one for next year."

"Are you serious?"

He nods.

"So . . ." I gulp, suddenly nervous that asking will jinx it. "Does that mean you're staying?"

He winces. "Not completely sure yet. My company said I

could telecommute for a couple months as a trial. Don't tell your grandmother, though. I only convinced her to let me have this stuff because I'd be here permanently."

Before I worry about what he thinks, my arms are around him. "You're the best."

He puts one arm around me, like he's unsure of how to do the parental-affection thing. "I can't wait to see your reaction when I buy you a car."

I pull away, eyes wide. "Don't even kid about that."

"Can't have you dependent on a boy for transportation."

I roll my eyes. "Seriously, Winn should be the least of your worries at the moment."

"Perhaps, but you've never been a teenage boy."

"Thank goodness." A sudden burst of worry rushes over me. "Does he really bother you that much? You bring it up like every time we talk."

He shrugs. "I suppose it's another reminder that you're already grown up, and . . ." He looks away, his eyes sad and distant. "I missed everything."

I bite my lip, unable to say how much I wish he had been there, too, now that I've met him. "We have photo albums. Maybe later we could watch something on this awesome TV, and I'll show them to you."

He smiles my smile. "I'd like that."

"I better talk to Nana. She's waiting for me."

"Right, of course."

Nana almost glares me to death when I enter the apothecary. Maggie is cradled in the small window seat, seeming positively bored. I sit in the chair and give Nana the rundown on Levi and Rose. When I finish she just sits there for a moment, her hands clasped.

"It seems very strange that he would not Curse you," she says. "Is he toying with us, or is he someone we can trust?"

"I don't know." I wrap my arms around myself. "Trusting him seems like a really stupid idea, doesn't it? He has magic when he shouldn't, and we don't know anything about him but his name."

"And the fact that he sounds like a total jerk," Maggie adds. "He almost killed Kat. How did he even know she was bound to you? That is super fishy, if you ask me."

Nana sighs. "He could have sensed it. If he can sense Josephine's magic, it must be a skill of his. Maybe that's how these men have been able to hunt down witches for centuries. And I do not like how he said he doesn't take what isn't offered . . . why would a witch offer to be Cursed? It makes no sense."

"Nothing makes sense anymore," I say.

"I know, dear." Nana looks so sad, so filled with regret. "But that boy has answers. I think he *does* know who killed Carmina, and he certainly knows how the Curse works. We need that information desperately to even stand a chance."

Levi's smug grin flashes in my mind. "I think he knows that, too."

"Certainly."

"Which means there will be a steep price to pay if we risk seeking his help." I put my head in my hands, unsure of how much I'm willing to sacrifice to survive.

TWENTY-FIVE

Friday evening, Gwen rummages through my armoire as I carefully apply a layer of eyeliner. I don't wear it often, but it's my first real date with my boyfriend. It seems like I should kick it up a notch. She pulls out my blue sundress, the one I was wearing when Winn saw me at the county fair. "You have to wear this."

I blink several times, my eyes itching from the extra makeup. "I don't know. Isn't that a little cheesy?"

"A *little*?" Kat sprawls out on my bed and opens her notebook.

Gwen puts her hands on her hips. "I think it would be romantic."

"It's stupid."

"Is not!"

Kat rolls her eyes. "Whatever."

I head over to Gwen. "It doesn't matter, because it's not what I want to wear anyway."

She hangs it back up with a huff. "Then what do you want to wear?"

I stare at my clothes, pursing my lips. "I don't know."

"Well, you better decide soon, because we have fifteen minutes to take out those hot rollers and get you ready." Gwen pulls my shoe organizer from under my bed. It kind of sucks not having a closet in my round room, but it has helped me learn organization. "Maybe picking shoes will help you narrow it down."

"I'll know it when I see it." I scan my clothes yet again, and nothing seems good enough. I wish I could have bought something new and perfect, but the closest mall is too far outside the barrier to risk. At least I have internet now—hello, online shopping. "Why are all my clothes so ugly?"

"They aren't!" Gwen holds up gold flats and red sandals. "Which ones?"

"Gold. I think?" I put my hand on my head, only to get burned by the curlers. "I don't know! I'm freaking out here."

"You two are ridiculous." Kat slams her notebook shut and stomps over to my armoire. She pulls out a pair of apple-green leggings and a short black dress, then points to Gwen. "With the gold flats."

I raise my eyebrows. "I . . . love that, actually."

Gwen folds her arms, probably hurt that I picked Kat's choice over hers. But Kat kind of has an advantage, since she can basically read my mood. I throw on the clothes and plop down in my vanity chair. "Gwen, please make my hair look good. I beg of you."

She sighs, though I'm sure she's happy to oblige. That is one thing she'll always beat Kat at. Gwen has magical powers with hair, I swear. She can curl it, straighten it, pull it up in fancy braids, and it always looks perfect.

"Your hair really does have a mind of its own, doesn't it?" She fiddles with a wayward curl, and it miraculously goes into place.

Seeing her do that makes me ache. I don't want to keep the grief in and ruin my date, so I take a deep breath. "My mom used to do that. She could always flip my curls and they'd fall the right way, as if they thought she was the boss."

Gwen smiles as she fixes another one, seeming appeased by the comparison. "Now I'm the boss."

I laugh. "That's for sure."

The doorbell sounds, and I can barely contain myself. As I head for the stairs, Gwen follows just behind. She tugs on my hair so hard I squeak. "That hurt!"

"One second! This one needs help, too."

I bounce like a kid hopped up on Popsicles. "Hurry! If I don't get the door first—" It creaks open, echoing through the whole house, and I freeze. "Crap it all."

"You must be Winn." My dad's voice carries from downstairs. Despite his convincingly friendly tone, I can imagine Winn's smile dropping right off his face.

"Nice to meet you, Mr. Johnson. I hope you're liking Willow's End," Winn says. I can tell he's nervous—he sounds too proper.

"Let me go!" I whine. "I have to diffuse a potential disaster down there."

She pats me on the shoulders. "Okay, you're good. Have fun and tell me everything."

"Of course!" As I bound down the stairs, both their faces go from fake smiles to real ones. I almost hug Winn, but then decide against it. "Please tell me you guys aren't playing out the awkward father-meets-daughter's-boyfriend scenario, because I expected so much more out of you."

"You're about to be sorely disappointed," my dad says. "There's no way around it, because I planned to be cool and totally failed."

Winn looks down, as if staring at me might get him in trouble. "Not doing so hot on this side either."

"Sad." I take Winn's hand, at which point they both turn back into cardboard. "Oh, for the love. I'll be back before midnight, okay?"

My dad manages a nod, and then we head for Winn's truck. He revs the engine, and we're off to the diner, which is really the only place in town for a nice meal. He lets out a low whistle. "Now that I'm sure we're out of your dad's hearing range, you look so hot."

I bite my lip. "Thanks."

When we get to the diner, it feels like everyone is staring at us. I try to distract myself with the never-ending array of stuff on the wall. The place is fairly popular with travelers, since this is the last stop before about a hundred miles of corn to our west. Travelers like stuff on the wall. It's eclectic, authentic, whimsical. At least that's why I think they keep adding old gas-station signs and mini rocking chairs and old tennis rackets.

Mrs. Holman, whose husband owns the place, shows us to our seats. She hands us menus with the most obnoxious "Well, aren't you adorable?" smile. "Can I get you two something to drink?"

We both order our whole meal, since everyone in town knows the menu by heart. That way she doesn't have to keep coming back to check on us.

"So." Winn taps my foot with his. "You think we'll actually get through an entire date with nothing bad happening?"

I laugh. "We probably shouldn't take bets on that. Our odds haven't been good so far."

"We'll still have fun, even if we do get hit by lightning." His smile still takes me off guard with its perfection. I can't wait to kiss those lips. It better be tonight. . . .

Focus, Jo, focus. "Don't go straight to lightning. Let's at least hope for something as trivial as breaking limbs, or maybe . . ." His face darkens, and I turn around to see what he's looking at. My eyes go wide. Even dressed in jeans and a T-shirt, it's easy to spot Levi and all his dark energy.

Levi. In Willow's End. Despite all our magical alarms and barriers. When he spots me, his mouth curls into a wicked smile.

"I'm sorry, but if he comes over here," Winn says, "I might have to beat the shit out of him."

My head whips back to Winn—I have never heard him swear, and it changes something. I didn't see him as the fighting type. When I put my hand on his, his expression softens slightly. "Winn, I appreciate the chivalry, but I can handle him. Without throwing punches."

He puts his other hand over mine. "I don't like how he looks at you. I know guys think you're hot—even Adam and Billy say it all the time—but that guy is different. He's . . . I don't know, but there's something off about him."

I purse my lips and study the sincerity in Winn's stormy eyes. It's as if he knows, on some deep level, that Levi is a threat far past "trying to steal my girlfriend." Only when Winn squeezes my hand too hard do I realize that Levi is standing right next to us. "That's a pretty big booth for two people."

"Go away," I say.

Levi puts his palm on the table, and my free hand automatically goes to my necklaces. "But all the other tables are full."

"Sit at the bar," Winn says.

"I'd really prefer company, and you two are such an electric couple. You light up the whole room, which is pretty difficult considering the loud decor."

I sigh. "What do we have to do to get you to leave right now?"

"Hmm." Levi rubs his chin, though I get the feeling he already knows exactly what it'll take. "If I could have five minutes of the lovely Josephine's time, I suppose I could eat pizza instead."

"Who the hell do you think you are?" Winn says.

Levi's eyes narrow. "Do you really not know?"

As they glare at each other, it feels like a fight is about to break out. Something about this *does* feel weird, but I can't put my finger on why. "Five minutes is fair," I say, trying to diffuse the situation.

Besides, Levi has information I need. If I can get rid of him *and* learn something? That's worth it right there.

I start to stand, but Winn pulls at my arm. "Jo, I don't think—"

"How else are we going to get rid of him peacefully? You hit him, and we'll be spending the rest of this date at the police station. Not romantic." I try to smile, though thousands of questions run through my mind. "Trust me. I'll be right back."

"Safe and sound," Levi says.

Winn doesn't look happy, but he backs down. "I'm coming outside in exactly five minutes."

"Fair enough." Levi holds out his arm for me. I glare at it, wanting so badly to set it on fire. Stalking past him, I head into the cool night. A nearby willow provides enough cover to keep people from noticing us or overhearing. "How did you get in here?"

He shrugs. "The spells keep out those who plan to harm your family. I don't have any intentions like that."

That can't be right. He had to have used a loophole or broken through the spells. "Perhaps you're so evil you don't see your goals as harming us."

He scoffs. "If that were true, *he* would have found you years ago."

"He? You mean the man who killed my mother?"

"That would be the one."

I ball my fists. If Levi really had good intentions, he'd tell me what he knows and solve all my problems. "You're sick, you know that? How can you stand here telling me you don't have bad motives when you already threatened to Curse me?"

His cocky smile twitches. "Like I said, I only take what's offered."

My eyes narrow. I feel like I'm missing something. "Why would any witch offer to die? That makes no sense."

"I'm not killing anyone."

I let out a wry laugh. "Don't you dare say that. I've seen it. I watched my mother hack up black blood. I watched her grow weaker and weaker until she couldn't even get out of bed, let alone cast a spell."

"Control can be difficult." Levi looks down as if he's ashamed, but I don't buy the act. "But the Curse isn't supposed to kill."

"Control? What the hell are you talking about?" I'm breathing way too hard. I try to stop myself, try to calm down. It doesn't work. "So you control the Curse to torture us for as long as possible?"

He rolls his eyes. "Damn, you're slow. You know what the Curse does, right?"

"Of course. It drains your magic, makes you weak, slowly kills you."

He sighs, and for some reason it seems sad. "And where do you think all that magic goes?"

My jaw slackens as this information clicks into place. No. It can't be. That is the most disgusting thing I've heard in my entire life. "You . . . your kind . . . you take it? That's how you can use magic—you steal it from us."

"I told you I do *not* steal," he growls.

I cover my mouth, horrified. Some man was leeching

my mother's magic for himself? "How dare you claim to be anything but evil? Magic belongs to witches, not to people who murder for it!"

He glares at me. "So you're going to judge me based on what others of my kind did? You think witches never do anything wrong with their power?"

"I didn't say that."

"You basically did, which is incredibly ironic, seeing as you're looking at one of the biggest mistakes your people ever made."

It feels like the wind got knocked out of my lungs. "Excuse me?"

He holds up his hands. "You know what? Screw it. You can find out the hard way. I wanted to help you—I came to apologize for showing up like that on Wednesday—but you're a stuck-up little brat. Find me when you realize you're not any better than I am, oh holy one."

I squeak, but that's the extent of my comeback. Levi walks away as I stand there trying to find the right insult. It never comes.

When I get back to the diner, my food is at our table and probably cold. I sit next to Winn on his side of the booth. Why do they always put couples on opposite sides? It's stupid. I pull my plate over and dig in to the mashed potatoes. "I don't think I've ever hated someone so much in my entire life."

"Good. Then we're in agreement." He slips his hand around my waist. "He didn't try to make a move on you or anything, did he?"

"No. I would have killed him if he did."

"Then what did he want?"

I pause, searching for a cover. "He thinks I have something that belongs to him, but I don't. He's totally insane."

Winn doesn't look completely satisfied. "I don't want to sound like a possessive boyfriend, but you shouldn't be alone with him like that. It'd be nice if you never saw him again, even. He seems really unstable."

He has no idea. Just the thought of Levi—of what he can do—makes me sick. I didn't think the Curse could be worse than it already was. I squeeze Winn's hand, looking him directly in the eye. "I know, and I'm not ever doing that again."

"Okay." He breathes a sigh of relief. "Let's get back to our date, then."

"Yes, please."

After dinner, we drive to Winn's house, which is so much more beautiful in the dark. The white glows a silvery blue in the moonlight, and the stained glass shines bright from each lit window. Winn parks in the gravel up front, since their garage is closer to the barn.

When we get out, my stomach twists at the thought of meeting his parents. Maybe I shouldn't have made fun of him, because it's kind of scary. I want them to like me, but at the same time I'd rather avoid them completely. Winn takes my hand and, to my surprise, doesn't head for the house.

"We're not going in?" I ask.

"Not yet. I wanted to show you my favorite place out here." He steps into the long grass, and a few fireflies flee at his steps. "You know, before my parents scare you away forever."

I laugh. "I don't think that's possible."

"I guess we'll see."

The evening gives up its last shreds of light as we walk hand in hand. It's quiet, which is when I realize Winn and I aren't usually quiet. It's nice, being together like this. Sometimes I worry the second I stop coming up with clever comments he'll get bored, but maybe not. He doesn't look bored, at least.

I like the trees here, mostly because they aren't willows, which get tiring in large quantities. Winn's trees are oak, and I imagine the person who planted them planned to be here a long time, since they aren't the fastest-growing tree. These are massive, their new leaves not big enough to hide the starry sky.

When I see the swing, I smile. It's wide enough for two and carved with flowers. Old things were always done with such care, and I immediately get why Winn likes it so much. "I haven't seen one of these in forever."

"My grandpa put it here." He grabs the old rope, and the tree branch creaks like my house. "I guess my grandmother loved to swing, but she died before I was born."

"It's beautiful. May I?"

He smiles. "Of course."

The tree protests when we both sit, but it holds our weight. I lean my head on his shoulder and watch the fireflies dance around us. The air is quieter since it's spring. There are crickets, but they are timid about their newfound voices. The bullfrogs sound young, the deepness of their croaks not quite there.

"I never brought Chelsea here," Winn says.

I look up at him, his profile strong in the remaining light. "What?"

"I hardly ever brought her to my house. It's weird, but everything wrong with her seemed to stand out when she was here. I guess I was in denial about it." He pushes the swing back, and we rock softly. "But you fit here so well it's scary."

Hearing him say that makes up for everything that happened at the diner. "Great. I'm scary."

Gently, he kisses my cheek. "Terrifying."

It sends a wave of warmth through me, and I hold my breath as I wait for what must be coming next. I study the lines of his face. The creases from his smile. The place by his eyes where laugh lines will someday show his age. We have so much life ahead of us, so many more experiences that will change our faces from young to old. And then something in my heart snaps.

This won't last forever.

I look down, trying to recover the water pooling in my eyes. *Now. Think about now. Enjoy it now.*

"Jo?" Winn puts his hand on my face. "Is something wrong?"

"No. Nothing." I look back up, smiling as best I can. "I just wish this moment could last forever."

He leans in. "But there are so many better ones to come."

"True." When our lips meet, it's unlike anything I expected. It's not "meh," as Gwen once described her first kiss. The power inside me tingles, growing stronger the more we kiss. It begs me not to stop, as if my magic has been waiting a lifetime for this moment.

Winn pulls away first, breathless. "Where . . . how . . . was that as amazing as I thought it was?"

I gulp as I search his eyes, confused not only by how strong our connection seems to be, but by his ability to recognize it. "I think so."

He kisses me again, and my magic sizzles at our lips, so addicting I can barely control myself. The only thing that stops me from unleashing it is my confusion over what it wants, why it would react to Winn. Maybe this is totally normal for a witch. If it is, I plan to be with Winn as long as

I can, even if I can't have forever.

After a long time swinging and kissing, we head for his house. I'm not as nervous as before. I do feel like I belong here, as if the place is familiar in some way. But it's not until we enter the house that I know why. I have to catch myself from falling because the magic is so strong and deep and warm, like a well straight down to the Earth's core. I know, with everything in me, where I am.

I'm in Great-Great-Great-Aunt Fanny's house.

TWENTY-SIX

I force myself not to panic, but I can't stop wondering about how on earth the Carters ended up in Fanny's house. Agatha did write that Fanny's house was bound to a family. Maybe it was Winn's.

But as I take in the spells, it seems impossible that any witch—let alone a normal human—could find this house and bind to it with such powerful barriers surrounding it. They are overwhelmingly strong, more so than any on our house. My head spins as it tries to decipher all the magic in the air.

"Jo?" Winn says.

I jump. "Huh?"

He seems really worried, like he thinks I might run and never come back. "Are you okay? You kind of spaced out a little."

"Oh, I'm fine. I just . . . didn't realize your house would be so beautiful inside." It's the truth. The simple beauty of the outside follows you in. White walls with striking, colorful art mirror the stained-glass windows. The soft navy blue area rugs mimic the shutters. The lush greens and browns bring the trees inside.

It's magical.

"I've always liked it." He tugs my hand, and I take a few steps forward only to stop again. A stunning array of old ceramic tiles covers the hall wall, carefully arranged so that it looks like a night sky with hundreds of colorful stars.

"That's amazing." I step closer. The pieces certainly don't belong to one another, but are chips from something else. "Who made this?"

He shrugs. "It's always been there. A lot of things have always been here. They're so beautiful that there's no reason to change them."

I touch the tiles, imagining Fanny herself putting them up. My fingers turn hot and then numb, and my wonderings are proved right. This is one massive spell—a spell of hiding, like a star among many. This is why Nana and I haven't found this place right under our noses. I can't make out all the complexities, but it seems like only those bound to the house can bring people in. So there's no way someone could have murdered Fanny unless . . .

Did Winn's ancestors do it? Maybe she let them in to give

them a spell, and they attacked her. But surely she would have defended herself.

"Winn?" His mother's voice echoes down the hall. "Is that you?"

"Yeah." He squeezes my hand once. "Don't be nervous. She'll love you."

I *am* nervous, but not for the reasons he thinks. "I hate your confidence—makes it so much easier to disappoint."

He shakes his head. "C'mon."

We pass by the spiral staircase and through a swinging door, which opens to a rustic kitchen, the old woodstove still in place. To our right is the living room, where a TV gives off the only light to see his parents by.

They look normal and non-magical, hanging out on the couch after a long week. Mr. Carter is a total farmer, hard work written in every line on his face. Winn's mother's grin is warm, and her hair matches Winn's sandy color exactly. I try and try to see if I'm missing something, but there's not a speck of magic in them that I can find. It doesn't make sense, but I'll take it. That is much better than discovering a witch or whatever Levi is in the house.

"Well, aren't you pretty as ever, Josephine," Winn's mother says with her soft southern accent. I'm not sure which part of the South she's from, but she and Mr. Carter went to school in South Carolina and that's how Mrs. Carter ended up all the way out here in Willow's End.

"Thank you," I say. "Your house is gorgeous. I'm still trying to take it all in."

She smiles wider. "It wasn't until I saw the house that I said I'd marry Jim."

"That's the only way any of us Carters manage to tie the knot," his dad says.

I laugh, but then stop short because I'm not sure if I'm supposed to.

"You'll hear that joke at least twenty more times." Winn pulls me to the couch. I try not to look as awkward as I feel, sitting so close to him when they're staring. Not that they seem upset, but it's weird.

His dad takes a swig from a glass bottle. "It's the truth. The Carters have only had boys for generations—my grandpa used to joke about us ugly mutts needing a nice house to convince any woman to live in Willow's End for the rest of her life."

As much as I don't want to, I have to ask. "Generations, huh? How long have the Carters been here anyway?"

"Oh, since around nineteen hundred," Mrs. Carter says. "You should see the attic, honey. Someday we'll get around to appraising all that stuff. We'd probably be rich."

My heart skips a beat. It's too close to when Fanny died. "Really?"

"We're not selling anything," Mr. Carter says. "But yes, my great-grandfather Phillip and his wife, Cordelia, moved here around the turn of the century. I remember my grandpa showing me their journals and letters when I was a kid—he loved exploring the attic."

"Wow." I don't want to go on, but Nana would be pissed if I didn't. "Do you know who lived here before that?"

His parents glance at each other. "No one did. My family built the house," Mr. Carter says.

"I see." I know he's lying. Which means they have something to hide. I don't want to think about what that might be.

"So, uh . . ." Winn clears his throat. "Are you guys going to bed soon?"

His mom laughs. "All right, all right, baby, you two be good. We'll finish off this movie in our room."

"The volume will be on low," his dad adds.

Winn covers his face. "We really need a movie theater within reasonable driving distance."

I offer a laugh, though it sounds halfhearted. When his parents leave, Winn gets up to put in a different movie. "What do you want to watch?"

I shrug. "I like anything. You pick."

He gives me this look, as if he knows something happened within the last few minutes but isn't sure what. "Okay, if you say so."

I watch him, wishing I'd never come here. I want to go back to not knowing that, even though it should be impossible,

Winn lives in a witch's house. A witch who was probably murdered. But it feels like I'm falling into darkness deeper than anything I've ever felt. I don't want to accept the most logical explanation: Winn's family is somehow like Levi.

Is that why my magic reacted so strongly when we kissed? Is Winn after it as well?

My stomach turns as I worry about whether or not Winn can sense my powers. I hate that Levi's claim about people lying has gotten to me. The way Levi looked at him when we first met screamed of recognition. Levi probably knows how Winn plays into this, and he's somewhere smiling that evil smile, thinking about how devastated I'll be when I find out.

I am devastated.

Winn sits next to me again, pulling me close. I hate how quickly his touch has turned from comfort into fear. Maybe he's like Levi—maybe he's not the kind who Curses immediately, but instead waits for the right time to ask for what's not his. Maybe he's waiting until I'm so in love with him that I'd do anything to keep him.

I should leave.

I don't want to leave.

"You're so quiet," he whispers.

I blink, realizing that the movie has been going at least fifteen minutes. It's a comedy, and I haven't laughed once. "I . . . sorry, I was falling asleep." I lean into him more, his scent enveloping me as I fight back tears. I have to be wrong. *Please, please be wrong.* "You're just so comfortable."

He kisses the top of my head. "There you go, calling me fat again."

My laugh sounds more like a mouse being squashed, but I cover it up by burrowing my head into his chest. He seems happy with that, and I wish I didn't want to be this close to him. Why can't I get myself to leave?

"So much for our bad luck on dates," he says.

One tear escapes, and I hope he doesn't feel it wet his shirt.

TWENTY-SEVEN

The waffles my dad makes aren't as bad as I thought they'd be, but I still can't bring myself to eat more than a few bites. When I woke up this morning, I tried to convince myself that last night was a dream, but it definitely wasn't. My dreams were worse—Winn drenched in blackness like Levi, losing our ivy-covered home, dying of the Curse like my mom.

"I really don't think Winn is bad," Maggie says through a mouthful of charred bacon. "There has to be another explanation, because I saw him and he felt totally normal to me, too. You can't hide magic if you have it."

I fight to keep my face from cracking. I cried enough last night. "But then how'd they get bound to the house, and not Agatha? Seriously, the spells over there have lasted over a hundred years, and they're still so strong. I can't imagine normal Phillip and Cordelia Carter just strutting in there on their own."

She frowns. "Then she gave it to them?"

"It's not impossible." Nana pulls a pudding from her fridge, which means this is a disaster. She's usually a no-pudding-before-noon person. "If Fanny was dying from the Curse and didn't tell Agatha, the hunters must have found her. Perhaps she bound the Carters to the house so whoever was hunting her couldn't have it."

"That's true! I could see that!" Maggie says.

I sigh. "Maybe."

"No use fretting when we don't have all the details, dear," Nana says. "As far as magic is concerned, Winn doesn't possess any. So he is not a direct threat. We'll find the answers in time."

"Yeah, because we have so much of that lying around."

My dad pats my hand. No words, just this simple gesture of understanding. I offer him a small smile and force myself to move on. "I guess there's nothing we can do but keep trying to stop our hunters. Since Levi has refused to help us and Winn is up in the air, we need to focus on our one actual lead—Stacia's mom in Georgia. We should pay a visit."

"I agree." Nana licks her spoon, her eyes rolling back slightly. That's what I call the Pudding High. It's pretty disturbing. "The only issue is getting there."

"Right." I purse my lips. Can't teleport to a place I've

never been, and we have no door connections in the area. "Are we really gonna have to drive or something? Lame."

Maggie raises her hand. "Thanks to Aunt Pru, I actually know a door in Georgia. So no road trip necessary."

I raise an eyebrow. "You speak as if Georgia is as small as Rhode Island. Your door could be half the state away from Blossom Ridge!"

She tips her chin up. "Better than half the country!"

I lean back. "True."

"Even though Anastacia should be a friend, I still want you to be extremely cautious. Don't let anyone know how much trouble we're in." Nana crunches her pudding cup like a beer can and, shockingly, goes for another. "What do you plan to bring as Stacia's possession we claimed to have?"

"I . . . forgot about that." It will have to be something that belonged to Mom, and I don't love the thought of parting with her things.

Nana gives me a knowing look. "I will find something. You and Margaret should locate this Blossom Ridge on Joseph's fancy computer."

He stands. "I'll go get it."

"Thanks." I put my plate in the sink, and Maggie and I rush for the TV. As two teens who've been deprived of media for all time, we've spent every free minute in front of the big screen. Seven hundred channels! Infinite, mind-numbing glory.

Maggie gets the remote first, and she turns on the Disney Channel. It's totally cheesy and should be too lame for us to watch, but we both love it. The utter non-reality is strangely soothing. The fake audience laughs. The hokey jokes and slightly oblivious characters. I could watch this all day, pretending that my problems could be resolved that easily.

"Here we go." Dad sits next to me, handing over the laptop.

I search for Blossom Ridge in Georgia. Of course, it appears to be completely out of the way, surrounded by orchards and not a major city in sight. "Where's your door, Mags?"

She leans over to see. "It's in Dublin. Aunt Pru had . . . a friend there."

"She has friends?"

"Ha. Ha." Maggie points to a dot I wish were closer to Blossom Ridge. "It could be worse."

"I guess, but we'll still have to take a bus or hitchhike or something."

"Whoa, there." Dad holds up a hand. "You are not hitchhiking. I can rent you a car, okay? There's no reason to get reckless."

I laugh. Because this whole venture is so safe. "Can you even do that? Don't I have to be like twenty-five?"

"We'll . . . bend some rules. Just this once. You can fake

your ID with a spell, can't you?"

"Yeah, but did you seriously just tell me to fake my ID?" I can hardly believe I'm hearing this from my father, who just last night freaked about me going on a date.

"Better than hitchhiking!" He finds a rental place in the area, and we're set to go in an efficient thirty minutes. Before Maggie conjures the door, Nana takes my hand. Something cool hits my palm. I look down to find a familiar pendant. Intricately carved gold surrounds a glass ball filled with swirling violet smoke. It was one of Mom's favorites.

"Tell her Carmina intended to give it back to Stacia, but then they lost touch and after the Curse it was impossible," Nana says.

I wrap my fingers around it, wanting to keep the precious token for myself. "I will."

Maggie conjures a boring, gray door that looks like it belongs to an apartment complex. Sure enough, when we go through, the place is tiny and messy, but there's magic there nonetheless.

A ragged witch sits on the couch, smoking a cigarette. She doesn't make a single move as she eyes us. "That you, Maggie?"

"Hi, Nicole." Maggie looks at her shoes. "Sorry for the intrusion. We needed to go to Georgia, and this was the only door we knew. I know you probably—"

She waves her hand. "Don't worry about it. Just because Pru and I aren't together anymore doesn't mean you're not welcome here."

My eyebrows raise. I'm surprised a dictator like her would have dated someone who seems a little haggard and lazy.

I've never seen Maggie look so uncomfortable. "Okay, well, we better get going. Sorry to bother you."

"Not at all. Safe travels, ladies."

As we walk to the rental place, Maggie is so quiet I'm not sure what to do. She seems upset, but I'm not sure why. "I'm not embarrassed," she finally says. "My mom told me about Aunt Pru when I was like four. It's just . . . they had a really bad breakup. Epically bad. I feel awful for showing up like that."

"I'm sorry."

She nods. "But this is important, too, right? Your family is at stake, and that's basically saying my family is. We'd hate to lose you guys."

I nudge her, grateful for the support. "Right."

Georgia is beautiful and warm. There are trees everywhere—so many that sometimes it's like we're driving through tunnels carved right through them. It's almost suffocating, like the corn gets in late summer. Finally, we find Blossom Ridge, which is the complete opposite of what I expected.

Basically, it looks like a rainbow threw up all over it.

As we get out of the car, I can't get past the multicolored picket fence. Something that bright and friendly shouldn't have such a menacing barrier spell on it. I stare at the pink plantation home, in awe of its similarities to a Barbie dollhouse I once had. If this is anything like our house, the barriers should warn someone that we're here, so all we have to do is wait for them to let us in.

A woman emerges from the house, her white hair the only plain thing I've seen thus far. The closer she comes, the more I see that her outfit makes up for it. Red polka-dot dress with a bright teal belt. Yellow stockings and purple shoes. Green and orange jewelry. She's a walking bag of Skittles.

"Hello there, darlings," she says in a sugary-sweet way, as if we're in preschool. "Are you looking for something?"

"Someone, actually," I say. "Sylvia Black?"

She puts her hand on her ample chest. "Why, you're looking at her."

Yes, yes, I am. I can't look away from all the color, in fact. "I'm Josephine Hemlock. You sent Rose to tell us about finding Stacia?"

"Oh, yes! Of course." She unlatches the gate. "So nice to meet you. I remember how much Stacia would talk about Carmina. They were so close."

"Really?" For the first time in a while, I feel hope. If

there are answers anywhere, they must be here.

"Come on in." Sylvia heads back up the path, which is lined with cheesy garden sculptures. Mostly bunnies. "I'll see if I can get ahold of Stacia for you. She's been traveling a lot, so it might take some time to track her down."

"We're fine waiting," I say, my heart pounding with excitement.

The house is as strange on the inside as it is on the outside. A large chandelier of glass eyeballs dominates the entryway. They stare down at me not in a creepy way, but as if they're curious. Everything seems to be made from eccentric components like this—a side table with taxidermy animal legs, a rug of what I'm sure is some kind of hair, and mosaics very much like the one I saw in Fanny's house.

"The kitchen is right through there," Sylvia says. "I'll go upstairs and see what I can do about tracking down Stacia. Have whatever you'd like to eat. You must be hungry from your travels."

"Thank you." I head to the kitchen, Maggie right on my tail. I try to stay on my guard despite the fact that Sylvia seems like your average head of house, complete with strange hobbies and appearance.

The kitchen is tiled with old glass bottles, their bottoms colorful and bumpy underfoot. We sit at the table, which is weathered wood with a sheet of glass over it.

"What do you think of her?" Maggie whispers.

I shrug.

She bites her lip. "That's the craziest getup I've ever seen!"

I restrain a laugh. "I know, right? But hey, if she's willing to help us, I don't care what she wears while she's doing it."

Maggie nods, and then we sit there staring at the clocks on the wall. Hundreds of clocks in all shapes and sizes. Only one of them ticks—a small brass one with black numbers.

We jump when a door slams beyond the kitchen, down a dim hall. Footsteps come closer, and I feel like a fool for not realizing someone else would live here. Maybe another daughter or a granddaughter my age.

The person appears, half dressed and hair messy. When our eyes meet, Levi looks truly surprised. My heart sinks, along with all my hope.

TWENTY-EIGHT

"What are you doing here?" we both say at the same time.

"Wait, who is . . ." Maggie starts to ask, but then she seems to pick up on all the shadows. "Holy crap, is that Levi?"

I shoot her a look. "Yeah."

"You didn't say he was freaking gorgeous; I was expecting pure evil!"

That cocky smile is right back on Levi's lips. "I like your friend."

"Shut up!" I stand, prepared to fight or run if I have to. "I can't believe you conned an old lady into letting you Curse her. What, did you charm her with a spell?"

"You're sick." He opens the fridge and chugs orange juice straight from the jug. I'm so glad I didn't get anything to drink. "And a total idiot."

I put my hands on my hips. "Then what is it? You obviously live here."

He gives me this look, like I couldn't be more dense. The magic in me boils. It begs me to do awful things, and I have to breathe deep to control it. Levi leans on the counter, his eyes glittering like chocolate diamonds. "Remember when I said witches aren't exactly blameless in all this?"

A lump forms in my throat. "Oh, no . . ."

Maggie swings her giant braid over her shoulder. "Can we stop being cryptic? It's really annoying."

Levi smiles wider. "That old lady she accused me of seducing is, in fact, my grandmother. She's evil, by the way, so you really shouldn't be here if you like being alive. This is what you would call a trap, and you idiots walked right into it."

Maggie snorts. "No way. She's helping us find Stacia."

He raises an eyebrow. "What?"

"We're here to see Stacia." Maggie stares at Levi way more than I'd like. "We were hoping she'd know more about who is hunting the Hemlocks, since she knew Carmina so well."

Something is wrong. I can feel it all around me now, closing in like a predator. The Blacks . . . could they really be in on this? Or is he lying? Levi crosses the kitchen and looks out the hall where we entered. "You need to get out of here. Right now."

"Then can you contact Stacia?" I try to hide how desperate I am. "I need answers. I've waited years for answers."

He looks down at me. "You won't get any from Stacia."

"And why's that?"

Levi's expression is dark, and the pause before he speaks is longer than normal. "Because she died years ago. From the Curse."

My eyes go wide, and I shake my head back and forth. She can't be dead. "You're lying. You're just trying to stop me from finding the truth, because then you'll have nothing to keep you safe."

He comes over to me, puts his hands on my arms. "I'm not lying. You want answers? Fine. The Blacks are the ones after you and your land—me, the others like me, are pawns in their game. They've been snuffing out other, more powerful families for hundreds of years using us. And if you don't go now you're dead."

He's not lying. It makes too much sense to be anything but the truth. This is the big secret we've been missing all these years.

"Why are you doing this?" I pull away from him, pissed because now I have to be grateful he told me.

He leans on the doorframe. "What do you mean?"

I take the opposite side. "You obviously hate me. And now you're saying you belong to a family that wants me and Nana dead so they can take my land. But you're ruining your grandmother's plan."

He looks at his feet, as if he's trying to stuff his emotions down, and then back to me. "Maybe I know what it's like to watch your mother hack up black blood, to be helpless to stop it, to hate the person who did it so much all you think about is revenge."

"What? Witches can't have sons!" But I know the agony on his face, hidden well to those who've never lost a close family member. "That's impossible."

"Not when your father has magic, too."

I can't breathe right. So much about this is wrong, and yet it feels true. "Stacia . . . was your mother."

He doesn't have to speak for me to know I'm right. It's all in his eyes. "You need to leave. She's calling him."

My blood turns cold. *"Him?"*

He nods.

Nana was right—witches were involved after all. The betrayal cuts into me. How could the Blacks do this? The Curse goes so much deeper and darker than I could have ever imagined. And still I say, "But what about you?"

His brow pinches, as if he's completely confused. "Huh?"

"It's just . . . will she know you told us? Won't you get in trouble?" I fiddle with my hair. Stupid boy, making me feel compassion for him.

"I'll be fine, Josephine, but thanks for caring." He smirks, and I regret giving him a second thought.

"Maybe I should make sure you have a good alibi, just in case." Before I can think better of it, the magic pools into my hand and overflows. With one flick, Levi is on the floor convulsing from the shock. I smile, enjoying it far too much. "You couldn't stop us from leaving, could you?"

He's limp, only his chest moving up and down rapidly. "I hate you."

"Good." I motion to Maggie. "Let's move."

We run for the door, and once we're out we don't look back. I'd teleport right there, but I don't want to risk them finding the way to our house through magical remnants. We need to get some distance first. I speed away, and Maggie keeps her eyes on the road behind us, silent with terror.

"Do you see anything?" I ask every five minutes.

"No," she whispers. "Not yet."

Everything seems worse in the silence—how stupid we were to think that Sylvia would help, how close we came to being Cursed and sucked dry, and how the only reason we're alive is Levi. Being indebted to him is not my favorite place to be.

By some miracle, we make it all the way back to Dublin without so much as a flicker of threat. Which is probably Levi's doing, though I try to pretend it isn't. Once the car is checked back in, we find the closest deserted alley and teleport back to my house.

The apothecary is empty when we arrive. In fact, the entire first floor is dark, save the glow coming from the living room and its glorious TV.

"Nana?" I call, though she can't possibly be watching television.

"She went to her room," my dad says. "How did things go?"

"Not as planned," I say, rushing up the stairs. I hope she's not writing more letters, because obviously that got us a lot of nothing. I open her door without knocking, and the world crumbles beneath me.

Black blood. On the floor. The sheets. Her quivering lips.

TWENTY-NINE

"Josephine," Nana says, her voice partially garbled from what I can only assume is more blood. I can't move. I'm not even sure I'm breathing. All I can do is stare at her while everything clicks into place. I knew something was wrong the day we cured my father—felt it deep in my bones—but I never thought it would be this.

Everything makes sense now. She let Kat know about witchcraft so I'd have someone to talk to. She allowed my father to stay so I'd still have a parent to care for me. She kept Maggie here because she was losing her power. She stopped harassing me about Winn because she knew I'd need someone with comforting arms to hold me when . . .

I lean on the wall, my knees threatening to give out. This can't be happening. It doesn't matter who else I have. How am I supposed to go on without her?

"It had to be this way," she says. I still can't get my lips to move, and she squirms in the silence like I usually do in hers. "I was careless, my child, hungry for revenge. When that shadow man appeared . . . I did what I had to do to make sure you survive."

Of course she sacrificed herself. I put my hand to my mouth, that moment taking on all new meaning.

She runs a shaky hand through her long, white hair. "I hoped the dagger and my magic would be enough to stop it entirely, but the Curse was far more insidious than I dared to imagine. The purity of that weapon wasn't enough, and it transferred to me."

I can't look at her anymore, the image too familiar and horrible to handle. So I pull my knees in and put my head to them. Something pokes my skin, and I put my hand to it.

Mom's pendant.

I pull it from my pocket, rubbing it with my thumb over and over. She used to wear it all the time, though it wasn't for any spell that I knew of. She loved the look of it, I suppose. It is beautiful, a never-ending storm swirling inside. Thank goodness I didn't give this up to our enemy. They've already taken so much.

"I'm not afraid to die," Nana says.

"Oh, that's good to know." Finally the tears burst through, hot on my cold cheeks. "I'm so glad that *you're* not afraid to die! That's makes everything all better."

"Josep—"

"You should have told me!" I yell. "We've wasted all this time trying to fight our hunters when we should have been trying to cure you."

She purses her lips. "We know very well that I can't be cured."

I stand. "No. We don't. Levi was at the Blacks' house, Nana—he told me they're the ones who created his kind and therefore the Curse. Now that we know where it comes from and what it really does, there has to be a way to stop the guy who Cursed you."

Nana shakes her head. "We don't have time. Whoever this man is, he is taking all he can from me as fast as he can. I assume in order to get to you and our land. All we can do now is protect you, the house, and hope he can't break through."

"No!" I gasp between sobs. "I'm not letting you die!"

She gives me that look, like I'm being completely unreasonable.

"I'll kill him first. Killing him has to break it."

"Even if you could, we still don't know which of these men Cursed me."

"Levi does. I could find him again. He wanted to help us—"

"No!" Her gaze turns angry. "You are not leaving the barrier, and he is too dangerous to trust. It's not worth the—"

"Don't you dare say it's not worth the risk." I ball my fists, so close to losing it that all I can do is believe there's another option. I can't do this without her. I can't be head of house at seventeen. I can't be the only Hemlock on the entire planet. "Your life is just as important as mine—you know I don't have a chance at survival without you."

Her dark eyes water. "You do not give yourself enough credit, my dear."

"If I have so much talent, then why are you giving up?"

She leans back on the headboard. "I can't lose you. I already failed Carmina . . . my sweet, strong, beautiful Carmina. Josephine, don't let me die worrying that you'll follow."

What little resolve I have left is gone. My face crumbles into sorrow as I rush to her bed. She puts her hand on my head, and I cry into her bony shoulder. Heaving, painful sobs that reach deep and far. Even the house groans, as if it shares our misery.

This is too close to another horrible day in my life. A morning and afternoon sitting by a bedside, then a night spent lying next to my mother, wide awake in fear that she'd stop breathing the moment I closed my eyes. I still remember the feel of her fingers going limp on my back, how I could sense her leaving. I cried like I am now.

"It's not fair," I say.

"I know." Nana continues running her hand over my

hair, and I feel like a child but I don't know what else to be right now. I wish I could go back in time and stop everything from happening. I wish my mom were here, so she could be in charge instead of me, so we could move on like we're supposed to, so we could sit on the couch together and reminisce about Nana and her pudding.

But no. I'm alone. My witching family is hanging by a charred hair, one breath enough to turn it to ashes.

"Take her."

I don't know how long I've been sleeping when I hear her voice, but it startles me awake. "Nana?"

"Right here, my dear." Her voice is soft, like she's trying to soothe a baby. "Joseph is going to take you to your bed, so you can sleep more comfortably."

"No." I lay my head back down.

"Jo," my dad says. "Dorothea needs to sleep comfortably, too."

"No."

He sighs, and then I feel his strong arms on my shoulders. Before I can stop him, he's carrying me like a little kid.

"Put me down!"

"Sorry." He pushes my door open and plops me on the bed. His stare cuts through the darkness, intent and yet compassionate. "I can't let you do this. I know it's hard, but we'll be okay."

My mouth hangs open for a moment. "Wait, you knew?"

His words catch in his throat.

"You knew!" Anger and betrayal swell inside me. "She told you before me! Why would she do that? How could you let her?"

He looks down. "I don't know why. The day after you fixed me, she just did. I didn't think it was my place to question her choice, being new to all of this."

"Were you going to let her die? Did you think it would be easier for me to handle if it happened one day and I had no clue?"

"We thought—"

I throw a pillow at him. "Neither of you thought at all!"

"We thought a lot. I promise you that." His eyes are sad, but they don't reach me. My soul is spent and desperate.

"You lied to me. She lied to me." I pull the covers over my head, ignoring whatever my dad says. I don't even hear his footsteps as he leaves, but the darkness after he closes my door proves he's gone.

Great Black Death, Levi was right—everyone is lying to me.

THIRTY

My phone keeps ringing—whether it's Winn or Gwen or Kat I don't care. I shut it off. When I can't sleep, I stare at my ceiling. A long crack begins at the chandelier, and it slithers out toward the window, stopping short of the frame. It reminds me of a lifeline. My nana's lifeline, almost out the window.

Stupid crack.

I burrow into the sheets, into the darkness that is at once comforting and full of sorrow. There's a knock at my door, but I've sealed it shut with my sense of taste. I don't need it anyway, since I'm not hungry. "Jo, it's time for dinner," my dad says softly.

I don't answer.

His footsteps trail off, the creaking stairs signaling I'm alone again.

I can't stop thinking about Mom, though I should be thinking about Nana and how to fix the mess that is my life. But I don't know what to do. Listen to Nana, who lied and sacrificed herself? Find Levi, who, despite his knowledge and presumed goodwill, probably wants to use me? Or keep fumbling around trying to find answers on my own, which I prefer even though it's probably reckless?

Nothing feels right anymore.

My pillows smell like Mom, I swear, even though her scent left the house long ago. Her soap was lavender, and it made me gag up until she died. Some memories are fuzzy, but that smell stands out against the haze. I remember the homemade lotion, purple like her pendant, and how her whole room would smell like lavender after she put it on. That scent still belongs to her, and each time I take it in it's like she's here. But she's not.

She never will be.

And now Nana . . .

I curl into a ball, trying to get that smell out of my head. The smell of missed hugs and motherly advice. Of moments never shared and dreams once bright. It seems like it's everywhere, so thick that it saturates my lungs and tastes bitter on my tongue.

"Carmina! Get down here right now!"

My eyes fly open.

A girlish laugh fills the air. It's familiar, but I don't dare believe it. I pinch my cheeks, trying to wake up from my crazy dreams. The stress has finally gotten to me—I'm officially insane.

"Carmina Lucille Hemlock, get your fanny on the ground this instant!"

I pull the covers off, recognizing that tone even if her voice has a younger sound to it. There, on my cracked ceiling, is a projector-like image. It's lavender-colored, a bird's-eye view of two women—Nana and Great-Grandma Geraldine. I know it, even at this distance, because of their voices. The other thing I immediately notice are the two scrawny legs perched on a broomstick. They wobble as a little girl tries to stay balanced in the air, and she laughs again.

It's Mom.

I can't breathe. This isn't possible. I shake my head, but there it stays, the scene playing out before my eyes. Mom soars out from under the interstate bridge, and the fields are endless before her. I can feel her sense of freedom, of having the whole world at her fingertips.

As she flies and flies, I notice a small wisp of purple smoke. It trails all the way to me, to Mom's glass pendant resting on my chest. I gasp when I touch it and the image disappears, like I put my hand over the projector light.

Luckily, I didn't ruin whatever spell I triggered. I'm not sure how I got it to work, but I hope it gives me something—anything—before it wears off.

The scene changes. Mom is outside the ivy house with

two young girls who look like Tessa and Prudence Craft, with their long, fair braids. They comb through the brush in a manner I quickly recognize as snake hunting. Prudence lets out a bloodcurdling scream, and Tessa laughs as Mom pulls a serpent from Pru's ankle. At a second glance, I realize it's plastic. Even I laugh at that. Prudence afraid of snakes? I have to use that information.

After watching a particularly homey Christmas, complete with chestnuts roasting on an open fire, I am pretty sure this is a store of Mom's favorite moments. I've never heard of such a charm, but I want to kiss it. I don't, because it might stop the reel of lavender memories.

The next is another familiar scene—a Halloween Ball, with witches packed into every corner of an old house. Mom is with the Crafts again, and they're laughing as they consume enormous caramel apples covered in chocolate and nuts. Mom stops, her sight focusing on a girl sitting in the hallway with her head to her knees.

"I'll be back in a second," she says to the Crafts.

Mom sits next to the girl in the hall, who jumps. Her eyes are watery, and I'm guessing blue from their pale hue. Her hair is fair as well, and stick straight. "Who're you?" she says to Mom in a timid, high voice.

"I'm Carmina Hemlock. What's your name?"

The girl's eyes go wide with what I think is recognition. "Anastacia Black. But everyone calls me Stacia."

I freeze. Here she is: the girl I'll never meet, but who clearly has everything to do with what has happened to us. And she's Levi's mother? But his hair is so dark, and his eyes are almost black like Nana's.

"Do you like caramel apples?" Mom asks.

Stacia wipes away her remaining tears and nods.

Mom plucks a rose from a nearby vase and turns it into a big, juicy apple. She hands it to Stacia, who offers the smallest smile. "That's the nicest thing anyone has ever done for me."

"That can't be true."

Stacia eyes the apple as if Mom gave her a purebred Persian kitten. "I've never had any friends."

"I'll be your friend."

"You really shouldn't." Her eyes are the saddest I've ever seen in my life. They tug at me, as if they've witnessed more than any little girl should. In that moment, I understand why Mom never let go of Stacia Black.

Mom tilts her head. "Why not?"

Stacia takes in a deep breath, the kind that comes before one shares a secret, but then someone bangs on my door and the lavender images are gone. I shake the pendant frantically, as if that'll reactivate the spell. Nothing happens.

Another knock.

"Go away!" Rubbing the pendant, I push back angry

tears. I lost the only connection I've had to my mother in years. I want it back.

"Jo, please." Though Kat's voice is muffled through the heavy wood, I can tell she's upset. "I know you're hurting right now. I've tried to give you the space you need, but something happened. And I don't think it was an accident."

She's not lying. When I let myself feel more than my own grief, there's something in her that is nearly frantic. I force myself up and break the spell on the door. Kat's face is tear streaked and tired. "What happened?"

Her lips quiver as she tries to keep it together. "Gwen's house caught fire in the middle of the night, and she didn't wake up."

I should say something, but the words won't come. All I can see is the picture Levi sent, his cruel words on the back. *I spy with my little eye . . .*

I can't ask if one of my best friends is dead.

THIRTY-ONE

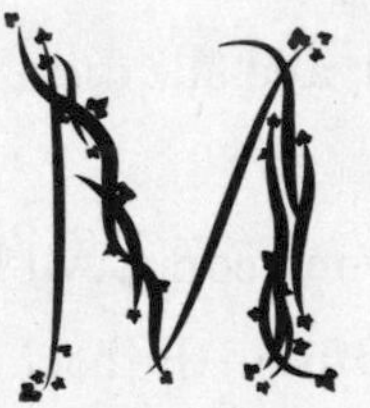

My knees give out, but Kat keeps me standing. "She's alive, Jo. I should have realized you thought she might be . . . she's not dead."

Hearing that gives me enough strength to pull it together. I take a deep breath, shoving the grief over Nana and my mom into a little box for later. Gwen comes first. "How bad is it? What happened? Is her family safe?"

"I don't know exactly." Kat goes to my armoire and riffles through my clothes. "Mrs. Lee called me from the hospital. I guess her parents and siblings escaped once they smelled the smoke, but then they realized Gwen wasn't there. Her dad grabbed a fire extinguisher and went back in for her. She wouldn't wake up even when he shook her, so he carried her out."

I grab my phone, feeling like the most selfish person in

the world for turning it off. Sure enough, when I listen to the messages, half of them are from Mrs. Lee, telling me they're at the hospital in Denison. "She's in a coma?"

Kat tosses me a pair of jeans and a shirt. "Yeah, but I have a feeling she would have been dead if it weren't for . . ." She touches her charms.

"The spell must have been really bad if it still put her in a coma."

She heads for the door. "Get ready. I'll ask Dorothea what we should bring to fix it."

Once I'm dressed, I rush down the stairs. My dad and Kat stand in the entryway. Their hushed tones obviously mean they're talking about me, and the accompanying guilty looks don't help their case.

Kat holds up a bag. "She said you'd know what to do with this."

I take it and peer in. This stuff should definitely help fix whatever has happened. Too bad I don't know the exact curse—it would make it easier to decide on the antidote. "So we have transportation?"

She gnaws on her lip. "I called Winn. He should be here soon."

"Oh." My stomach does all kinds of flips. I'm not sure if they're good or bad ones. I haven't talked to him in a few days—not since I found out he's living in my great-great-great-aunt's house.

"Be safe," my dad says when Winn's lights shine outside.

I don't answer, but instead give him a long, pained look. What am I supposed to say? *Sure, we'll be safe trying to save Gwen from a botched murder attempt. Nothing will go wrong.* I'm never assuming I'm safe again. Not even among my own kind.

Winn is headed down the path as we leave the house, and an unexpected wave of relief crashes over me when I once again see no magic in him. I hold on to that fact like my life depends on it. When we meet, he scoops me off the ground; I'm too exhausted to resist. He whispers into my ear, "Where have you been? I missed you."

How can he still make me want to smile? "It's been kind of hectic around here, getting my dad settled and all."

"I guess I can accept that." He puts me on the ground, and his beautiful mouth turns down. "So, how are you doing with all this?"

I know he means Gwen, but it feels like it applies to everything. Searching his eyes, all I can see is concern. No blackness or cunning like Levi. It can't be fake—he can't be trying to trick me. Or have I already been tricked? I lean on his chest, the comfort of his arms too strong to ignore. If it is a lie, I fell for it a long time ago. "I'm so tired."

"You can sleep on the way there," Kat says. "We should get going."

"Right." Winn guides me to the car, and we head for

Denison. As I doze off on his shoulder, I decide I'll deal with his part in this whenever it comes. For now, I need him too much to let go. He's the one thing in my life that hasn't gone totally wrong yet.

Gwen's family looks ragged, half of them passed out in the hospital's waiting room. My heart aches for them even more when I realize they don't have a home to stay in. Mrs. Lee, who Gwen takes after almost completely, hugs us. "Thank goodness you came. We're hoping that having friends here might . . ."

She chokes on a sob, and I put my hand on her shoulder. "I'm so sorry I didn't hear sooner. I feel horrible."

"No. It's only been two days. . . ." She puts a hand to her chest. "My, it feels like so much longer than that."

"I know exactly what you mean."

It's silent for a moment, as if we're all too tired to make polite conversation.

"Do you need anything?" Winn shuffles back and forth, seeming antsy. "You guys must be hungry, and hospital food is awful. I could run out and get you supplies. Maybe some blankets and pillows?"

"Oh . . ." She shakes her head. "That is so sweet, but I don't have any cash and—"

"It's on me." Winn looks my way, his eyes full of understanding. "I'm sure Jo and Kat want to see her on their own, and I like to be useful. What do you want?"

Mrs. Lee seems hesitant to accept his offer, but she relents. "Anything would be great."

"Say no more. I'll make sure you're fed." He kisses me quick on the cheek. "I'll be back in a few."

I grab his arm, realizing how far we are from the safety of Nana's spells. If anyone in the group is next on the list, it's Winn, my last shred of happiness. I take my strongest protective charm and drape it over his neck. "Be quick. And careful."

He smiles, and with one more kiss he's gone.

"So how is she?" Kat asks.

Mrs. Lee's eyes water. "She has some serious burns on her arms, and her hair . . . they had to cut so much of it off. The paramedics thought her passing out was smoke inhalation at first, that maybe the fire started in her room so she was the most exposed. But she won't wake up. They've run a bunch of tests, and nothing."

"Can we see her now? Or is it too late for visitors?" I ask.

"We'll tell them you're family," Mrs. Lee says. "I'm sure they'll let you in."

They do, though the nurse explains that we can't take too long. The moment I see Gwen, it's exactly what I feared. Her aura is black—she's under some kind of spell, but I don't recognize it. If Levi did this, I don't care what he knows anymore. He will pay.

I walk over, and the spell reacts to my presence with a

hiss. It doesn't come for me this time; it only works harder on its goal, which must be to murder Gwen. This spell isn't for killing me—its sole purpose is to cause me pain, to break me, to terrify me.

To my own surprise, it only makes me want to fight back.

"Is it bad?" Kat asks.

"Really bad. This spell was supposed to kill her—it's still trying to. It's a good thing she didn't take off the charms. The one place there isn't darkness is around them, but it won't last long."

"What do you mean?"

"It means if I can't get this thing reversed, she'll be dead before daybreak."

Kat gasps. "No."

I pull the bag out of my purse. "Hurry, I need your help mixing this."

"But I don't—"

"I need to concentrate on the potion; all you have to do is hand me what I ask for when I ask for it." I search for a makeshift cauldron. It's between a pink barf bin or the bedpan. I hold them up to Kat. "Which is the lesser of two evils?"

She cringes. "Unless it'll erode the plastic, I say the pink one."

"Hmm, I didn't think of that. Bedpan it is, just in case." I set it on the counter and get to work. "The rose oil first."

She rummages in the bag. "The clear water-looking one?"

"Yeah." She hands it to me, and I pour it into the bedpan. Holding my hand over it, I infuse the floral liquid with a heavy helping of magic, straight from my heart. "The dove eyes next."

It's quiet as I go about creating the purification potion—only the occasional beeps from the machines Gwen's attached to. Lizard tails for regeneration. A lion tooth for battle. Sunflower petals to purge the darkness. Before I know it, I'm almost finished, and the potion is a good one, full of power and love.

"And last but not least." I hold my hand over it. "The blood of a loved one."

"So that's what the knife's for." Kat pulls it out, eyeing it. "Can I do it? Or does it have to be from a witch?"

I smile, knowing how much she wants to contribute. "You can, if you'd like."

She cuts her finger without so much as a flinch, and the blood drips into the potion, making a stark crimson flower against the pearly white liquid. It spreads and spreads until I can feel the potion's full power rise.

"That's good," I whisper, concentrating on sealing it all together. The magic tingles through my fingers, and I'm tempted to give it a little more than it needs. But I don't. When I open my eyes, the potion is a bright red-and-white flower. I pluck it from the silver bedpan and bring it over to Gwen. Placing it on her heart, I wait for the spell to banish the darkness.

But instead, the shadows consume the flower until it's nothing but blackened ash.

THIRTY-TWO

I look to Kat, whose horrified expression must mirror mine. This has never happened before. My spells always work, and so do Nana's. How could it not cure Gwen? I collapse by the bedside, clutching my mother's pendant.

"What do we do now?" Kat says, her voice shaky. "We can't let her die. We can't. Gwen can't die."

"I don't know." I take Gwen's hand, even though the shadows burn and hiss.

"Can't we sacrifice something else? You gave up your voice to purify your dad's letter, and you burned your hand for me. There has to be something!" She paces the room, panicking enough for the two of us. "What about a kidney or a lung or an arm?"

"It's too much risk with no assurance that it'd work. I

can't take an arm without knowing with one hundred percent certainty that it would stop the spell."

"We can't lose her!" She yells far too loudly for a hospital.

"I know! But I'm not all-powerful. I don't even know what spell this is—I knew with you. I've done everything I can."

"Do more!"

I don't answer, because she's crying and too frantic to reason with. My tear ducts must be tapped out because my heart aches, but nothing will come.

Gwen is so lifeless and dark that I can't help but realize how much she usually moves. All the time I've known her, she was the one bouncing her knees or skipping when everyone else walked. She used to dance, back when old Mrs. Collins taught a jazz class for the girls in town. Gwen was amazing at it, and you couldn't stop her from practicing wherever there was enough space. What I'd give to see Gwen move a finger, let alone bounce around my room again like a butterfly.

The door clicks, signaling the end of our time with Gwen. I don't move. It can't end this way. I can't leave her to die. "Just one more minute, please; I beg you."

Someone lets out a low whistle. "That is one nasty death call."

I bristle at the voice and turn to see my worst nightmare. Levi actually has the gall to be smiling. He shuts the door, and I wish I hadn't used half my magic on that futile antidote. "You would know, since you're the one who put it on her."

"I would never," he says. "Death calls are way below the belt."

I'm not sure I believe him. "How did you find us?"

Levi sits on Gwen's bed, way too close to me. "When she lived through the fire, I figured you'd show up at some point."

"You've been waiting for me?"

He shrugs. "Basically."

"If you're on my side, you could have at least made yourself useful and fixed her."

"Dear Josephine, you know magic doesn't work that way." His smile is so smug I want to strangle him right there. "We Shadows may not follow all the rules, but payment is something no one can avoid."

"Shadows?" Kat says.

He rolls his eyes. "That's what we call ourselves. It's obvious, but fitting."

I shove him. "Do not disrespect her. I'm ready to kill you as it is."

His eyebrows raise at my touch. "You keep saying that, and I'm still not dead."

"Quit it, okay?" I restrain myself from stomping my foot. "My grandmother is dying and my friends are at risk and after they're gone, I'm next. So do what you came here to do and stop pretending like you're all mysterious and cool."

Levi frowns. "You're no fun."

"I used to be, until you ruined my life."

"My kind may be at fault, but not me personally. Stop blaming me for the actions of someone I don't particularly like either." He fiddles with a stray thread on his shirt. "Your life isn't the only one he's ruined, you know."

"He?" I ask, hoping he'll just tell me already.

"Yes, he." Levi bites his lip, seeming to hesitate. "My . . . superior, you could say. If you want to blame someone, that's the guy to blame. I'm just trying to do what I can for you without getting caught. My life might suck, but it's better than being a dead traitor."

I'm not sure what to say. Maybe I feel a little sorry for him, but I'm not about to let him know.

"So . . ." Kat breaks the silence. "Can you two set aside the hate for a second? If Levi can help, I don't care what he is or what he did."

Levi and I glare at each other, but she's right. "Fine."

Kat stands between us like the mediator in a peace negotiation. "Okay, so Levi wants to fix Gwen, right?"

"Right," he says. "She's been called to death—summoned by a Shadow to the darkness that awaits us all. No witch can remove it. It's a Shadow thing."

Kat shudders. "And what do you need to stop it? You

need something from us, right?"

"Yes, and you won't like it."

I fold my arms. "Try me."

"You have to kiss me."

My eyes go wide. "No freaking way. Kat can take that hit. Sorry, Kat."

"Fine," she says.

Levi shakes his head. "No, it has to be you. I need your magic to save her, and I can get some through a kiss so I don't have to Curse you. Unless you'd prefer the Curse—that would make everything easier."

I glare at him, the choice already made. If I have any chance to save Gwen, I have to take it. So I square my shoulders, determined to look stronger than I feel. "I guess one kiss is better than being Cursed. Barely."

"You have to give it. I don't take." At least he has the decency to look slightly uncomfortable.

I force myself forward, though I'm terrified of what this will feel like. Levi's eyes are dark, full of anticipation as I come close. Desire oozes out of him. I'm not sure if it's me or my magic he craves, but I don't like either option. Tipping my chin up, I close the distance and pray this won't hurt too much.

Levi's lips press against mine, soft and yet urgent. I want to stop—despite the fact that he is, undoubtedly, a very good kisser—but he puts his hand on my face, as if to say, "Not yet." I close my eyes, trying not to get lost in this . . . this chemistry.

Then it happens, and my eyes go wide in terror. My magic drains from my body so quickly I have to grab his arm to stay standing. He holds me up, though all I want to do is push him away. He's taking a part of me, and I hate that I let him.

When he's taken almost all of it, he guides me to the one chair in Gwen's tiny room. I can barely move, and tears drip down my cheeks. He wipes one away, the shame in his eyes crystal clear. "I'm so sorry, Josephine."

"Just save her," I whisper.

He goes to Gwen and puts his hand on her chest. The shadows around him flare, fueled by my magic. He winces as the spell fights him, but it retreats quicker than I expected. I don't want to admit that my magic seems stronger under his command, but I can't deny what I feel. There's no way I could have done that, even if I were full to the brim. Within seconds, Gwen is back to her normal, non-shadowy self. When her eyes flutter open, I can't regret what I did.

Gwen takes in the room and her visitors. "Jo? I saw you trying to stop t-the . . . I wasn't just sick or hurt, was I? There was s-something . . ."

I force the lump in my throat down. "Yeah, but don't say anything, okay? I promise I'll explain later. You were in a coma—that's what everyone thinks."

She nods, but her lips quiver. "The shadows . . . they were everywhere, pulling me down into a black pit. I thought it was over." She looks up at Levi. "Then this guy pulled me out. Who are you?"

"Uh . . ." Levi shoves his hands in his pockets. "No one."

The door clicks open, and I want to die when Winn walks in.

THIRTY-THREE

"What the hell is he doing here?" Winn growls, glaring at Levi like he'd start a fight if we weren't at a hospital.

This would be one of those times where it'd be really convenient if I could tell Winn the truth. But I can't even get my mouth to move, since I'm so low on magic and terrified of what Levi did to me. That kiss was how the Curse must feel, except the Curse is permanent. This is how my mother died, how Nana is suffering, but a thousand times worse.

But what Levi did with my power—he magnified it somehow. What could he do with even more of my magic? I hate that a little part of me is tempted to give it to him, to let him fix all my problems. But the price . . . it's too steep. I can't forget that.

Levi rubs his neck, apparently useless now. He does look drained, though, having used up what I gave him to fix Gwen.

"Um." Kat glances at me, as if I have the answer. Too bad there is not a single logical explanation for Levi being here.

Winn shakes his head, opens his mouth to say something, but then his eyes go to the bed. "Gwen! You're awake!"

She gives him a half smile. "Looks like Kat and Jo saved me."

Levi sighs, and I feel kind of bad that he can't take credit for saving Gwen's life. No matter what else comes, I'll always be grateful he did that.

Winn seems to calm at her words and comes over to me. "You look awful." Taking my hand, he glares at Levi. And I swear it seems like he understands what really happened. "Did he do something to you?"

I close my eyes, tears welling up at another shred of proof that Winn might be lying to me, too. If he was totally normal, wouldn't he have assumed I'm like this because I'm worried about Gwen? Yet he immediately blames Levi.

Levi's eyes meet mine, sad and penitent. "Yeah, my fault. Sometimes I don't realize when I'm going too far. Gwen, I'm glad you're awake. Hope you have a quick recovery."

"Tha—" Gwen starts.

And he's gone, leaving me with a million questions about the Shadows. Not to mention one seriously angry boyfriend.

The nurse comes in immediately after him, and her eyes pop when she sees Gwen awake. She shoos us out of the room, calling for a doctor frantically. Winn helps me to a quiet spot in the waiting room, while the Lees hug and cry over Gwen's miraculous recovery.

"Jo, I need you to be honest with me." He rubs my hand with his thumb. He's clearly upset, and I know he's not stupid. "Why does he keep showing up?"

I hate this. I don't want to lie to him—I want to share everything with him. And I can't. When Nana said this would be hard, I didn't realize how much she meant it. How can I really be with him if I can't tell him everything about me? But at the same time, it'd be wrong. He's already in so much danger, and there's still a chance he's normal. I must protect him from this horrible world I live in until I know for sure he's part of it.

"Levi is . . ." I pinch the bridge of my nose, not wanting to think of him right now. "My mom had a very close friend in college. Her name was Stacia, and Levi is her son. She died when he was a kid, like my mom did. It's this weird connection—we share the same grief—but I swear you don't have to worry."

Winn purses his lips, searching my eyes. "Why didn't you tell me that?"

"I don't know." Here come the tears again. "I didn't want you to think he was . . . he's important, but not like you're important. You're the only guy I want."

The truth of it hits hard, the guilt fresh and raw all over again.

He offers a small smile. "I'm not gonna lie—that's good to hear."

"I'm sorry I didn't tell you."

He brushes my hair from my face. "You know you can tell me anything, right? I don't want you to be afraid of how I'll react. You don't have to keep me happy—you just have to be you."

That's when I start blubbering like a fool. He holds me, and all I want to do is tell him everything. After several minutes of crying, I finally compose myself. Slightly. Winn has me cradled in his lap, and I run my finger back and forth over his prickly cheek.

"I must look pathetic," I say softly.

"Hey." He touches his forehead to mine. "You've been through so much lately. I'd be freaking out if Billy or Adam were in that room."

"And crying?"

"Well, maybe not in public."

I pinch his cheek, and he laughs. Then the sound is gone, and I know he's going to kiss me. I don't deserve it, but I want it.

His lips brush against mine, and my whole body remembers how perfect Winn's kisses are. I pull him closer, kiss him deeper than I have before. The little magic I have left tingles at my lips, but it's not going anywhere. This isn't giving and taking; this is sharing—sharing something better than anything Levi could offer. Winn moves to my neck, and goose bumps cover my skin.

It takes a second for me to get my head on straight, to realize we are full-on making out in a hospital waiting room. It feels so good, like I can finally breathe again after days of only getting by. Against every instinct, I push him back. "You won't cry in public, but you'll do that?"

He grins. "Right, public. I forgot."

I laugh. "Me too."

"You hungry? I bought enough for us. Figured we might be here awhile." He rubs my legs, which are in his lap, and for the tiniest moment all is right with the world.

"Starving."

I watch him go, feeling far too content considering the circumstances. Mom's pendant is warm against my skin, and I put my hand to it. I may have missed my chance to find clues in those lavender memories, but Gwen is alive and that is what matters right now.

THIRTY-FOUR

y jaw actually drops at the sight of Gwen's house, which is barely more than a pile of ash on a cement foundation. I'm sure no one else can see the tendrils of smoke still clinging to the few upright beams. They are too black, too marred by magic. My guilt swells up anew. If only I had been paying attention instead of wallowing in my own grief.

Kat puts a gentle hand on my shoulder. "Let's get to work."

I nod, unable to speak with my tongue caught between misery and fury. Revenge is all I can think about, and for the millionth time since yesterday my mind goes racing back to Levi and his power. I shake the thoughts away. There has to be a way I can stop this Shadow on my own. Too bad I don't know what that is. I spent all night trying to make Mom's pendant work again, but nothing happened.

Kat hands me a pair of gloves, and we join in the cleaning efforts. All of Willow's End has shown up to help Gwen's family. As we toss charred wood into a giant trash bin, trucks arrive with new lumber and building supplies. Gwen's dad seems to be overwhelmed with gratitude as he hugs Mr. Svaboda, the local contractor.

"Jo?" Kat says as we sweep ash off the foundation.

"Yeah?"

She leans in close to whisper. "Promise me Gwen gets to know what I know. It's not fair that she's on the outside, and I'd hate it if you erased her memory of this. She belongs with us."

Nana may not be a fan of the idea, but deep in my gut it feels right, important. Gwen, Kat, and I have always been bound together by friendship, and that should never change. "I promise."

She smiles. "Good, because I hate keeping secrets from her."

"Me too." As I think of her so far away at the hospital, I wouldn't mind having her bound to me. Then I would know if she was safe. "When she gets out of the hospital, I'll tell her everything. Hopefully she won't freak out."

Kat laughs. "It's Gwen. She'll have to freak out a little."

I smile. "True."

Her expression turns serious, and I'm not sure I want to hear what she has to say next. "What Levi did—"

A truck honks, and I turn to see Winn pulling up next to the fleet of pickups. I run over, happy to avoid whatever Kat was going to say. I don't want her to know how tempting using Levi is to me, because I'm sure she'd kill me for it. I wrap my arms around Winn's neck and kiss his cheek. "There you are."

He kisses me back. "Sorry, my mom took forever picking what I should bring."

I look to his truck bed, which is filled with furniture. A dining-room table, a hutch, and an old rocking chair. "Is that from your attic?"

"Yup." He pulls me off and starts unhooking bungee cords. "And this isn't even half of it. Still have a few beds and an entire living room to haul over."

I help him with the cords. "There's really that much up there?"

"You wanna come see?" His face is full of hope, and my heart flutters. His attic . . . there could be something helpful up there, since it would have been where Great-Great-Great-Aunt Fanny kept her history. For all I know it could still be there hiding, waiting for me. It could help me solve her death, and hopefully clear Winn of any responsibility.

I look to Kat, and she waves her hand as if she knows even from a distance that I'm about to ask her if I can leave. After we help with putting the furniture under the donations tent, we hop into his truck and drive to his place.

"You look better today," Winn says as we head inside. The magic is as strong as I remember. I can't help but take a little, though I'm already full. "Had me pretty worried last night."

I sigh. "It's been a crazy couple weeks, but helping at Gwen's took my mind off things."

"That's good." We climb the stairs to the second floor. The hall is tall and narrow, and I wonder which door leads to his room as we walk to another set of stairs.

"It's quiet. Are your parents gone?" I ask.

"Mom went to visit Gwen and Mrs. Lee at the hospital, and my dad is trying to round up extra seed so they can still plant on time."

"I see." Perfect. Alone.

When he opens the door to the attic, it's obvious to me that this place was meant to hold histories like any witching house. The ceilings are vaulted, and windows let in good reading light. The floors are finished in fine wood, and there is plenty of room for bookshelves. Except Winn's family has chosen to use that space for about a century's worth of old furniture, piled haphazardly for as far as I can see.

"Do you guys throw anything away?" I ask.

He smirks. "Not if it's still in good condition."

"I guess since it's helping Gwen, I'll overlook the pack-rat tendency." I take a few tentative steps inside, worried that if I breathe too hard it'll all come crashing down. "No wonder it took your mom forever to decide what you should bring."

"No kidding." He points to a nice-looking lamp with a pink ribbon tied to it. "The bow means we can take it."

I scan the room, noticing that some of the ribbons are attached to pieces that are practically buried. "We're gonna be up here for a while."

His smile turns mischievous. "Is that a problem?"

I shake my head. "Let's get to work before I regret not bringing a chaperone."

He bites his lip, like he wants nothing more than to spend the day kissing me in the dark corners of this dusty attic. I wish, but trying to find Fanny's history in this could take weeks. I need it now. Yesterday. We start gathering the marked furniture, taking the smaller pieces downstairs to get them out of the way, and then begin the task of unearthing beds and sofas.

"Wow." I hold up a beautiful lamp that I swear is Tiffany. "This is an antique dealer's heaven."

He laughs. "I know, right?"

We've been working for a while, and I still haven't found anything Fanny might have written in. Sighing, I sit on the nearest couch we've dug out, its plastic crinkling at my weight. "So, have you ever found any family stuff up here? Pictures or journals?"

"Oh, yeah." Winn sets down the large vase he pulled off

the nearest bed and sits next to me. "My great uncles fought in World War II. My dad dug out their albums and medals when he was a kid. We keep them downstairs now."

"Anything older?"

He gives me a curious look. "Sounds like you're looking for a particular answer."

I shrug, already hating the lie on my tongue. "Nana said that back when she was a girl there were really strange rumors in town."

"Really?" His brow furrows, and I can almost feel his nerves. "Like what?"

"Just about weird stuff happening in Willow's End. I've always been curious about it, and I was hoping there might be something up here that could tell us more."

"Hmm . . ." He rubs his chin as he looks around the attic. It seems the more we've "cleaned," the less organized it's become, as if more things keep appearing from the nether. "I don't *think* so."

"Well, it sounds like some of the town thought there really was a . . ." Suddenly I can hear my heart thumping, and the word catches in my mouth. I look at Winn, his eyes curious but not at all cunning like Levi's. He doesn't ooze desire or reek of darkness. He's just a guy, and part of me wants to keep it like that. "Never mind. It's stupid."

I stand, deciding to get back to work, but Winn grabs my hand to stop me. "C'mon, Jo, you can't leave me hanging like that." He tugs at my arm, and when I don't sit back down he gets up. "I promise I won't laugh."

I roll my eyes. "We should get more stuff to Gwen's."

"Tell me. Please?" He pulls me so we're facing each other, and his eyes bore into mine with a kind of hope that is so intense I have to cave.

"Nana says there really was a witch in town back then. That it wasn't just a myth, and people were being cursed, but then someone killed her." I don't blink, don't breathe, for fear of missing a key reaction. "Have you ever heard of something like that?"

Winn's eyes flicker with recognition, and for a second I think he might tell me what he knows about this house and what happened here. But then I see fear cross his face, and he tries to brush it off with a low chuckle. "Is that all? I've heard that myth, but I don't think it's true."

"You said you wouldn't laugh." My heart races because it feels like he's lying—like he might know all about the very world I hide from him—but he pulls me closer and gently puts his hand on my cheek. His palm is rough but warm, and it sends a jolt of tingles down my spine that may or may not be magic.

"Can I kiss you now?" he asks. "Because I don't think I can take this anymore."

He doesn't wait for my answer, and his lips against mine are insistent. I wonder if this might be a distraction tactic, but then he pulls me right up against his chest and I forget everything. I let myself get caught up in him. His kisses and all the magic up here make me dizzy and giddy. I'm moving purely on instinct now, craving to be closer to him. I push my hips into his, and he guides me to the sofa.

I gasp when his weight presses me against the cushion, and he pulls back. "Did I hurt you?"

I shake my head. Biting my lip, I can feel my face flushing at the thought. "Just, um, can you kiss me . . . harder?"

"H-harder?" His smile is drenched in shock. "Did you seriously say that?"

I nod, pulling him closer again. "Can't I like it, too?"

"Best. Girlfriend. Ever." Winn's lips smash against mine, and his fingers are tangled in my hair. I can't help but slide my hand under his shirt. His skin is warm and comforting, and I wonder if maybe Nana had the right idea about protecting the house and hiding. I could hide in this protected house with Winn . . . have my own daughter . . .

"Winn? Are you up there?" his mother calls.

He pushes away from me, scrambling for his shirt. "Yeah! One sec! Crap, what time is it?"

"I have no idea." I sit up, breathless and surprised to find myself shirtless as well. I seriously don't remember that happening. "Talk about bad timing."

"Tell me about it." He shakes his head, his eyes running over me. "Do you think we really would have . . . ?"

I can feel the smile stretch across my face. "Maybe."

He whimpers, and I laugh. Holding up a finger, he says, "Be right back. I'll get my mom to leave."

"Okay." I rake my fingers through my hair, and he runs down the stairs with loud, quick steps.

It feels weird sitting in Winn's attic without a top, so I put my T-shirt back on and start digging through more stuff to distract myself from my pounding heart. He doesn't come right back, and I start to worry his mom knows I'm up here.

As I continue toward the far corner, I finally feel calmer, but the magic keeps buzzing. Then I realize it's getting stronger back here, and if that's the case . . .

I push through piles of stuff as quickly and as quietly as I can, trying to follow the spell's trail. Reaching that corner, I know the magic surrounds something in the wall. It resonates in my blood, and because of that I'm sure it's a Hemlock enchantment. Fanny must have put something here.

Placing my hand on the wall, I try to figure out the spell. It's a code of some sort, but it doesn't feel very complex, especially in comparison to the rest of the spells on the house. I push some magic into the wood and am rewarded with an image in my mind:

Pointer fingers and thumbs placed on four knots in the wood.

I follow the instructions quickly, afraid that Winn will

come back any second. A small opening appears in the wall, and I hold my breath as I realize there's a book in there. And not just any kind of book, but a history. Hope floods through me. There must be something in here that will save Nana and me from the Curse. But as I read the title, I wish I'd never found it. It can't be true, and yet the proof couldn't be any clearer.

History of Cordelia Black.

I shove it back into the little compartment—afraid that it'll unleash a spell on me—and the wall reseals. Shaking, I make my way back to the couch and pace as the reality sinks in.

Winn is related to the Blacks. His family must have killed Fanny. Even if I can't see the shadows around him, he's probably like Levi. Has he been lying to me this whole time? I wish my gut didn't say yes. His hatred for Levi is way more than being protective of his girlfriend—I just didn't want to see it. I still don't.

"Okay! She's gone." When Winn rounds the corner, his smile drops. "Are you okay?"

Everything feels wrong, like I'm falling down a dark pit I'll never be able to get out of. I don't want to, but I have to give him up before he has me completely. I head for the stairs, unable to look at him. "I better go. Sorry. I'm so sorry."

"Wait! Can you tell me what's going on?"

I hear him following me, but I don't turn around. Instead, I rip out a tuft of hair and use it to teleport the second I have cover. When I appear in my room, I lean against the wall, shaking.

THIRTY-FIVE

"Ugh!" I almost throw Mom's pendant out the window, but restrain myself just in time. The stupid thing won't work no matter what I do. Toppling onto my bed, I stare at the crack in my ceiling. I even tried that as a pendant trigger, and all I got was a nice afternoon nap. But after yesterday's miserable revelation that my boyfriend is probably a Shadow, this pendant is my best option. A long shot, but at least I can't get Cursed while hiding in my room.

My phone buzzes on my nightstand, and I don't dare look at it because it's probably Winn again. The thought of talking to him fills me with panic. I'm too tempted to answer it, to fall deeper into whatever trap he's laid. But then I think of Nana dying, and my resolve grows stronger. I can't let her down like that. I have to focus on saving her.

"Jo?" my dad calls from the hall. When I don't answer he taps on the door, and then he cracks it open. "Can I talk to you?"

I shrug. I'm still mad at him for not telling me about Nana, but part of me wants to cry on his shoulder and tell him all the horrible things that have happened in the past few days.

The door swings open, and that's when I notice the sleek white box he carries. It's my computer. I suck in my excitement, trying to look as indifferent as possible. He can't buy me off. I mentally repeat that as he sets it on my bed. I want so badly to reach out and touch it, but I hold back. "You think this will fix everything?"

"No, but it arrived and I thought you'd like to have it. Just because you're mad at me doesn't mean I'll keep a gift out of spite."

Ugh, how am I supposed to resist when he's so nice? "You should have told me about Nana."

"Perhaps." He looks at his hands. "We weren't sure how it would progress, Jo. Your mother had it for a few years, and Dorothea didn't want to raise the alarm if she had that long to figure it out. If we'd known this guy would drain her so quickly, yes, maybe the decision would have been different. But she didn't know."

I put a finger to the glossy box. "Even if we had a few years, you still should have told me. I'm not a little girl anymore, and I'll be the next head of this house. I have a right to know when my family members get hurt."

He purses his lips. "You'll have to talk to your grandmother about it."

"I . . ." I haven't talked to Nana since I found out. Every time I think about it, my stomach gets sloshy and sick. There is so much to tell her, but I can't watch her die like I watched Mom.

"She keeps asking about you, and Maggie is already tired of being grilled for updates." He stands. "I can't imagine how hard this is, but don't forget that this isn't only about you. Dorothea deserves much more than a cold shoulder, considering all she's done for you."

Watching him go, I'm stunned by the reproach. He shuts my door, but I continue staring at it, baffled that my dad is . . . a dad. How did it happen so quickly? That guilt trip made it feel like he's been parenting for years. I glance at my pretty computer box, but I can't get myself to open it. Instead, I flop back into my pillows, the remorse cutting straight to my heart.

He's right. Of course he is.

I shouldn't punish Nana, but I can't help thinking about how long she kept my mother's illness from me, too. Apparently, Mom had been Cursed around the time I turned four. I was too little to remember or to even know she was sick, so they hid it from me.

Nana didn't tell me until I was six and a half, and by then I'd already noticed how quickly Mom got tired and how often she needed to go to the bathroom. I just didn't know it was to throw up the black blood. It was bad enough learning Mom was that sick, but worse to know she'd been that way for a long time while I lived like nothing was wrong. I took her for granted, not knowing how little time I'd actually have with her.

I squeeze my eyes shut. No more crying. I'm so tired of this emptiness, this constant ache in my chest, as if I've lost part of my soul.

Grief is such a strange thing. Sometimes it seems to be gone entirely, but then one smell or sound or memory and it's as if it was waiting there, in the shadows, until you noticed it following you.

Lavender envelops me, and I tense. My lungs can't seem to get enough of it; they beg to breathe in more to make sure the scent is still there.

That's when I realize only a moment of true grief can trigger the pendant. The voices kick in, but these sounds make me wonder if I want to look. I venture a peek and quickly shield my eyes again. Yup, that's my mom and dad doing it. Apparently, the memories don't come in order. Good to know. I really wish I could plug my ears, but I want to know when it switches.

This is way too much information.

"I love you, more than anything in the world." Dad's voice is surprisingly the same as it is now.

"And I love you forever," Mom says.

As awkward as it is, I can't help feeling sad, too. They were so happy, and she left because of me. Because of her duty to this house. She used to get this far-off look in her eyes, her smile sad and wistful. I wonder if all those times she was thinking of him.

"Mom!" My mother's voice bursts with excitement, and I figure it's safe to look if Nana's there. My heart stops at the sight of her belly, so large I can't see her feet on the other end of the living-room couch. Her breathing is ragged, and her arms glisten with sweat. "I think it's time!"

Nana comes into view, her face much younger than I ever remember it. She hands Mom a rag. "Bite down on that; don't want you harming your jaw when the pain really kicks in. You think the contractions hurt? Well, you're in for it."

"Hardly comforting, Ma."

I snort. Ah, Nana.

She checks Mom out down there, which I'm really glad I can't see. "She's ready, darling. Next time you get a contraction, push like you have to pass a—"

"I know!" she yells. "We've gone over this for nine months!"

And then she pushes. For a long time. Mom screams and snaps at Nana anytime she tries to give direction, and I start to wonder why this ended up in the Good Memories category because it scares the crap out of me.

"One more, Carmina. You're almost there." Nana takes hold of a goopy lavender blob I can only assume is me. So relieved this is not in color. Baby Me lets out a wail, and Nana holds me up for Mom to see. Even through all the nasty and monochrome, my hair is jet-black. "You did it, honey, and she's beautiful!"

Mom's hands reach out, eager to their fingertips. "Let me hold her."

Nana cleans me and wraps me in a blanket. Then Mom takes me in her arms. I can hear her sniffling as she says, "Hi, beautiful. It's so nice to finally meet you." She kisses my forehead. "Oh, I wish Joseph were here to see you. He would love you as much as I do."

She feeds me, which is kind of awkward, but I'm mesmerized by Baby Me, by how crisp this memory is, making the others seem a little hazy. Her joy is so intense I can feel it through the spell.

The scene changes, and it's the first one I recognize. She's in her bed, holding on to this very pendant, as I come bursting through the door in all my awkward childhood glory. My frizzy hair is worse than I remember, and I'm covered in dirt. No, those are my freckles. Mostly. I proudly hold up a massive bullfrog. "Look what I caught, Mom!"

"Wow!" she says, her voice not betraying how sick she was at this time.

"Nana said that if I found a big one it would make a stronger spell for you." I kiss the frog. "I think this one will make you all better!"

She laughs. "I think so, too."

I come over and give her a big kiss . . . with my frog-slime lips. "I love you, Mommy. I'm gonna give this to Nana now."

"Come back when you're done?"

I nod, my hair bouncing wildly with the action. "I'll bring you a pudding!"

She laughs loudly as I skip out the door. I'd forgotten how perfect her laugh was, warm and sincere, never mocking. It filled you with sunshine, made you want to do anything to hear it again. I never thought about it, but even when she was sick, she didn't stop being that happy person I remember.

The scene changes again, and my eyes go wide. I know this one, too—she's in San Francisco with Stacia, when she meets Dad for the first time.

"Don't worry, Carmina," Stacia says. "They're nice. Well, except Jeff, but I'll protect you from him."

She gives her sunshine laugh. "Thanks."

"There they are." One of the other girls points to a group of guys outside a café. Dad's there, but he's not the one I can't stop looking at. Next to him, tall and brooding, is a boy that looks exactly like Levi.

THIRTY-SIX

Stacia grabs the Levi Guy, who I guess is Jeff, before he says even one word to Mom. She's already so engrossed with Dad that she's not paying attention. Everyone else goes slightly hazy, as if her memory only sees my father, but I can tell Jeff is looking at my mother. Stacia whispers something to him. He may not be drenched in shadows and evil, but his glare makes me tremble the same way the Curse did when I cleansed Dad. In my gut, I know Jeff is the guy who killed my mom, the guy who killed Stacia. And I would bet a thousand dollars that he is Levi's dad.

Stacia and Jeff whispering is all I get before Mom and Dad walk ahead of them into the restaurant. And then we're back to a making-out memory, which is even more motivation for me to run downstairs to find my father. The moment I'm not alone, the pendant turns off. Dad has commandeered the dusty study for his office, and there he is, talking to someone on speakerphone. He holds up a hand to stop me, clearly in the middle of work.

I turn around and head for the living room, plopping down next to Maggie.

"Jo, you will not believe what Autumn did. She was totally flirting with this cute guy at a beach party and she's all making fun of Callie, and then the boy is Callie's older brother and Autumn gives him this blank look like, 'Oh, crud, there goes my chance.'" She laughs. "It was awesome."

I can't help but grin. Maggie must be relaxed if she's finally blabbering away like her normal self. "Has she learned The Very Important Lesson yet?"

"After the commercial, I bet." She stuffs a wad of Cheetos in her mouth. The Crafts are big on all-natural food, so whenever Maggie visits she spends the whole time gorging on processed goods. "Now, are you going to tell me what's going on? Because you seem different today—don't think I can't tell."

I put my hand to the pendant. "I think I know who killed my mother."

She coughs on her mouthful, and I hand her the liter of orange Fanta on the coffee table. She takes a few sips and then stares at me with her big, bright eyes. "What?"

"I saw him in—"

"Did you need something, Jo?" My dad stands in the study's doorway.

"You had a roommate named Jeff, right?"

He raises his eyebrows. "How'd you know that?"

"What was he like? Did he seem interested in Mom?" My heart pounds in anticipation of his answers, even if I already know partially who he is. This is Mom's killer we're talking about, and I have a first-person source right here, one Jeff probably planned on getting rid of once he served his purpose.

Dad scratches his head. "Jeff Anderson? He was an average guy, kind of quiet, kept to himself. If he was interested in Carmina, he never said anything. Actually, he and Stacia were dating when we moved in together. We kind of lost touch with them after that, since we relocated closer to San Jose for my job."

"I knew it." Jeff probably Cursed Stacia first. Then he went for my mom once Stacia was dead. Why he'd use a Black, I'm not sure. But that must be how Levi came into being, and I'm pretty sure he's the only one who knows the rest of this story.

"Knew what?" Dad asks.

"Jeff? He looks exactly like Levi, who is Stacia's son. Stacia was killed by the Curse, too, so . . ."

Dad's eyes widen. "You think he . . . ?"

I nod.

"But he was a totally normal guy!" Dad leans on the doorjamb. "I lived with him for months, and he never did anything bad. He didn't seem like a killer."

I give him a flat look. "How long did you live with Mom without knowing she was a witch?"

He deflates. "I never had a chance, did I? There was no way I could have protected her."

I stand, never more determined to end this. "Nope. Honestly, you're helpless, just like Kat and Gwen and everyone else. That's why Mom protected you, not the other way around. And you have to be okay with that, because that will never change."

His jaw slackens, but I keep talking. "That's why I have to know everything that happens here. I am the protector—I'm the only one who can keep us safe right now. If I'm missing information, I could fail. And that means we're dead. That's why I'm mad. I'm tired of everyone thinking I'm the one who needs protecting. I am protecting you, and that'll be even more true if Nana dies. So don't ever forget it."

I rush for the stairs, the power of knowledge pulsing through my veins. I can't wait to tell Nana. She won't give up if she knows how close we are. We have a name for the first time in a decade. We know what he is, what the Curse does—hell, we even know who he works for. That only leaves one thing: how to kill him.

When I push through her door, a little of my fire extinguishes. Nana's brittle hand hangs past the bed, her wrist dripping black blood into a basin. Her face is pale, and I know too well how close she is to death.

"Oh, Nana . . ."

She startles, her other hand going to her chest. "Josephine, there you are."

I let out a long sigh, forcing myself to the basin. It's practically full, so I take a cloth from her nightstand and cover her wrist. "That's enough for today."

"It eases the pressure," she says. "I hated when Carmina would ask me to do this, but now I understand. The Curse is wicked, my dear. It doesn't just drain your magic; it makes you crave it even more."

"Shh." I take her hand, not at all surprised that nothing needs to be said for us to pick up where we left off. "Don't waste your strength."

"Once I knew someone was taking my magic, I tried not to fill myself. But it hurts not to, worse than it normally does. I still try, but sometimes the pain is too much. The blackness builds in my blood, swells in my veins. Letting it drain . . ."

"Stop," I say, unable to hear the finer details. "It'll be over soon."

"Don't I know it." She laughs a little. "That bastard will get as little from me as possible, even if it does kill me."

"No, that's not what I mean." I tell her everything I've learned, from the Blacks' treachery to the Shadows to Winn to how Mom's pendant holds all her good memories.

Her black eyes glisten. "Jeff. How strange to have a name, and such a normal name, too."

"Please hold on, Nana. I'm going to save you, and you can't say no because if you're this incapacitated that means I'm in charge." I fight back the tears, determined to prove that I can do this, trying to convince myself I can. Seeing her like this puts everything in perspective—all that matters right now is saving her and our bloodline.

Her lips, barely there in the first place, disappear, like she's trying to keep her protests from coming out. "And how do you plan on doing that?"

I crawl into bed next to her. She seems so small and weak, barely a bump in the queen-size bed. "I don't exactly have that figured out yet, but Levi . . . now that I know about his parents, I'm sure he has the answers I need."

Her furrowed brow says she doesn't like the idea. "You're not talking to that Levi boy again. I don't care if he claims to have principles or if he has information. It's too risky. He could Curse you anytime he felt like it. You understand that, don't you?"

"Fine. I won't." The lie feels awful on my tongue, but she doesn't seem to notice. I know she's thinking of my safety. Problem is, I'm only thinking of hers. "He once said

Shadows were the worst mistake we ever made, which, to me, means that a witch somewhere in time made them. And if we made them . . ."

"We can unmake them," she whispers. "Their power is an extension of our own, so we should be able to do anything they can."

"Exactly. We just need to figure out how." Which I'm pretty sure Levi can help me understand as well.

Her smile is weak, and yet warm. "No problem."

I touch her silver-white hair, which I hardly ever see down. It's softer than it looks, the ringlets not nearly as tight as mine or Mom's. Whoever Nana loved, he must have had crazy curls. "What was my grandfather's name?"

She eyes me. "You take to leadership and audacity far better than you think, dear."

"Well?"

"Carlo," she whispers. "I met him in Italy when I toured Europe and the old magic sites. He was a beautiful man, with a voice that made women throw themselves at his feet. But he came to me, and we spent the next few years in Florence, blissfully happy. You can imagine the rest."

I can, and it hurts even for me. "Carlo, Carmina. Joseph, Josephine. Is this a tradition I wasn't aware of?"

Her smile widens. "My father's name was Theodore, so I suppose so."

I laugh. "So much for us not knowing anything about our fathers."

"It's a natural curiosity."

"Yeah." I stare at her chandelier, all crystal and pearl, trying to focus as much as possible on this moment. "So I'm part Italian. That's cool."

"I'll hang on, for you." Nana's hand goes limp in mine, and even though I know she fell asleep it feels like preparation for what's to come.

THIRTY-SEVEN

When everyone is sleeping, I sneak down to the apothecary. The house threatens to betray me at each creak, but I manage to get there without waking anyone up. Sitting in Nana's chair, it hits me—this could be my place soon unless I do something. Something possibly desperate. I shake it off, searching the drawers for the right ink and parchment. Grabbing a quill, I dip it in the enchanted purple liquid and write:

We need to talk.

I'm surprised how quickly a message appears underneath my messy line.

Is this who I think it is?

Under the magic willow tree.

That's barely within our protective barriers. If Levi

doesn't intend to harm me, he'll be able to get there like he got in last time. And more important, anyone at his house who might see this message won't.

See you soon.

My heart pounds as I slide on a sweater and creep out the front door. Willow's End is pitch-black at night, save a few lamps that mark street corners. I avoid the light, knowing this path by heart. I walk under my favorite willow, soaking in the faint magic as I do. Levi is already there, leaning on the thick trunk. He has his hands in his pockets, like it's totally normal to be out in the middle of the night with shadows dancing all around him.

He smiles when he sees me. "How's Gwen?"

"None of your business." I stay a good distance back, the memories of that kiss begging me to run. If I get Cursed, it really is over.

His grin disappears. "I should have known you'd be afraid of me after that."

"More like disgusted."

"Was it that bad? Because at one point I could have sworn you were into it."

My cheeks burn, not a single comeback on my tongue.

"If I were a regular guy . . ." He folds his arms, smug. "I have a feeling you'd like me."

I shake my head. "You aren't a regular guy, so what does it matter?"

He doesn't have to say anything, because I can see it all over his face. There's no denying he wants me, and not just my magic, though I'm sure that's a big part of it. "Doesn't seem like regular guys interest you, do they?"

My heart twists at the thought of Winn, so badly that I have to put my hand to my chest. "Look, I didn't call you here to fight. I want answers, and I know you have them."

"And why would I give them to you?"

"Because . . ." I search for something, but what incentive does he have? He doesn't have to help me, and doing so would probably get him in big trouble long-term. But there is one thing. "I know you want him destroyed as much as I do, Levi Anderson. You want to avenge your mother's death—you want to kill your own father."

I kind of can't blame him, but it's still creepy.

His eyes go wide. "How . . . ?"

"You really thought I'd need you to find out? Jeff Anderson was my dad's roommate in college, and a Shadow. You're the spitting image of him."

"Shit." He kicks the ground.

"But I don't understand it all, and I want to." I take a few steps closer. "Please, Levi, tell me why he'd kill a Black, if they are the ones using you. Why would he go to such lengths to hunt the Hemlocks down and never stop?"

Levi's face softens slightly. "My dad is the worst of our kind—a Shadow without a leash, a madman completely lost to the Consumption. My grandmother, who's also Consumed, really likes him because he's willing to do what a lot of us won't. She and some of the other Blacks hate witching families that are more powerful than them."

"Why do they think we're so powerful? There are only two of us. The Blacks are a massive family in comparison to the Hemlocks."

"Numbers don't matter as much as you'd think. Having used Black magic and yours . . ." He bites his lip, seeming embarrassed. "Let's just say you have more power in your little finger than any in-control Black witch. You're like ten of them."

"I thought the only difference in magic was location," I whisper, the idea of me being so powerful hard to wrap my head around.

He shakes his head. "Different bloodlines hold different magical strengths. Of course, the Blacks are the only ones who know that, since they have Shadows to tell them. The Yarrows, Nightshades, and Hemlocks are the top of the hit list—since your magic is the best."

It sounds so petty, and yet it somehow doesn't surprise me. "So they've been trying to get rid of us because . . . they're jealous?"

"Pretty much."

I grit my teeth. Oh, Nana will be pissed when she hears

about this. "But what about your mother? Why would he kill her, then?"

"Yeah, uh . . ." He scratches the back of his head. "She was protecting your mom."

"What?"

He lets out a tired sigh. "My mom made it so I'm the only one who can read her history. She wrote a lot of stuff that probably would've gotten her killed even sooner. She was assigned as my dad's steward—the witch who decides when a Shadow is ready to have magic. The first witch we Curse. Mom knew my dad was bad news from the second she met him. Like every steward and Shadow, they were ten years old when my grandmother assigned them to hunt the Hemlocks."

I gasp, remembering Mom's first memory of Stacia. They were probably about that age. Could that have been why Stacia was crying? Why she told my mom they shouldn't be friends? "Their whole friendship was a lie."

"No. It wasn't." Levi's glare is defensive, and I realize I'm insulting his mother. "She didn't think it was right—she wanted to protect Carmina. She did for a long time by refusing to give my father magic, even though it pissed off my grandmother. He was ravenous for power, and she knew he'd have no control once he had even the smallest taste."

I venture closer to Levi, leaning on the tree with him. "He didn't just take it?"

"It would have been hard. The first time . . ." He cringes. "We're only born with enough magic to sustain us. If we use it up without having a steward, we're screwed. He could have tried, but my mom would have overpowered him. And my mom spent most of her time traveling, so her mother couldn't make her accept my dad through a spell."

"So that's why he didn't look magical when my mom met him," I say, though my thoughts are all on Winn. This explains way more than I'd like it to.

"Yup. By the time they were in San Francisco he was desperate and my grandmother was practically hunting my mom down. My father wanted to follow orders, but he was pretty much a normal person without his steward giving him magic. Grandma finally gave up on her daughter and told him to risk everything to Curse Carmina without my mom's help. Since Carmina didn't know what he was, he could have taken her off guard and used what little he had to do it."

I wrap my arms around myself, pain surging through me. "So Stacia gave in, on the condition that he didn't touch my mom."

Levi nods, his eyes cold. "And like she guessed, he didn't hold back in taking magic from her. She died because of his greed, but then he had enough to go after Carmina. Of course, my grandmother was happy to have her useless daughter out of the picture. It would have ended like this, either way, with both of them dead."

Silence swallows everything as Levi and I watch the willow branches sway in the light breeze. I don't want to ask him, of all people, and yet I have to know. I force the words out. "So is Winn . . . like you?"

He purses his lips, and it feels like he's wrestling himself over what to say. "I really want to lie and say he is, because I know you'll leave him over it. But truthfully, I'm not sure, and I'll admit I'm curious about it."

I raise an eyebrow. "What do you mean?"

"Shadows can recognize each other, even if they haven't taken in magic yet. I'm sure I felt that when I met him, but at the same time he didn't appear to recognize it in me. At least not in the right way—he sees me as a threat, not someone he shares an identity with.

"On top of that, he doesn't seem to *need* magic like us. I *crave* it, like always being hungry. He doesn't seem to be bothered in the least by all that power coursing through you." Levi sighs, looking at me like I cause him physical pain. "And it's not like there are more than a couple dozen of us. I thought I knew all the Shadows. It doesn't make sense."

I gulp, not wanting to say it out loud. "He lives in my great-great-great-aunt Fanny's house. I found a history in his attic, hidden in a magical compartment. It belonged to Cordelia Black."

He actually looks surprised by this. "Really?"

"Yeah, but like you said, things don't seem to be adding up. I think he knows something, but he's trying to hide it. And if he is like you, he's had plenty of opportunities to Curse me if he wanted. Why prolong it?"

"Good question. This is definitely weird. I'm not aware of any Blacks living around here either." He looks at me, his smirk in place. "Do you want me to investigate?"

"Would you?" I don't like the idea of being in his debt even more, but I have to know whether I can trust Winn or not. Because even after everything I've discovered, my heart won't let him go without a fight.

"Sure. I do have a nice side, you know."

I roll my eyes. "Whatever."

We both laugh, and in that moment I realize Levi and I have always been after the same things. He wants this to stop as much as I do.

"I'm sorry, for everything," I say.

"Me too." He gives me this look that sets my face on fire. "You know, I hated your mom for so long. You too, of course. In my mother's history, she said that Carmina wasn't sunshine—she was the sun. Everything couldn't help but orbit around her, but nobody minded because she warmed them all up. I think I'm beginning to understand why she felt that way."

I can't stop staring at my ratty old tennis shoes. "So now that we kind of understand each other, how do we stop him?"

"That is a complicated question," he says. "Legend goes that an ancient Black witch fell in love, and she told the man what she was. He asked to share her power, and she was so blind that she did it. But it was never enough; he found a way to take magic from her. He passed on that ability, just like witches pass on theirs."

"I can't believe . . ." It's horrible, stupid beyond insane. "And no one tried to stop him?"

"That's the thing. Shadows can store a lot more magic than you can; we need to since we can't take it from the ground. The Blacks tried to stop him, but he'd Curse them and take their magic before they even had a chance, until he had so much no one could stop him. Compromises were made to satiate him until he died from Consumption, but he had seven sons. The Blacks became their stewards and remain so—they allow us to use them as payment for their mistake.

"Most of us don't enjoy being what we are and only use our steward's magic, but there are always a few like my dad out there. Consumed, insatiable, pretty much pure evil. The Blacks spend a lot of time trying to hide all this, but they can't always control all their family members or their creations."

It feels like he's rambling, like he's avoiding the real answer. "Are you saying you don't know how to beat him?"

"I do." He gulps. "I'm just giving you some background

so you know how big a job this will be. He's been sucking up all your grandmother's magic—he has so much I can hardly stand to be in the same place as him—and he plans to use it to break through your house's barriers so my grandmother can have it. You? He wants to keep you for a long time. He's gotten quite a taste for Hemlock magic, so you'll get to be his pet for as long as you survive."

I shudder. The thought of his father leeching off me is too much to bear. "How are we supposed to beat him if he has a huge store of my nana's magic? She's majorly powerful, Levi, which means he's . . . godly."

He chews his lip, much like Kat does. "There's only one way."

"Which is?"

His eyes meet mine, and suddenly I don't like where this is going at all. "A few kisses won't do it. I'd need a lot more than that. Like a year's worth of kissing, which we don't exactly have time for. So . . ."

I take a few steps back. "Are you saying the only way to beat him is to Curse me?"

"You saw what I did with your power at the hospital, and that was using the little you had at the time. I wouldn't ask if I didn't think we could do it. Your magic is incredible and truly unique. I could—"

"I'm such an idiot!" I kick the ground, though maybe I should have kicked him where it hurts. "It's what you've wanted all along! That's your big plan, isn't it? Get your dad out of the way so you can have my power instead."

"No! All I want is to stop him." He tries to grab me, but I shock his hand. "Damn it, Jo! I would never let you die because of it. I would . . . I would always take care of you. I would be indebted to you forever. How many times do I have to say that I don't want to hurt you?"

"A million, at least. What makes you think I'd ever say yes?"

His face hardens. "Because you know I have the skill to get the job done."

"No offense, but if that's your only plan I'd rather figure out how to kill your father myself."

"You'll fail." His jaw sets, and I can feel him fighting to stay still. "You're just going to let your grandma die?"

"Charming. I'm so convinced now." I turn, heading back toward my house. Maybe I'm walking away from my big chance to fix things, but this can't be the right path. I should have listened to Nana—Levi might have answers, but they come at too heavy a price. There has to be something else, and I will find it.

THIRTY-EIGHT

Three days later, I pace the apothecary floor in a fit of nerves. Gwen texted me an hour ago, saying her parents are finally sure she's not dying, so she's on her way over. I don't know why I'm so jittery, but I can't help myself. Promise to Kat or not, I shouldn't be doing this. But then again, Nana and I have practically murdered every witching tradition in the last few weeks, so why not add to the pile?

"For the love, Jo!" Maggie says. "I've had two liters of Mountain Dew and you're still beating me on the hyper scale. Sit down!"

"Gwen will be fine," Kat adds. "In fact, she'll probably be ecstatic."

"Still, she has no clue what she's getting into."

A loud bang sounds from the hallway, and in walk Tessa

and Prudence. Just in time. Maggie doesn't quite have the skill level to perform a binding, and I have to participate, so I asked them to help.

Tessa wraps me in a hug, "How is Dorothea?"

"Not good," I say, pushing back the lump in my throat. "But she would love to see you, I'm sure."

She offers a tight smile. "We'll visit her after we help with your friend."

Prudence eyes Kat. "Are you sure you want to bring more outsiders into this? With your father and Katherine in the house, it seems you've forgotten the old ways."

I tip my chin up. "And since when is the head of house questioned, oh rule keeper?"

Her eyes narrow.

"Considering the circumstances, Pru, I need to protect the people closest to me as best I can. Gwen almost died because of this man—the charms and enchantments I gave her weren't enough. I won't let it happen again."

She puts her hands on her hips. "Fair enough. Where's the spell book?"

"Here." I turn the heavy, old book so she can see. A flicker of doubt runs through me. It's a hard spell—maybe they won't be able to do it either.

Pru scans the page, then looks back to me. "You have what we need?"

"Yeah. But be careful with the golden eagle tears; there

aren't enough for mistakes."

"There won't be any." She gives me the crustiest glare, but I'm not offended. Pru is Pru. She's always been the one who is dead serious about everything. I'm half tempted to pull out a plastic snake to lighten things up.

The doorbell rings. "That should be her." I head for the door, but am taken aback when the blond hair I see isn't Gwen's. "Winn."

"Hey." He barely looks at me before his eyes find the ground. "Your phone . . . seems to be broken. Are you busy? I wanted to talk to you about the other day."

I bite my lip, feeling like the worst person alive. He might have no clue why I haven't answered his calls, and I still can't face him. "Actually . . ."

He tries not to frown, but it doesn't work very well. "So you're avoiding me."

"No!" I can tell he sees my lie, but what else can I do right now? I have a whole gaggle of witches to tend to. "It's just that Gwen is about to get here; otherwise I would."

"Right. Of course. She comes first." He nods too much, which sends up all sorts of warning flags. I've really hurt him. He needs me to be there for him, and I don't know how to do that anymore.

"I'm so sorry, Winn. Things have been crazy since we were up in your attic. I've been setting everything up for Gwen. Kat, Maggie, and I had this slumber party all planned out. You know, trying to make it feel kind of normal for her."

He smiles, but it's not the same bright grin he usually gives me. "You are such a good friend."

"You are such a good boyfriend." I mean it, even if I still don't know what role he plays in all of this. I want so badly to be with him, but even though we're right next to each other it's like there's a universe between us. It feels like if he leaves, things will never be okay for us again. The thought of really losing him slams into my chest, and I find myself saying, "Maybe I can sneak away for a second."

"Really?" His voice is small, skeptical.

"I miss you," I admit, even though I shouldn't. He could be the enemy, and I don't have any more chances to take. "I'm sorry I ran like that. I . . . I guess I got scared once you left."

"It's okay, figured as much. I kind of got carried away—sorry for pressuring you." He sighs as his hands find my waist, and I can't resist his touch. "I miss you, too."

Someone clears their throat, and we jump apart. I really hope it isn't my dad. Winn's skittishness doesn't seem so silly anymore. Luckily, it's Gwen, whose golden hair now brushes at her collarbone. I've never seen it that short, but it's gorgeous and mature.

"Sorry to interrupt," she says, readjusting her large duffel bag.

"Gwen!" I walk past Winn and down the stairs to give her

a hug. "I love your hair. Seriously, you look amazing!"

She smiles. "I thought I'd hate losing it, but it's kind of hot, isn't it?"

"So hot!" I turn to Winn. "Right?"

He smiles, and this time it's real. "How am I supposed to answer that?"

I roll my eyes. "You can be honest with me, too, you know."

Our eyes lock, and for a second I think he might understand I mean that in a different way as well. But then he blinks it away. "Fine. Gwen, you look beautiful." He comes down the stairs and pecks my cheek. "Have fun at your girls' night."

"But didn't you want—?"

"Just promise me we'll hang out later."

"I promise," I say, though part of me never wants to have the conversation that's coming. Why did I have to find that stupid history? I want everything to go back to before that moment, when it was only me and Winn stealing kisses in his attic.

"Call me, okay?"

"Of course." I wave and smile, but inside it feels like I'm falling apart.

Once he's out of earshot, Gwen grabs my arm and pushes me back toward the house. "You better spill, because I can't take another day of nightmares without knowing what the hell is going on."

"This way." I point her down the hall.

As she takes in the apothecary, with its various skeletons and ceiling-high cabinets of mysterious bottled things, she doesn't seem so excited. "Is this for real?"

Prudence rolls her eyes. "This will be exhausting."

I spit in my hand and use it to conjure a snake, which I toss at Pru. She lets out a pleasing scream, shaking it off, and I make it disappear. "So you're still afraid of snakes."

Pru says nothing, just straightens her hair and goes back to the book.

Tessa tries to hide her smile. "How did you know that?"

"Mom said something once." I turn to Gwen. "Sit over here."

She takes the chair, its heavily carved wood and burgundy upholstery contrasting against her light hair, and looks at me. "You're not like that guy who cured me, are you? Because when he was killing the shadows in my head . . . Whatever that magic was, I can't see you being like that, Jo."

I lean on the desk. "No, we're not like Levi, but that doesn't mean what we do is pleasant. Magic is dark. But we don't let it consume us—we are in control of it, or at least any respectable witch is."

She nods. "So what's going on? Did . . . is that why my house is gone?"

I cringe. "It's my fault. The people hunting my family did

it to hurt me. I should have been there to protect you, but I wasn't paying attention because Nana is dying, and—"

"Wait." She puts her hand to her chest, as if hearing that was a physical blow. "Why didn't you tell me?"

Our eyes meet, and I know I don't have to speak.

"It's like what happened to me, so you couldn't say anything?"

"Along those lines." And then it all floods out—how my mom really died, my dad showing up, Kat finding out, the threats on my friends, Nana being cursed, Winn being a witch's descendant, Levi, the Blacks, and Jeff, the man who killed my mother. By the time I'm done, my whole body trembles, exhausted from the seemingly endless chain of darkness.

Gwen is silent for a long time. "You should have told me," she finally says. Then she turns to Kat. "She should have told us, right?"

"Yes!" Kat throws up her hands. "Can you believe her?"

Gwen laughs. At me. Definitely not with me. "Seriously, Jo, why do you have to do everything on your own?"

Prudence puts her hands to her hips. "Because outsiders aren't permitted to know of us. Josephine is breaking time-honored traditions that have kept us safe for generations."

Gwen raises an eyebrow. "What? You really think we'll burn her at the stake?"

Pru's eyes flare with anger. "How dare—"

Gwen stands. "Look, no offense, okay? I get the idea of the rule, but I don't think she's breaking anything. She isn't risking anyone's safety; she's only trying to protect her friends. I know you might not think we belong here, but Kat and I are Jo's family. I don't care if we're not witches. We care about her more than you can understand, and it's really shortsighted of you to overlook that."

We all gape at her, and I have this overwhelming urge to hug my adorable mother hen of a friend. Gwen looks my way. "So what next? I'll do anything to help you—save Nana, kick this guy's ass, whatever."

I can't help but smile, even as I grab the pliers. "First, a spell and a hell of a lot of pain. Then? Pudding."

THIRTY-NINE

Our attic has never been so crowded. I make Dad carry Nana up, though I don't let him stay. The thought of a man reading about our past is too much even for me. I open dozens of histories, and I hand each person a stack. If I can't think of a way to beat this Shadow on my own, then I will rely on my Hemlock ancestors for help.

"We need more power, so let's learn everything we can," I say. "There has to be something in here, somewhere, about the oldest of old ways, before the spell books were written."

"And what would you have us do when we find something?" Prudence asks from the nearest desk, where she already has her first book open.

"Read it out loud, I guess. Anything you think is important."

"Yes, ma'am." Gwen holds up her monocle, and her smile widens. "Wow! That's amazing."

"That's what I said." Kat sits next to her on the couch, and I love the sight of the two of them together, here with me. Same with Maggie and her mother, cuddled in the window seat. And Nana, head still held high, as she reads in the plush chair. Somehow it fills in a little part of what I've been missing all these years. Having the house full makes me realize how empty it was before.

I put my hand over my heart, its warmth overwhelming. Despite the world caving in around us, I haven't felt this whole in ages. Not since before Mom died. My skin prickles with the realization:

Now is the time.

I rush to Mom's history. Its gold lettering glitters in the last slivers of evening sun, and I hold my breath as I put my hand above it.

"Josephine . . ." Nana says quietly, her voice reeking of pain, as if she doesn't want me to be disappointed if it doesn't work.

"It's okay, Nana. I . . ." Mom's pendant is warm on my skin, and her memories swirl around me like wisps of lavender. She's never been gone—not really. Her mark lingers on everything in my life, and it's not a mark of sorrow, but one of love and life and perpetual sunshine. "I can do this."

Slowly, I lower my hand toward the book. Tendrils of

lightning meet my fingers, but what was once a shock is now a tickle. I close my eyes, focusing on the spell she placed on her book. It wants me to do something, but I can't quite catch it. My fingers are going numb. This is the trap now, not the repellent for those unprepared to read. The tingling slowly travels up my arm, will continue if I don't figure out how to open it soon.

It's not a reagent. I know that for sure. The puzzle hums through my brain as I detangle the magic. Not an action or gesture. I try to shake out the needling sensation, but it only makes it worse.

Not a spell.

No . . . a password.

Great. I have no idea what it is, not even a good guess. I don't dare say anything, since the spell might punish me for uttering the wrong words.

The numbness is almost to my shoulder, making it difficult to keep my hand over the book. I can't lose now, not when I'm so close. All these years I thought that if I was ready it would be easy to open. Stupid me. Mom was an incredible witch—she even made things not in the spell books, like her pendant.

The answer is right there, like a word on the tip of my tongue. I can almost feel Mom scowling down at me, because I've forgotten something. What is it? Racking my brain, I go through every memory I have of her. There's no way I could have forgotten her giving me a password—I've worked so hard to remember everything about her. I pause, realizing there's one thing I try to forget:

The moment she died.

Pain fills my heart as the memory floods my mind. I can almost see it, and I can certainly feel it. Her bony arms encircled me, and I clung to her as if that could make her stay. She smelled of lavender and death, but her touch was still the most comforting thing in the world.

"Don't die," I whispered to her.

"Shh." She kissed my head. "I'll always be here, even when you can't see me. You know why?"

"No." My voice cracked on the word.

"Because when you truly love someone, it's forever. They never leave you, because they're part of you. Love is forever, sweetie." She squeezed me as tight as her arms could. "Say it for me."

"Love is forever," I cried.

"Don't forget it. Promise me."

I nodded into her chest, and I listened as her heart slowed and finally stopped.

I gasp at the pain, raw and new all over again, but I know these are the words I must say. "Love is forever."

The numbness is gone immediately. I look down, and there on the black leather is my hand. I move my fingers across the soft grooves, savoring the feel. The spine cracks as I lift the cover, a satisfying sound.

"Josephine, you wonderful girl." Nana's voice is reverent, and she pushes to get out of her seat.

I hold up my hand. "Don't get up. I'll read it out loud."

Mom wrote a lot. I had no idea how much would be in here. She has pictures glued in—her and the Crafts, Nana, Great-Grandma Geraldine, Stacia, Dad, and little baby me. There are locks of hair and pressed flowers and postcards, letters and sketches and newspaper clippings. Her entire life: she put it in this book.

"What are you looking for?" Maggie asks as I flip through the pages. I wish I could read each one, but there's only one thing that matters right now.

"Here," I say, my hand running over the page. "When she noticed she was Cursed."

I read it, my voice surprisingly steady:

Something is wrong. I can't keep magic inside me like before. One little spell and it feels as if I've used my entire store. I have to fill up more often than I used to, and leaving the house is like leaving my life source.

I asked Mom if this was something that came with age, and she gave me one of those suspicious looks. I think she knows I'm keeping these worries from her, but I still don't want to admit what I did. I never should have gone. I am sure it happened when I went to San Francisco. How selfish of me, to have put us all in such danger because I couldn't forget him.

I stop. "Maybe I should go back one." I look at Nana. "I was like three when she wrote this. Did you know she went to San Francisco?"

She shakes her head. "She never told me."

I flip back a few pages to the previous entry.

I can hardly believe what I did today. Everything started out normally, and as I sit here now it all seems like a dream. This morning, I made Jojo pancakes. That girl could eat pancakes for every meal if I let her. She was so excited she kept saying, "I love you, Mommy! You're the best Mommy! I love you!"

It killed me. I couldn't stop thinking about my other Joe, how much he would have loved this little girl of ours. Sometimes she's so much like him that it takes my breath away. I ache to my soul, I miss him so badly.

I had a momentary lapse in judgment. It didn't seem fair to keep them apart. He should know he has a daughter. So when Mom went out to collect rodents, I took Jojo to San Francisco. I wanted to show her where we fell in love, where we would have lived if things were different. More than that, I wanted to relive it, to be in the places that hold some of my most cherished memories.

We had gelato, which Jojo loved. And we walked through Chinatown. I bought her a little doll, and by the afternoon she'd already lost it. It didn't matter, though. I was having the time of my life. We both were.

And then I did it. I went to our old apartment. Tears streamed down my cheeks when I saw him through the lighted window. I couldn't believe he still lived there, as if he was waiting for me to come back to him. And here I was, more in love with him than ever, so desperate to touch him that I could barely contain myself.

I carried Jojo across the street, since she was tired and a little cranky from the long day, and the second I touched the curb something strange happened.

All my magic—it was gone. This darkness encircled me like death, and I was stranded with no way to defend myself. I looked in every direction for something threatening, but there was nothing, at least that I could see. But I felt it watching me, waiting for what I would do next.

I couldn't see Joseph now. I cried, knowing I shouldn't have tried to meet him at all. It was a sign—this is why our traditions exist.

If it weren't for Jojo, I don't know what would have happened to us. She still had her magic, and I quickly explained to her how to make a teleporting spell. She did it! I know she's only three, but she amazes me with her abilities already. She knows magic. It's in her heart and mind and soul, as natural as breathing. She saved us tonight, and she will probably never know until she reads this history.

I barely catch my tears before they hit the page. I can't believe I was there when it happened—I have no memories of it—and it breaks my heart that she missed Dad so much.

"If only I'd welcomed Joseph into our house eighteen years ago," Nana says. "She would have never gone. We would have all—"

"Don't start that." I refuse to even think about what could have been. "Now we know. Jeff must have been waiting for her; sounds like she set off some kind of alarm when she went there. He knew them, how much they loved each other, and he used it against us. First to get Mom, then me. He will have hell to pay for—"

Nana's eyes fill with horror, and she puts her hand to her neck like she can't breathe. I run to her side. She trembles as she takes my hand, and tears spill from her eyes. This scares me more than anything, because Nana doesn't cry.

"What is it? Are you in pain?" I ask.

She shakes her head. "He's coming. I can feel his presence at the town's barrier."

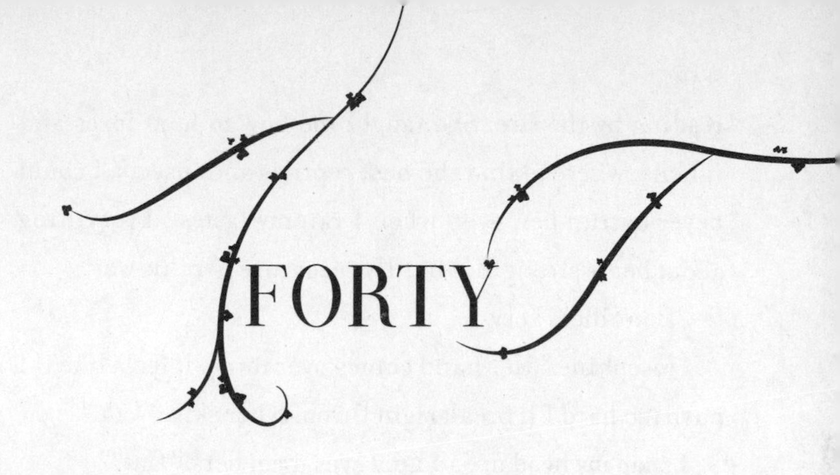

FORTY

"No . . ." But one look out the window proves Nana's right. The light is changing to an unnatural, sickly orange. Thunder rumbles, and with it comes a strange noise that sounds like someone is torturing animals. Then I realize what it is. "The alarms."

"He's trying to take—" Nana puts a handkerchief over her mouth. And then she coughs, so hard and so long I worry she'll suffocate. The speck of black on the white cloth grows until it stains her fingers. Her hand shakes in mine, frail and exhausted. Death waits for her, so close it seeps through the cracks in our house and chills even me.

I wish I could force back the tears. Nana has never really looked young, but she's always been strong. As a child, I remember her carrying me to my room if I fell asleep reading by the fire. She taught me how to hunt foxes and rabbits, where to find the best reptiles and insects. I could never outrun her, even when I ran my fastest. Everything about her is strength. I hardly recognize her this way.

"Don't die!" I cry.

"Josephine." Her hand comes over mine. It feels like if I push too hard I'll break right through her skin. "Cut."

I snap my head up, and my eyes meet hers. "Cut?"

She nods.

I gulp down another sob and take the letter opener from my desk. Sliding the trash can up next to us, I take her wrist but then hesitate. It feels wrong to hurt her, to let her bleed, but she said it helps ease the pain. She deserves at least that, even if she . . .

The knife slides across her wrist with little resistance, like cutting into whipped cream. Black blood bursts from her veins with an unpleasant gurgle. It spews far too quickly, as if there is more than her body can hold. The smell is sickly sweet and bitter at once, sugar and bile, life and decay.

Nana lets out a long sigh. "Better."

"What do you feel, Nana?" I ask.

She purses her lips. "It's not good, my dear. We must maintain the barrier. If he uses all his magic on that, then you can make sure he doesn't get any more by—"

"Wait." I shake my head, already knowing where she's

going. "No. I won't do that. I can't do that. No one here can do that."

"What?" Gwen says, her voice quiet.

I close my eyes, the idea too horrible. "She wants us to kill her, so he can't get any more power."

Everyone gasps.

"That would be unpardonable," Prudence says. "To kill our own."

"It won't work anyway," I say. "He already has more than enough." The sky screams again, as if to emphasize my point.

Nana's eyes fill with tears. "This will not do. He can't have you."

No one speaks, even after she lies back, spent. Prudence has her hand over her mouth, horror in her steely eyes. Maggie holds on to her mom, and Tessa blinks back tears. Kat and Gwen stare at me, waiting.

I force down the freak-out. I don't have time to freak out. I have to fix this before it's too late. Stand tall. Focus on the task at hand. Treasure the time I have. "He won't win. We'll figure this out. Keep reading."

Blank stares.

"I said keep reading! We need to find an answer *now*."

They go back to their books. Every page flip sounds frantic, and I push as fast as my eyes will go. There has to be something. This can't be the end. But as the hours pass, the storm grows worse, and the alarms at the barrier are the only other sound in the attic. My mind keeps going back to Levi, to his claim that Cursing me would be the only way.

Please don't let him be right.

"Here!" Prudence about jumps from her seat, and hope blossoms inside me. "In Astrid Hemlock's history, it says: 'There is far more capacity to hold magic than some realize. As I have studied and grown in magic, it has grown in me. The body is only one way in which we can store magic, but there is another, more powerful way: storing it in your soul.'"

"In your soul?" The wheels turn, Levi's shadowy aura at the forefront of my mind. He said Shadows were born with a little magic. Witches aren't—we immediately absorb it from the ground when we're born. Maybe that's why his is stronger, because it's stored in his soul. "Does she say how to do that?"

"Not in detail." Prudence turns the page. "All she says is: 'Once I found the seat of my soul, it was a simple matter to transfer my magic there. My power is unmatched, and no witch challenges our family's stake in this land.'"

I sigh. It's not much information, but it's better than nothing. At least it gives me some other option that doesn't involve Levi Cursing me. "Maybe I can figure out how to do that."

No one seems very convinced, but Nana smiles. "If any-

one could do it, you could, my dear."

I try to smile back. "Just have to find the seat of my soul, right?"

"What does that even mean? Like where your soul is inside of you?" Gwen asks.

"I guess." I sit on the floor and close my eyes, focusing on the magic that permeates every inch of this house. It's dark and warm, like melted chocolate coating my lungs. I let it fill me until I'm practically buzzing on it.

"What are you doing?" Kat asks.

"Absorbing magic," Maggie answers for me. "Are you full yet?"

"To the brim." I put my hand to my head, dizzy from trying to get more than I can hold. "There's no where else for it to go."

"Try to put it in your heart?" Gwen offers with a cringe. "Aren't souls in your heart or something?"

"Yeah . . . don't think so," Kat says.

"Give me some time," I say. "Tessa, Prudence, Maggie, if you could try to fortify the barriers . . ."

"Of course." Prudence stands with her sister and niece. "He won't get through on our watch."

"Thanks." I close my eyes. The magic swirls around me, but all I can do is breathe it in and out. I'm so full I feel like I could burst. Try as I might, there doesn't seem to be a way to put it in my soul.

Levi's magic bounces all around him, like an aura of power. Maybe that's what it looks like when it's in your soul, so I try to push it out while hanging on to it. Doesn't work. Then I attempt visualizing it in my soul, all comfy and powerful. I even get desperate enough to try stuffing it in my heart like Gwen suggested.

Hours go by. I smell dinner, salty and savory, downstairs. They try to get me to go with them, but I stay in the attic, determined to find a way. Because if this doesn't work, then all I have is Levi. I'm already out of time as it is.

My head doesn't feel right from breathing in magic for so long. I lay back, exhausted. "This is ridiculous."

And then I'm laughing, because "ridiculous" sounds hilarious. *Which rhymes!* I think.

Josephine.

No one spoke my name, but I know I heard it. I hold my breath, straining to listen for it again. Desperate to hear it, as if it means I've made progress.

Josephine.

Whatever it is, it sounds as old as the earth itself. It comes from all around me, in the air and the walls, the furniture and histories. It even comes from inside me, and that's when I gasp. I know this voice like I know my mother's.

This is magic.

My heart leaps as I feel its power crackling everywhere, like a million mini lightning storms and tornados in constant motion. It smiles at me, knowing that it has my full attention. This has to be it. I've somehow gotten the magic to my soul, and now I'll be able to save Nana and avenge my mother and make everything all better.

Come.

It calls, wrapping around me like a queen's mantle. Promises—it has promises of power and safety and happiness. Here are my answers! This is true power, and with it I will destroy the Shadows and make the Blacks pay for their crimes. I will teach every witching family not to mess with the Hemlocks.

Mine. Forever.

I pause, realization washing over me in all its cold truth. Before I can talk myself out of it, I force myself to leave the room. Rushing down the iron stairs, I rub my arms, which are ice. I sit at the kitchen table, silent and hopeless. This is not how it's supposed to end, not after how hard we've fought and how much we've learned.

"Give up?" Prudence asks.

I shake my head. "I found the power Astrid was talking about."

Gwen looks so hopeful, and it breaks my heart. "Does that mean you can—?"

"No. I can't beat him. Letting the magic into your soul . . . that's Consumption, total loss of control to the darkness. It almost had me." I hang my head, ashamed. "I almost let it take me so I could stop him."

Everyone at the table slumps. Even the house seems to sag a little. Nana puts her hand on mine. "That, I will never allow you to do. Not to save mc or anyone."

I nod, though in my heart I know there is no way I can let Nana die. Maybe I can't be Consumed, but there is still the Curse.

FORTY-ONE

Astrid Hemlock was not a good witch. I pore over her history all night, hoping to find some glimmer of hope, something to convince me that I don't have to find Levi. Maybe she just did it wrong. Maybe there is a loophole, a way to be *un*Consumed. But it only gets worse and worse with each page. She was obsessed with her land, with the idea that people were trying to take it. She even thought the nearby settlers would kidnap her daughters if they stepped a foot out of her tightly woven magical barrier. But it was never enough. Never.

The villagers are gone, consumed by plague. They won't bother us anymore.

I had no choice but to burn down the castle. No one claims my land.

An old man begged for food, but I knew he was a spy. I used his eyes to guard our gate.

I cursed the ground to only grow weeds, that way no one will settle here.

I poisoned the water.

I found a child in the gardens . . .

On and on it goes, Astrid laying waste to the European countryside ages ago. I can't help but feel shame that I'm related to this woman, this monster. It isn't any wonder that people feared witchcraft, what with this kind of stuff going on. Why is it always the bad apples that define a group?

Then I feel horrible, because I judge Levi based on his father all the time.

When Astrid's pages end, I search for her daughters' histories. I find Persephone's first, and after a quick sleeping-spell reversal I'm in. This book is worse.

Mother is mad. She has not had a sound mind for years, and I know from reading other histories that she's succumbed to Consumption. She doesn't notice how it's eating her away. Her once-beautiful hair is thin, nearly gone. Her fingers are black and rotting, as are her feet and teeth. In her sleep, when she sleeps, she moans and cries in pain. I suspect the magic is eating away her insides in return for taking more than she should.

Nothing in the world is worth her agony, and yet she won't see reason.

Demeter and I hide in our room most days now. We know there is nothing we can do but wait for the magic to kill her. Then we'll be free, and perhaps we can heal this land after she is gone, though it may take the rest of our lives to do it.

Eaten alive by magic. This does not sound at all pleasant. Nor does the evil, murdering insanity part. I may as well hand myself over to Jeff Anderson.

Or Levi.

The thought makes my heart shrivel. This should not be the better option, but as I watch Nana sleep in the recliner beside me I can't imagine my life without her. And honestly, I have no chance of survival anyway, even if she wants to believe it. The Blacks probably wouldn't let any witnesses live, which means Gwen, Kat, my father, and the Crafts are dead. I would be forced to live on, because I don't doubt what Levi said about his dad wanting to leech off me for as long as possible. And the idea of Sylvia Black in *my* house . . . it makes my blood boil.

Surely being Cursed by Levi would be better than that fate. If anything, at least my friends would live. Nana would kill me if she knew what I was thinking, but what else can I do?

In the silence of early morning, my phone chirping sounds very loud. It's a text from Winn.

Can you come over?

"Shit."

"Who is it?" Kat asks.

"Winn. But I can't leave now. . . ."

"Go," Gwen says from the floor, where she, Kat, and Maggie passed out a few hours ago.

"But—"

"Go." Kat rolls over. "Sometimes the answers come when you stop looking for them. Go work things out with your boyfriend. Relax a little. We'll call if Nana gets worse, okay?"

I nod slowly, but only because this is the perfect excuse to go find Levi. If I tell any of them my plan—they'll try to talk me out of it. But my decision is made.

"We'll scour the spell books for anything that might ease her pain," Tessa chimes in from the window seat, where she and Pru are still reading. "We might not be able to cure her, but maybe we can give her more time."

"Take a little break, sweetie," Nana whispers. "I'm not dead yet."

"Okay." I suck in the tears as I text Winn.

Sorry. Sick again.

My stomach twists at the thought that these could be my last words to him, that everything is about to change. I care about him so much, but how can I possibly be with him when I'll be tied to Levi for the rest of my life? It's not fair to Winn, even though it feels like my heart is crumbling inside me.

When I get downstairs, my dad is at the kitchen table nursing a cup of coffee. He looks concerned as he takes me in. "Did you sleep at all?"

I shake my head.

"Here." He gets up and grabs a clean mug from the cabinet, pouring some for me. "I know you're busy trying to save us all, but you need this at least."

Giving a half smile, I lean on the counter next to him. "Thanks, Dad."

His eyes go wide, and I hope my calling him that doesn't bother him. I have wanted to from day one, but it didn't feel like I could say it right off, even if I thought it. He smiles. "That's strange, but I think I like it."

"Good, because it'd be weird to call you my name."

He laughs. "True."

I sip at the coffee, savoring this moment with him. I hope my choice makes it possible to have many more mornings like this. That's what I have to focus on—I might be losing myself, but everyone else wins.

I head to the apothecary after I finish my drink, pull out the ink and parchment, and try to steady my hand as I write, *Where are you?*

Levi answers quickly. *At the Main Street park, waiting for you.*

He knew. He always knew it would come to this, that I wouldn't have time for anything else. As much as I don't want to, I send one final line:

Okay.

FORTY-TWO

The Main Street park isn't more than a block from my house, and I walk slowly, savoring my last moments as myself. The willow trees blow like angry spiders as I pass them. The storm is right overhead, its bruised clouds hungry to break through. Lightning cracks, and it's alarmingly loud, so loud it seems to cut right through me. The park is empty. Surely even normal people can feel how evil the weather is, a bad omen hanging overhead. It fights to get in, to come for me, but for now the barrier holds.

It's too soon when I spot Levi sitting on a park bench. He wears all black, like the death he is, and his hair flies wildly in the wind. I hate him and need him all at the same time. I want him to fix this. I want to be saved. Our eyes lock, and his are sadder than I expected. Maybe he doesn't want to do this either. But now I understand it was inevitable for both of us, determined long before we met.

Sitting next to him, I ask, "Will it hurt?"

His fingers tighten around his knees. "Not in the traditional sense. You felt it already. It's like that, but I would never take that much at once. At least not after we finish off my father. I'll need a lot for that."

I shudder at the thought of his kiss—it was as if I lost part of myself. Feeling like that all the time will suck, but it's better than Nana dying. Better than Levi's father taking me instead. "And it's permanent?"

"Unless I die, which I really prefer not to do."

I gulp. "I don't want to."

His hand is tentative as he places it over mine. "I know."

"Why does it have to be this way?" My tears run against my will.

"It's not fair," he says. "I wish there were another way. I really do."

"That's not true—this is exactly what you want."

"Could I be inside the barrier if that were true? Maybe I care about you and want to protect you." His dark eyes look right into me, and his wanting pours all over my skin, full of hunger and desperation. As he leans in closer, I wonder if I could be okay with this someday. He is beautiful, the kind of boy that girls drool over. And maybe when we're on the same side we would get along.

Maybe I'm making a bigger deal of it than it is.

That doesn't stop me from pulling away, though, thoughts of Winn swirling in my head. "No. Just because we have to work together doesn't mean we have to kiss."

His breath is cool on my neck as he sighs, and it gives me goose bumps. "Maybe I just want to kiss you."

"Well, I don't." I put my face in my hands, the full weight of this crashing over me. I have to say yes. I have to look him in the eye and tell him I want to be Cursed. And then he will always be part of my life. Always. And what if he does lose control someday? What if he turns into his dad?

"That's a lie. You definitely wanted to kiss me before. . . ." His voices fizzles, and I look up to find him staring at something over my head.

It's Winn. And he's holding a bouquet of flowers.

My breath is gone. My lungs are gone. I know what this looks like, but I never wanted him to see it. He turns to go, and I stand before I can think. "Winn! Wait!"

No answer.

"Please!" I run, but he doesn't stop. I grab his arm when I catch up, but he pulls out of it. "Let me explain!"

He turns on me. "Explain what, Jo? That you were cheating on me? That you were lying to me about everything even when I *asked* for the truth?"

I shake my head. "That's not—"

He throws the flowers on the ground. "I'm such an idiot!

I knew something was wrong, but you didn't seem like the type. And here I was worried about you. I went out of my way to get you flowers and wanted to make sure you were okay . . . forget it."

"I never cheated on you."

He scoffs. "Care to explain why you kissed him, then?"

"I had to!" I cry, hating to see him so hurt even if I'm not the only guilty one here. "It was the only way to save Gwen."

He raises an eyebrow, his gaze all judgment and no compassion. "What? That doesn't make any sense!"

"Doesn't it?" I can feel the glare on my face. "I'm not the only one lying here—you don't think I know you're keeping secrets from me, too? And yet I never asked, always hoped that you'd explain it to me."

He doesn't move, doesn't breathe, but I can see the fear in his eyes. "I don't know what you're talking about."

"You do! And so do your parents—I know they were lying, too." I hate that I'm yelling at him, but pushing him away is the only way to keep him safe. "We both have secrets. I guess the question is whether I'm more important than what you're hiding, and vice versa."

He purses his lips, and I think he might be holding back tears. "Even if I told you, I don't think you could ever forgive me."

His words hit me right in the chest, and I can't breathe right. He really does know where he came from and what his family did to mine. He knows I'm a witch. He knows about magic. All this time . . . he knew. "See? We're both liars."

"How I felt about you—how I still feel—was never a lie." Winn's eyes, stormier than ever, meet mine. "But I was selfish to want you, and stupid to hope that you wouldn't figure it out."

I hug myself, wishing I didn't feel exactly the same way. "Just go. Levi and I have a job to do, and you better not interfere."

"Fine." His face hardens, and I know this is the end of us. I don't want it to be over. I want to erase all my memories and stay in blissful ignorance. So I can be with Winn, laughing and kissing and falling in love. As I watch him leave, black rain begins to fall, coating the earth in darkness.

FORTY-THREE

The cement is cold and wet against my face, but I don't care. I lie there in a ball, holding Winn's flowers, now marred with oily droplets. I'm pretty sure normal people can't see the black, but that's all I can see. Endless darkness. Death. Evil. It's all around me, and it will never leave. It's driven away and killed everything I love.

I hate magic. I hate being a witch.

Levi's shadow hangs over me, though he doesn't say anything. His shoes scrape against the path as he kneels down next to me. When he puts his hand on my shoulder, its warmth proves how cold I am.

I don't have the strength to push him away.

"Don't be sad. I swear I'll protect you, because that's what my mom begged me to do."

I turn to him. "What?"

He won't look back, as if the shame of his words is too much to bear. "You're going to get sick, lying here in the rain." His arms come around me, and he picks me up off the ground. He carries me to an old, shaggy willow tree where the rain can't break through. As he sits at its roots, he doesn't bother to put me down. "Better?"

I'm so tired. Of fighting. Of this life. I lean my head on his shoulder. "Finish your story."

He gulps. "This is my fault. I waited years to earn magic, years to see what my mother had left in her history, and you and your mom were in it more than I was. She knew my dad was sucking her dry so he could break the protective barriers she put around Carmina. She knew Carmina would only leave your dad if she was pregnant. She wanted more than anything to protect you both, but by then she was too weak to break free from my grandmother's house.

"The last pages of her history are all letters to me, telling me to protect you, the innocent, from him. She said we owed you because of Carmina's unwavering friendship. And . . ."

He leans his head on the tree, squeezing his eyes shut so tightly they wrinkle like raisins. "I didn't listen. I was mad that she sacrificed her life for you and then asked me to do the same. She should have been there for me—she was my mother—so I ignored everything she said and tried to live my life."

I bite my lip, the weight of his pain familiar. "What changed?"

He sighs, and it's heavy with guilt. "When he Cursed your grandmother. He was so pleased with himself, laughing at the kitchen table about how it would break you into a million pieces. I couldn't help but think of my mom, wonder if he enjoyed putting me through that pain. It was then, finally, that I realized it wasn't your fault my mother wasn't there for me. It was his. It was always his.

"But by then it was already too late to protect you like I should have. I messed everything up." He puts his hand on my cheek, and I look into his eyes, filled with regret. "I'm sorry this is all I can offer you now. I've made too many mistakes to count, but I swear I will make it up to you for the rest of our lives."

My voice catches, so many what-ifs running through my brain I don't know what to say. What if he had come earlier? Warned us? Told us what we were up against? We could have prepared. We could have been ready to fight. What if I had met him years ago, not as an enemy but as a friend? What if . . . I had fallen in love with him?

"Tell me about your steward," I say.

He looks surprised. "What?"

"You have a steward, right? A girl you take magic from?"

"Yes." He looks away. "Of course I do."

"I was just wondering . . . I mean, Stacia and Jeff had

you, and you had to kiss me to take my magic. Is she your girlfriend?" The idea makes me squirm. He shouldn't be holding me like this if she is, and I really, really don't like the idea of sharing. I'm not a good sharer.

"She's ten years older than me," he says. "Her name is Abigail. Some of the Blacks encourage a relationship, the ones who like these power games. But the more prudent part of the family overruled the Consumed ones and deemed me 'too dangerous to reproduce,' thanks to my father."

"I see." My heart pounds at the thought that even the Blacks consider Levi dangerous.

"Abby is nice, I guess." He shrugs, and his cheeks go slightly pink. "She's kind of like a big sister, and she's proud of how I turned out, all things considered. I don't see her often these days."

I nod. Everything seems surreal all of a sudden. Levi isn't so bad—he was just dealt a crappy lot in life. He really is trying to make the best of his situation, and I can respect that.

"I know this will totally kill the moment." He takes my hand, his hold gentle and yet strong. "But we don't have a lot of time."

I jump. "Oh, right."

"So?" His eyes plead with me, full of hope and longing. "Will you help me stop him? Will you give me your magic?"

Fear washes over me anew. My magic curls up inside, as

if to say it's perfectly happy where it is. Deep down I don't want to give it away again. I don't want to feel empty and ashamed and powerless. But what choice do I have? I'm out of options and out of time. Levi wouldn't do it if there were another way. He's only trying to make amends for his past, too. We both have a stake in this, and who am I to refuse him his part? Maybe I'm being selfish, wanting to keep it to myself.

I close my eyes and take a deep breath.

Just say it. Say it, and everything will be fixed.

But my mouth won't work! *Why can't I say it?*

Someone clears their throat behind me. I tumble out of Levi's lap as I attempt to see who it is. My brain feels like it's melting under Kat's and Gwen's furious glares. Gwen puts her hands on her hips, and I shrink a little more. "This is pretty much the stupidest thing you've ever done, Jo."

FORTY-FOUR

"We're taking you home. Right. Now," Kat says in a flawless imitation of Nana.

"Damn right we are." Gwen grabs my arm, pulling me up with surprising strength. "What the hell are you thinking? Your grandmother is dying, and you're out here with *him*?"

I resist her hold, but she won't release me. "I can't go. This . . . this is the only way to stop him. I won't let her die, so let go of me."

Kat eyes Levi. "What do you mean, this is the only way?"

I can't say it out loud. They'll be beyond angry I didn't tell them, and I don't need any more people mad at me right now. All I'm trying to do is make things better. I don't care about anything else.

Levi stands. "She can't get rid of my dad on her own, and

neither can I. We need each other to do it, so get out of the way."

Their eyes go wide. Then Kat shakes her head, her little frame filling up with a confidence I've never seen before. "No. You are not doing that to her again! There has to be another way."

"There isn't!" I cry. "Would I be doing this if there were?"

"Then you're not thinking hard enough!" Gwen turns me to face her, her deep blue eyes fierce. "Take a second and really think, Jo. Past today or tomorrow. Past the pain and fear. Can't you see this is a trap?"

I shake my head. "No!"

This will work. I have to believe that. If I don't, that means there's nothing I can do but watch Nana die and wait for my own painful death.

I tear myself from Gwen's hold, going back to Levi. He puts his arm around me protectively. "It's not a trap," he says. "I want him dead as much as anyone."

Kat looks like she's about to rip his heart out, but she takes a deep breath and tries to calm herself. "Jo, please, don't do this. I might not know a lot about magic, but watching you go through all this has taught me one thing: nothing good can come from giving a guy magic. You know that's true. I know you do."

A lump forms in my throat. I try to tell myself she's wrong, but all I can think of is the story about how the

Shadows came to be. The woman gave away her magic for love, and that one decision is still killing witches today.

"You don't even know him," Gwen says, her voice sad. "You shouldn't be relying on a stranger; you should be relying on your friends, on the people who love you."

Levi spins me around to face him. "Don't listen to them. They don't have a clue what they're talking about—they don't even have magic."

The anger in his voice makes the hair on my neck stand. I look back at them, their fear obvious. They are my friends, my best friends. I've spent most of my life with them, and I don't like seeing them this scared. "They may not have magic . . . but they do know me."

Kat takes a few daring steps closer. "If there isn't a way, we'll make a way, okay? You can do anything. I truly believe that."

"You don't need him," Gwen says. "You don't have to make this sacrifice."

"Shut up!" Levi's arm tightens around me. "We don't have time for this shit! Have you not seen the sky? He is at her doorstep, and you want her to throw away her only chance at survival? You guys are the evil people here."

"Your way isn't survival—it's a slower death!" Gwen screams.

I tense, her words washing over me like freezing cold water. What am I doing? I don't want this—I know I don't want this, and yet here I am ready to do it anyway. I'm crazy. No, just desperate. And afraid.

Neither of which is a good reason to be Cursed.

I push him away, my heart pounding a thousand times a minute. "I can't do this. I couldn't even say the words."

"Josephine," Levi says through his teeth. "Don't be stupid."

I look him in the eye. I'm not angry—this is all he knows; of course there's no other way to him—but my brain is finally working, and so is my gut. "I'm not being stupid. I . . . I think I have an idea, thanks to my friends."

"It won't work."

I hold my head up high. "Won't know until I try, and if you can't trust me then maybe they're right about you. If everything you said was true, you'll let me go, Levi."

His eyes go wild, to the point where I'm waiting for a shadowy Curse to spew out of him. It scares me, the fury he holds inside. His deepest, darkest desires ooze out of him, the shadows around him intensifying. He tries to be good, but there is a part of him that wants to take me and be done with it, that wants to consume every bit of me as his own.

He falls back on the tree, his head cradled in his hands. The shadows dim. "You are such a pain in the ass."

I glare at him, angry that he would have taken me despite knowing all the evil he keeps inside. I feel like such a fool for even considering the risk. "The feeling's mutual."

"It's not my fault if you die," he says.

"Nope. But if I die, at least I know I had control to the end. I am free, unlike you."

As he curls up on the ground, it's as if I can see the shackles that bind him. He's a prisoner to magic. "Leave. Before I change my mind."

I rush home with Gwen and Kat by my side. Once I reach the porch, I stop to catch my breath, and they hug me. I let out a sigh of relief, somehow at peace though I've made this a thousand times harder on myself. But I won't let anything control me, not magic or fear or even a beautiful boy.

"What's the plan?" Gwen asks, our faces still close.

I gulp, not even sure I can do it. But I have to try. "Are you really willing to do anything for me?"

"Of course," Kat says.

Gwen rolls her eyes. "Duh."

"Okay. To the apothecary, then."

FORTY-FIVE

The Crafts come in as I heft the biggest cauldron we have onto the table. "How's the Willow's End barrier?" I ask, searching for the tools I need. Pliers. Knife. Scissors. Lots of cloth bandages. This spell has to work; otherwise the rest of my plan won't.

No pressure.

Maggie cringes. "It's not looking good."

"We did the best we could," Tessa says. "Hopefully it will buy us time."

Prudence raises an eyebrow at the materials I've gathered. "And what are you up to? This doesn't look like any spell I know."

"Because it isn't." I pull out the chameleon scales. Definitely need something to denote transformation. While I'm at it, I grab a jar of cocoons. "I'm making it up as I go, and no, I don't need to hear how crazy I am. I'm well aware."

Pru holds up her hands. "As long as you know."

"Okay . . ." I survey what I have, knowing it's not enough. "Mags, grab me a mother-bear heart and a cub stomach from the cellar. Tessa, I need a lock of Nana's hair. And Pru, I need the Hemlock braid from the door to the histories."

As I wait for them to return, I pace and pace, focusing on what I want my magic to do. I am in control. It will listen to me.

"Jo?" Kat startles me out of my trance.

"Huh?"

"You still haven't told us what you're doing."

Gwen looks at my supplies. "It looks scary."

I take a deep breath. "It is, but we need more power. We need to intensify the next spell as much as we can, and we do that by channeling a spell together. With many witches."

Kat raises an eyebrow. "Wait. Are you saying what I think you're saying?"

I nod. "I'm going to make you and Gwen Hemlocks."

"As in . . . witches?" Gwen says. "Can you do that?"

"I don't actually know. You both got me thinking about it back there with Levi. Giving magic to guys definitely isn't good, but what about giving it to other girls? Girls I love as much as my own family, no less. I can rely on you. I always have." I bite my lip, suddenly worried this is too much for them. "Like you said, I should turn to the people who care about me, not a complete stranger. So, what do you think?"

They exchange glances, and both their mouths slowly stretch into smiles.

"You're serious?" Kat asks.

I nod.

Gwen laughs. "Nah, no magic for me. Who'd want *that*?"

"What are we giving? A toe? A finger?" Kat eyes the tools. "A tooth?"

I shake my head. "Nothing so serious. This is mostly me. We're already bound together—you've done your—" My eyes go wide when my dad comes through the door carrying Nana. "What are you doing? You need to rest!"

"She insisted." Tessa comes in behind them. "I thought it might be a good idea to have her close, considering you're about to make up a spell."

I purse my lips, forcing myself not to feel childish. "True."

"The chair will do, Joseph. Set me there," Nana whispers.

He shakes his head and sits in her chair, the one she once commanded this house from. The one that will be left empty forever if I fail. "I think I'll hold on to you. Carmina would want that."

She pats his chest. "You dear boy. I should have liked to have met you sooner."

"Here you go." Maggie thunks the animal parts on the

table as Prudence comes down with the family braid, glittery with beads and gems.

"Thank you." I take a deep breath as I venture a peek outside. The black-and-purple clouds hang so low it's as if they're creeping under the freeway. I can feel their weight, like particles of iron.

We don't have much time.

"Pru, Maggie, Tessa, I have no idea how long this will take, but make as many protection charms as you can before I'm done. Use whatever you must—it doesn't matter how rare the reagent at this point."

They nod, heading for the ceiling-high cabinets, full to the brim with powerful potential.

I grab a bundle of oak twigs, their age suggesting permanence and history. After setting them in the cauldron, I sprinkle willow leaves over them for place. This place. Which has become as much a part of us as we've become part of it. I pluck a pair of black swallowtail butterfly wings from a case and put them in the center of my little nest.

Black, fragile wings—for the freedom and beautiful darkness magic is.

"Here goes nothing," I whisper as I put my hand over the cauldron. I close my eyes and let the magic surge through me. It sings my name, calling for me to get lost in it, but I call back.

Not this time. You are mine to wield.

The reagents spark with fire, the flames blue and red as everything melts into the beginnings of my potion. The transformation reagents come first. Then I unwrap the mother-bear heart, its love and protectiveness radiating from the frozen tissue already. The potion absorbs the heart the second I place it in the iridescent blue liquid. The bear-cub stomach comes next, its need and trust adding to the mix.

I grab a bundle of dried hemlock to seal this phase of the potion, but then I hesitate. I'm missing something . . . something else in the mix for family.

It's not loyalty—that should be taken care of because of the binding.

"What's wrong, Josephine?" Nana asks.

"I . . ." When our eyes meet, warmth envelops me. I look to my dad, his face creased in concern. They are everything to me. They make me so . . . "Nothing. I've got it." I almost knock Maggie over on my way to the herb cabinet. Searching the various jars and bottles, I finally find it: gardenia oil.

For joy.

A few drops, and the cauldron bubbles with glee. I pour more of my magic into it until it stabilizes. Then comes the dried hemlock.

"Isn't that . . . poisonous?" Kat asks.

I give her a flat look. "No comment on the bear heart, but this concerns you?"

Gwen smirks. "Bear heart won't kill us."

"Neither will this—it's a way to mark our family. It has certain powers for us. For you. Now *shh*—I need to concentrate." Putting both hands over the potion, I pick out each ingredient, weaving together the magic and place and family, making it permanent.

"Good, good," Nana whispers. "I see what you're doing."

I nod, relieved to have her input. "Now the payment."

I cut a tuft from the bottom of the Hemlock braid, the hair of every generation giving its power. Then I come over to Nana and clip a lock of her silver hair. She takes my hand. "You can do this. I believe you can do this."

I kiss her forehead. "I needed to hear that."

After her lock, I offer my own. Then comes the bigger stuff—the painful stuff. I'm not sure which to offer first, so I close my eyes and let my hand come down on something at random.

Pliers.

I let out a slow breath, the thought of pain making my heart pound. I run my tongue along my teeth. Which can I live without? How hard will I have to pull? Settling on a top right tooth—not too far back or front, hopefully concealable—I clamp the pliers down. The metallic taste makes my mouth water when it should be dry. My hands shake, and it sounds as if I'm not the only one who has stopped breathing.

I hear myself scream, and a shot of pain radiates through my cheek. The tooth, its long root white against the blood, sits between the pliers' tongs. My head spins, and before I know it, Gwen has me by the shoulders.

"Steady." She holds out some cloth. "Put it in your mouth. You're drooling blood."

"Oh."

Well, *that* hurt. It was probably good to start there. Maybe the rest won't be so bad. I put the tooth into the mixture, bracing myself for the next act.

"More?" Kat says when I put the pliers to my fingernail.

I nod. "I'm asking a lot—I must give a lot."

A fingernail.

A toenail.

A chunk of flesh.

By the time I run the knife over my hand, I'm in so much pain it hardly registers. I let the blood flow into the concoction, waiting for the liquid to settle. I don't know why, but I know it has to settle before I stop the flow. It's like the bubbling cries for more payment, more pain, more sorrow.

And then, in an instant, it stops simmering. I pull my hand away, dizzy and tired, and the battle hasn't even started.

Breathing in the magic, I fill up only to pour it into the

spell. It needs more. More. I'm terrified by how much it needs. This will take time, which I don't have. Lightning flashes so brightly I can see it through the green velvet curtains. The screams are on top of us, and the house moans back as the wind pushes at it.

I can feel him near; his greedy, evil wanting swirls overhead. He has broken through the outer barriers, and he stands before our house of ivy, fighting his way in. I don't have to look to know.

"Everyone!" I cry. "I need your help to finish this off."

Their hands encircle the pot, and they pour their magic into my spell. We weave and weave the elements together, use our magic to knit them until they cannot separate. Little by little, the potion shrinks and forms. Into what, I'm not sure, except that they are round, about the size of an Olympic medal.

The color changes to a sandy brown, with flecks of black. As I peer down at the two circles, I try not to laugh. I hold them out for Gwen and Kat, who eye them warily.

"A cookie?" Gwen asks.

I smile. "Nothing says home like a chocolate-chip cookie, right?"

Kat grabs hers. "Guess we should be happy it doesn't look like bear heart."

"True." Gwen takes a bite. "Huh, it actually tastes like home."

Kat nods in agreement. "Except I don't feel any different."

"Me eith—" Gwen falls from her chair and Kat follows. Their eyes don't close, and when I put my finger to Gwen's neck, I can't find a pulse.

FORTY-SIX

"No. No, no, no." I pat Gwen's cheek, my head flooding with all the things I could have done wrong. They are totally limp, not breathing, and I can't see anymore because my eyes are filled with tears. They can't be dead. *Please don't be dead.* "Gwen, sweetie, I can't do this without you or Kat. I can't live without you guys."

Prudence kneels next to Kat. "They shouldn't have died. The spell may not have worked, but you paid more than enough. This could not be the consequence."

I'm still crying. I did this to them—I should have never been so reckless. "What do we do?"

Prudence gives me a sad look. "All we can do is wait."

"Wait? For what? For him to bust the door down?" I lay down next to Gwen, hugging her. I can't look into her dead eyes, so I close them. This can't be happening, but I can't hear her heart.

They both look dead.

Dead.

"This can't be right," Prudence says again. Her disbelief is surprising, what with her initial assumption that I was crazy to even try. "Your composition was well conceived, and we poured everything into it."

"I must have missed something," I whisper.

"I don't think so." She puts her hand on Kat's stomach, presses as if it'll wake her up.

"But we are missing something now, perhaps," Nana croaks, and then goes into a coughing fit.

I force myself to look at Gwen again, searching my mind for anything that might fix this. We can't raise the dead—or rather, the sacrifice is too heinous to even consider it. And there isn't time anyway. I can feel his magic pressing in all around us, hungry and excited for the pain he'll soon inflict.

"I'm so sorry, Gwen." I take her hand, trying to pretend that she's still here. "I don't know what to do. I just wanted to give you magic. I never thought . . ."

I gasp when I feel it. Magic is leaving my body, being drained like when Levi sucked it out of me. I jump up, scared that he found a way to Curse me, but the feeling disappears as quickly as it came. I search the room for the threat, but I see nothing. No Shadows.

"Josephine?" Tessa says, as if I'm on the doorstep to insanity. "Are you okay?"

"I thought I felt—"

Gwen's finger twitches.

I put my hand over my mouth. Of course! Rushing back to her, I grasp her hand and push my magic into her. If I feel bad without magic for even a few minutes, how awful would it be for a body to suddenly need it and not know what to do? They're empty. New.

Her hand tightens around mine, and I let out a joyful squeak. "Pru, take Kat's hand and give her some magic."

Her eyebrow raises. "What?"

"They're not dead! They're empty."

"Ohhh." She grabs Kat's hand and gets to work. "C'mon, sweetheart, time to wake up."

Gwen moans. Her eyes flutter open and fix on mine. "Did I die? I have a feeling I died."

"You did." I can barely breathe as I look at her, a strange and unreal recognition rushing through me. My blood . . . it's in her now. I can feel her power. She is definitely a witch, and more than that, she is a Hemlock. Not just in name, but in blood.

She's my sister.

Gwen pulls herself up, rubbing her eyes. "And now I'm back?"

"I think you were . . . reborn."

Kat groans as she comes to, and I feel it again. Sisterhood. True, perfect sisterhood. "You said we wouldn't die, liar."

"I didn't know!"

"Whoa." Kat puts her hand to her head. "Is this magic? That tingling in the air?"

"Yeah. Can you breathe it in? Hold it inside you?" I'm terrified waiting for their answer. What if I made them like Levi? What if they have to feed off us for magic? That would be worse than death, to have turned them into monsters.

They both close their eyes, and after a few deep breaths they smile.

"That's . . . fantastic," Gwen says. "I feel like I can conquer the world if I wanted to."

I let out a relieved sigh. They're real witches. There are more Hemlocks in the world, and having four in one room makes me realize why the Blacks want us gone. We are powerful, and we can stop this. I tackle them both into a hug, relishing all the family surrounding me.

"We don't do that whole world-domination thing, Gwen." Maggie bounces over to us. "But maybe we should tell you the rules after we kick the shit out of that Shadow."

"Margaret!" Tessa says.

She rolls her eyes. "C'mon, Mom, I know you want to. And now it's six on one! We just have to go out and get him."

"No," I say, the happy moment already gone. "We're not going out there—he has the advantage."

Maggie tilts her head. "Huh?"

"He has a massive amount of magic. Hundreds of times what we can store." I stand, pacing the room as I think. "If we leave our property, we only have what we can hold. That's not enough. We have to do this on our turf. Here, on this land. We have an infinite well of magic if we stay here. All he has is what he's stolen."

"He won't get any more from me. I refuse to take it in," Nana says, her voice so weak it hurts my soul.

I offer a sad smile. "Strong to the bitter end, aren't you?"

"Of course, dear. I will do what I can."

Prudence makes a disapproving face. "But take down the barrier? Let him on this land? He would taint it with all that perverse magic."

"No, he can use up his magic trying to get it down. It'll give us a little time to—"

A deafening crack shudders through the house, and we cover our heads as the jars and bottles rattle against the cabinet doors. Once everything is still, I rush to the window.

At the gate stands an older version of Levi, his eyes as wild as his smile. And yet his suit is crisp, as if he's here to talk realty. Which, in a sick way, he kind of is.

When his eyes find me, my entire body goes cold under

his cruel gaze. I can't help but feel terror—Jeff is so much worse than I expected. A million times worse than Levi. I'm not even sure one could call him by his human name—he is that Consumed by the darkness. I recognize the feeling immediately—it's exactly what I felt when I cleansed my dad.

He wants to take everything I have.

He will enjoy slowly destroying me.

He puts his finger to the gate's latch, and even though no one uninvited can enter, it opens.

FORTY-SEVEN

"Looks like our planning session is over." I head for Nana's desk, where the lion-jaw dagger sits on its stand. I pick it up, the bone smooth and cool against my sweaty palm. It's not much, but I'm taking anything that may even remotely help. "Where are the charms?"

"Here." Tessa holds up an arm's length of necklaces. "Three for each of us."

"I wish I had time to discuss my plan in detail," I say as Tessa passes around our meager protection.

"Kill him before he kills us?" Maggie asks.

I shake my head, my need for vengeance suddenly broiling. "No, I want him alive . . . and in pain. Basically, we need to restrain him. Then you guys need to form a pentagram around him and tap into the spell I cast to make it stronger."

Kat frowns. "Do Gwen and I know how to do that?"

"You'll know," all the Crafts say at the same time. Tessa places the last of the charms over Kat's head. "It's intrinsic. You will feel Jo's energy and power—all you have to do is match it."

Kat and Gwen nod.

Taking a deep breath, I look out the window again. He's standing inside the gate, smiling as if he knows what we're planning, as if it's futile, as if he's already won. *Ugh, so that's where Levi got all that ego.* Before I head for the door, I whisper in Nana's ear, "Take it all the second you can."

Her eyes go wide. "Okay."

I turn to my family, my friends, their eyes set with determination. My hand automatically goes to Mom's pendant, and I hold my head up high. No matter what happens, she would be proud of me for doing all I can. She would have expected nothing less. "For Carmina."

"For Carmina," everyone says.

And Stacia. I don't say it out loud, but I ache for Levi's mother. I'm grateful for what she tried to do for us. She deserves to be remembered and avenged as well.

I head for the door, footsteps clomping behind me like a death march. As I unlock the dead bolt, the house of ivy's black door seems more fitting than ever. Its creaking sounds more like a growl today, like it, too, despises the suffocating darkness this monster brought with him.

Everything is drenched in shadow, and not because it's almost night. His aura has transformed our entire yard—the grass, the trees, the ivy, and even the house—into inky gloom. We spread out, surrounding him without a word. He doesn't move, all the time his eyes trained on me.

But then he startles, his gaze flicking between Gwen and Kat. His laugh is quiet, but the insanity still comes through. "Josephine, you sweetheart. You didn't have to make me more treats."

I bristle at his voice, too gentle to be anything but deadly.

"You wish," Gwen says. Her magic is surprisingly powerful already, and her anger makes the air sizzle with electricity.

He takes a step toward me, and my fingers tighten around the dagger. His eyes are beyond wild, as if I'm looking into the depths of magic itself. "You are the spitting image of your mother, you know. Except you might be prettier."

Prudence's anger flares. "Why you—"

I hold up my hand. His eyes scare the hell out of me, but I force myself to look right into them. I will not give him the pleasure of seeing my fear.

"So quiet." He smirks. "You don't strike me as the silent type."

"You don't deserve words." My voice is flat, and my palms are full of magic. I point the dagger at him and release everything I have.

My lightning is red as it crackles through the shadows, magnified in strength and purity by the lion jaw. He holds out his hands, and a barrier blocks my spell. His grin is clearly unhinged, and I can tell he enjoys this though he struggles to fight it off. I breathe in more magic, letting it flow and flow. Maybe he can fight me off, but he has to use up magic to do it. That's just as good a result.

Gwen and Kat stay at my side, obviously shell-shocked, but I can tell they're trying to help with my spell. It could be so much stronger, but I'm proud they're doing as well as they are, being witches for a whole five minutes or so.

Thankfully, Prudence picks up on my diversionary tactic and comes at him from behind. She grabs both of his arms, and his eyes go wide. My spell is inches from his face when he holds out a hand to Tessa, and she screams in agony. All her fingernail beds run bloody as he catches her nails midair.

Prudence cracks at her sister's pain, and he uses the moment to get her by the neck with Tessa's bloody nails. "Nice try."

I drop the spell, my mind blanking as I watch the nails dig into Pru's pale skin. He won't hesitate to kill her; this I know for sure. Her eyes plead with me, and her lips mouth something I can't quite catch. Something that starts with a *B*.

She tries again.

Braid!

I hold out my dagger, telling the magic to cut Pru's hair. It frees itself from her, writhing in the air. It springs for his neck, wrapping around like a noose. I let it squeeze hard, hard enough that the nails fall from Pru's skin. He drops to his knees, and her impossibly long hair coils around his arms and torso, binding him in place.

Phase one complete. I can hardly believe . . .

He laughs, the sound strangled and disturbing. I try to go on with the next spell, but he seems too happy about being bound. That can't be good.

The air grows cold, so cold that I can see my breath.

His image blurs, the shadows around him flaring and pulsing as they leave his body. My fear becomes a crippling force that leaves me numb with panic. A black Shadow man—the same as when we freed my dad—forms next to Prudence. It smiles at her, and its wanting pours out everywhere.

"Eenie." He points to Gwen. "Meenie." To Kat. "Miney." To me. "Moe." The shadow turns to face Maggie, whose hands are frozen by her side. He pounces, and she's too far out of reach for me to stab the shadow and take the Curse instead.

FORTY-EIGHT

Tessa screams as she runs for Maggie, her horror overcoming the pain of lost fingernails. For a moment I'm back under the willow, watching Nana come to my rescue. Except Tessa isn't fast enough, and none of us can stop it. Even if we could, it still wouldn't help. He'll have another magic well to use when we are finally chipping away at his enormous store of power.

In a last-ditch effort, I chuck the dagger at the shadow. It sticks in the grass, barely missing. Maggie tries to make a barrier with a handful of orchid petals, but it only provides a second's worth of defense.

It's just as Levi said—he'll Curse us one by one until we're all drained.

As much as I want to, I can't do this alone.

Maggie braces herself for the Curse, but right before the

shadow touches her, a figure tackles it to the ground. I can hardly believe my eyes. Another shadow. They struggle in a mess of black smoke, and there's only one explanation.

"Better hurry." Levi's voice comes from behind, and I turn to find him on our porch, sitting there like I should have noticed him sooner. His smile is blinding against all the darkness. "I can't hold him off for long."

"Right." I focus on Jeff's other body, the one still trapped by Pru's hair. His glare is fierce, but it's not directed at me. It's Levi he's furious with.

"Traitor," he croaks.

"Murderer," Levi says back.

"Everyone, circle up!" I put my hand over my heart, determined to give what needs to be given. I have no idea what it'll do to me, but it's the only thing strong enough that I can think of. Closing my eyes, I dig into the earth's magic. I pull it toward me. I command it to listen.

Come, it hisses. *Ours.*

No, you are mine, but I will offer you a piece of me in exchange for a spell.

The magic simmers with excitement. A piece of soul. I imagine witches don't often give such a valuable payment. *For a piece, you may bend us to your will.*

"Josephine," Pru says in a warning voice.

"It must be done. I won't lose myself." *A deal it is.* I search deep down, to the dark place I found before, the place Astrid gave over to magic entirely. I section out the smallest portion I can and force it to leave me. It rips through my body, and I can't control my screams. It feels as if a knife cuts me from the inside out. I want to stop, to keep this small piece of my soul, but I push forward.

This is a worthy sacrifice.

My hands instantly warm when it emerges. The sliver is like a white firefly fluttering in my palms, beautiful and vibrant and much purer than I ever thought my soul would be. Magic surges into it, turning it red. I pour more in, telling the spell what it must do to earn this shred of my soul. I can feel my sisters add to it, intensifying and hastening its creation until my soul shard brims with power.

"Do it now!" Levi's voice is strained, and one glance at the battling shadows makes it clear he's losing ground fast.

I step forward so that I stand directly over Jeff. He glares, but I can see the fear in his eyes. I like it far more than I should. Slowly, I set the glowing red spell on his forehead, and it seeps into his skin until I can't see it anymore. But I can feel what it did, and I smile.

He laughs. "Nice try, but it seems even your soul can't kill me."

"I didn't ask it to kill you."

His eyebrow raises.

"She asked for something better." Nana stands at the porch, her tiny frame rattling.

"Better?" he says.

She nods as she holds out her hand. He screams when he feels what's happening. I can't hide how much I enjoy my success, watching him suffer like he made my mom suffer. His magic drains and drains. Nana takes back every ounce she can hold. Then she throws it away, gives it back to the place it belongs.

The ivy turns green again.

The house smiles.

The air sighs happily.

Nana stands taller, already looking better. "She reversed your Curse. Now I can take from you. And if you touch another witch, you better bet we'll do this again."

He collapses to the ground, gasping in panic. He's so empty of magic the shadows are gone, and without them he doesn't look so scary. Just a man. A weak, helpless man ravaged by Consumption. "Kill me."

I release the hair that binds him, and it turns to ash. "Sorry, I'm not that merciful."

We stand over him, as if no one can believe we actually did it. I certainly can't. I keep waiting for him to pounce and Curse someone, but all he does is shudder. He can't even get up. Levi stands next to me. "What are you going to do with him?"

I pull a frog eye from my pocket. "Send him back to your grandmother."

"She won't be happy."

"And I'm supposed to care?"

He smirks. "No, but I'll be out of a home."

I conjure a door to Blossom Ridge, and we roll him through and shut it. Old Lady Black should find him soon, but she's no match for us Hemlocks. Maybe she'll think twice before messing with us again.

Once Jeff is gone, my whole world tilts for a second. What now? But one look at Nana, her smile free of pain, and I know everything will be fine. She holds out her hands, and I run into them like I did when I was little. She strokes my hair, now streaked with white, and her tears wet my shirt. "You wonderful girl."

"No one will take you from me," I say. "No one but time, at least."

She laughs. "I think this calls for pudding, don't you?"

I nod. "Lots and lots of pudding. And maybe even cake."

Everyone heads inside, but I can feel Levi's eyes on me. He lingers by the gate, waiting, wanting . . .

Hoping.

I walk toward him, my head held high. He bites his lip, his dark gaze soft. There's something different about him. Something missing. His shoulders aren't as tense anymore, like the weight on his conscience has been lifted.

"Seems like you needed me after all," he says.

"Just not in the way you wanted." I look at my feet and

stuff down my pride. "Thank you. For letting me go, and for protecting us when the time came."

He sighs, and all the hope goes out with it. "I'm too late, aren't I?"

I glance up at him, and he's so beautifully sad I almost want to tell him it's never too late. I want to take his hand and make it all better. I want him to smile. But I can't forget the darkness he holds inside, the shadows that would haunt us forever. I have enough darkness to deal with already—I can't shoulder his burden as well. I don't want to.

"I'm afraid so." My heart aches, the full reality of Winn leaving finally breaking through. "I want Winn, Levi. I really do. I've known him for years. I've adored him for months. That's not something I can magically get over, even if I can't have him. Even if he lied to me."

He sucks in a breath and nods. "Well, it was worth a try. Hate to say you're probably making the right decision."

I snort. "What are you going to do now?"

"Probably start by visiting Abby. I'll be safest there."

"Makes sense." It feels weird saying good-bye to him, but right, too. "Take care, okay? And if you're ever in a bind, you're welcome here."

He hugs me, but this time all the sparks are gone. He's just Levi. The boy whose fate is tied with mine, but not the boy I want to be with. "Thanks, Jo. For everything."

I wave as he passes through the gate and disappears.

FORTY-NINE

Even under the freeway, we can't escape the summer heat. Gwen, Kat, and I lick at Popsicles. The cool grass tickles my arms. A mosquito flies overhead, and Gwen zaps it with a flick of her finger. She giggles. "That will never get old."

"Seriously," Kat says.

"I would say it's already old, but I don't miss the mosquito bites." I throw my Popsicle stick at her. "Though I'm kind of jealous the white-hair side effect looks like highlights on you. I just look middle-aged."

"No way." She shoves me. "It looks like you had a few chunks bleached."

Kat pulls out more grass, her hands unable to keep still. "You look punk."

I laugh. "Yeah, I'm so hard-core."

"Hey," Gwen says. "You are pretty badass. Don't tell me you already forgot what happened a few months ago."

I sigh, wishing they wouldn't bring it up. I am proud of what I did. I mean, I love having real sisters, that I get to share my whole life with them, that we get to learn and grow together. I adore having my dad around. I'm grateful every day that Nana is still alive and well. But there's something missing. Some*one* missing. I'm not sure the feeling of loss will ever leave now that I've given up a piece of my soul.

"Hello?" Kat waves a hand in front of my face.

I jump and then cringe. "Crap, was I doing it again?"

"Longing for Winn?" Gwen lies down and crosses her legs. "Yup. Aren't you ever going to talk to him about it?"

Now I'm the one picking at the grass. "What am I supposed to tell him?"

"Uhh, the truth?" Kat says.

I want to talk to him. I really do. Nana said I could, that we shouldn't blame him for what happened in our shared past. But every time I try, I can't even make it up the lane to his house. What if he's already moved on? I'm too afraid to find out. "I wish—"

"Jo!" Dad calls from the house. "Get in here! You have a letter."

"Coming!" Dad has been trying his best to cheer me up with favorite foods and, yes, even a car, but I think he knows that I won't ever be the same. "What is it?" I ask when I get inside.

He holds up the envelope. "I don't know, but it's from an L. Anderson."

My eyes go wide and I grab the letter, ripping it open. I can't imagine what he'd send, but it must be important.

Dear Josephine,

I know I'll hate myself for this, but it will make you happy and that will have to be enough for me. I looked into Cordelia Black, and it turns out she's listed as a traitor in the Black records. There's no death date, but she and her Shadow, Phillip Carter, ran away after refusing to hunt down—wouldn't you know it—the Hemlocks.

I'm thinking that clears lover boy, but it still doesn't answer my questions about why he's different. I think you'll have to get the rest of the story from him. That's all I got.

Take care,

Levi

P.S. You so owe me for this.

I put my hand to my heart, its pounding threatening to break down my rib cage. Winn. He said I'd never forgive him, and yet Levi's words prove that his family was on our side. Clearly, I am missing something huge.

"Jo, are you okay?" Dad asks.

I walk past him, nodding. "I'm going to Winn's."

"It's about time!" I hear Nana call from the apothecary. "Bring him back when you're done so I can hear the story, too."

"Fine." I roll my eyes, though I guess I should be glad she isn't going to spy on us.

I take my car, mostly so I have time to compose myself. When I pull up in front of his house, I still have no idea what to say, but my feet walk forward until I'm standing at the doorstep. Somehow I manage to knock, and I know those are his footsteps coming to answer.

The door opens, and his stormy blue eyes meet mine, shocked. He's tanner, probably having spent every day in the fields since we parted. His mouth is still the most beautiful in existence. He doesn't speak, and now that the surprise is gone all that's left is sadness.

"Cordelia didn't kill Fanny?" I say.

He gulps. "She may as well have."

I frown, holding out Levi's letter. "But the Blacks say she was a traitor, that she refused to hunt us and ran away."

"That part is true." He sighs, as if being in my presence is painful. It makes me want to cry, because seeing him makes me want him more than ever. "C'mon, let's go to the swing."

"Okay . . ."

We walk next to each other, close enough that I want to reach out and grab his hand. Many of my daydreams have looked a lot like today, him and me and the late summer

sun peeking through the trees.

He leans on the trunk of the oak tree and gestures for me to take the swing. It's hard to sit there, the place where we first kissed, but I do.

Winn takes a deep breath before he starts. "My great-great-grandmother Cordelia *did* run, and she even found Fanny and told her the truth about what the Blacks were doing. She and Phillip didn't want any part of it—they were so in love that Phil wouldn't even take Cordelia's magic. Your aunt Fanny, she was more concerned about protecting them than herself. She was worried they'd be punished for divulging Black secrets."

"So she stayed here with them and put up all those spells?" I ask.

He nods. "A lot more than that. Fanny, well, she became obsessed with trying to stop the Blacks. She kept it very secret, because she knew they'd all be dead if word got out. Once she created a spell she thought would work, Cordelia and Phil became the test subjects."

All I can do is nod because I'm too riveted by his words to speak.

Winn looks away, shame flooding his features. "It worked. Fanny was able to seal Cordelia's and Phil's magic. It's still sealed. I can't use it, but all of us Carters can feel it a little. It worked out great for Phil and Cordelia because they were pretty much regular humans after that. Except for one thing . . ."

"Fanny died," I whisper. I put my arms around myself, the truth filling me to the brim. Cutting two people off from magic? Of course she did. How reckless, and yet noble at the same time.

"I'm so sorry, Jo. They never meant for it to happen, but after it did they were helpless. Cordelia was afraid to go to Fanny's sister, and it seemed like she didn't even recognize her as a witch. They couldn't tell others what happened without the Blacks coming for them, and they had nothing to defend themselves with. They were scared—hell, I'm still scared. So it became a secret."

"Why are you scared?" I ask, the information still sinking in.

"Because you deserve to seek vengeance. In Cordelia's history it says killing a witch is unforgivable. She always felt horrible for what happened and said we should never forget the price that was paid for us to be free."

He crouches down and puts his head to his knees. "I don't have to be what Levi is because Fanny *died*, Jo. At first I thought I could tell you—was even excited to tell you—but then I saw the fear in your eyes when you came into the house. It scared me, and then I didn't *want* to tell you and lose you. But you found out anyway."

"You're such an idiot." I gulp back tears. Stupid, stupid boy.

He looks up at me. "What?"

I stand, furious. "You should have told me! I thought you

were a Shadow—I thought you were the bad guy. You made me break up with you over something that doesn't even matter!"

"It doesn't?" Finally, I see hope in his eyes, and it fills me with courage.

"No! I'm *glad* Fanny sealed your powers. I'm sorry she died, but she gave me a huge gift because now I can have you." I shrink back, my face suddenly warm. "I mean, if you still want me."

He's already on his way over, and I gasp when he grabs me. His lips meet mine, hot and urgent and so happy I can feel them stretch into a smile between kisses. We fall into the grass, his weight on me the most exhilarating sensation in the world. He pulls back enough for us to look at each other.

"I can't believe that's even a question." He pushes a strand of hair behind my ear. "Of course I want to be with you. I thought you didn't want to be with me."

"Ridiculous." I laugh and kiss him about a thousand more times.

We lie there, hand in hand, watching the stars come out one by one. And with them, the fireflies, just as alive and twinkling. I put my hand to Mom's pendant and pick a particularly bright star. With all my heart, I promise to live my life like she did, treasuring every perfect moment.

ACKNOWLEDGMENTS

I owe so much of this story to the legacy of my grandmother and the example of my mother, who taught me how to pick myself up after grief tore through our family. Mom, thank you for your unfailing love, your quiet strength, and your endless understanding. We may have lost grandma too early, but I see her in you everyday.

I wouldn't have been able to write about friendship without having friends I'd give everything for. To Kiersten White and Kasie West, thank you for being my Kat and Gwen. (In writing this, I totally just realized how apt that comparison actually is. Dude.) To Michelle Argyle, Renee Collins, Jenn Johansson, Sara Raasch, Shannon Messenger, Sara Larson, Stephanie Perkins, and Candice Kennington, thank you for always listening and laughing and sharing a piece of your lives with me.

My family is everything to me and my husband most of all. Nick, thank you for supporting me through thick and thin, for your undying patience, and for making me laugh at the most random times. To my Benji, Kora, and Gil, thank you for being such good kids and letting me squeak in writing-time.

I've been so lucky to have the amazing Curtis Brown agency looking after me all these years, and I particularly have to thank Anna Webman for selling *House of Ivy & Sorrow* and Ginger Clark for being the amazing agent she is. I have never felt so well taken care of. I'm the luckiest writer ever!

Speaking of incredible luck, I also have the best editor alive—Erica Sussman. Thank you so much, Erica, for falling in love with Jo and her story as much as I did while writing it. Thank you for helping me find the missing pieces I'd tried so long to discover, and for helping me take this book to the next level. It's everything I ever wanted it to be. And thank you to Tyler Infinger, too, whose happy faces and giddy comments always make me smile just as much as Erica's.

And finally, a big thanks to all the people at HarperTeen who have helped turn my story into a real live novel. I never stop being grateful that you have let me live my dream.